Wake Me In t

The Cryogen Chronicles
Book 1

Alex Oldham

Published by

Cryogen Publishing

Copyright © September 2011

This edition published December 2025

Cryogen Publishing

ISBN: 978-1-4478-3665-0

Cover design by nessgraphica.com

Prologue – Betrayed and Forgotten

The body stood there, rigid and unyielding, like a statue carved from the hardest stone. Its skin was as pale as the dim light that bathed the cavern around it. An ethereal glow seemed to mock the lifelessness of its form. No breath had filled its resting lungs for nearly a century, and its veins lay silent, devoid of life's crimson flow. To the casual observer, it would have appeared to be nothing more than a lifeless corpse, a relic of a bygone era…

But it wasn't.

Not quite.

Because this was my body, suspended in a state of cryogenic stasis, a desperate attempt to defy the inevitable, to cheat death itself. True, I bore none of the usual signs of life, and I was unable to conjure a single thought. My body was totally devoid of sensation, a mere shell of the man I once was. Yet, unlike the countless souls who had been buried or cremated before me, I was different. All the physical matter that once constituted the person I used to be was now trapped in this frozen prison, waiting for a future that might never come.

And as for the absence of thought? Well, if I could have, I would have been thankful for my current state, since it meant I didn't know what was unfolding around me.

The metal containment pod that I'd been placed in soon after my death had been removed from its foundation and encased in a larger, shiny steel one. And along with its frozen content — me — it was being moved for an entirely different reason than the one I'd dreamt about during those final days of my first life. This wasn't yet the time for my resurrection, the moment when everything was supposed to be in place to unfreeze, restore, and cure the aging body that had been frozen a hundred years before. No — thankfully, I was totally oblivious to my surroundings. But the two human figures that glided silently and weightless through the sprawling parade of semi-dead were fully aware of what they were doing.

"I'll tell you something," one of them said, his voice crackling through the comms link in his helmet. "It's a good thing these poor souls aren't conscious. They'd be bored out of their minds after a few hundred years."

"Make that a few million," his colleague replied, her tone laced with a mix of amusement and disdain. She peered through the visor of her protective helmet, surveying the rows of silver pods that stretched endlessly before them, each one a tomb for the forgotten. "Once this place is sealed, I doubt they'll ever see the light of day again."

As graveyards went, this one was unlike any other. It was on the Moon, for a start, far removed from the comforting embrace of Earth. No chiselled blocks of marble or stone lined its deathly aisles. Instead, row upon row of towering silver pods stood on polished marble plinths, glistening under the dim lights of the dusty cavern. Deep underground, far enough away to be forgotten by a race that had moved beyond this outdated and failed approach to its search for longevity.

After all, where better to discard Earth's unwanted than on the far side of the Moon, forever shrouded from its eternal partner? Though my dormant mind was blissfully unaware, I, along with countless others, was among those unwanted.

The rumbling vibrations from the nearby water processing plant accompanied the last of the incoming containers. As the technicians positioned it in its final resting place, it rocked slightly, a gentle reminder of the life that once thrived within. Until silently, it stood among the hundreds of thousands of other pseudo-headstones.

"That's it, then," sighed a voice, tinged with relief. "Finally done after two years. Boy, will I be glad to get back to Earth."

"You volunteered for this, Robert," his colleague shot back, a hint of sarcasm in her tone. "If it's bothered you that much, maybe you should request an easier assignment next time."

"Okay, okay," he replied defensively. "I know you're a hard-hearted witch, Sal, but I can't help but feel for these people."

"They're not people, Robert. They're just frozen cadavers—nothing more than the meat most folks have in their freezers." Her words dripped with disdain.

"Don't be disrespectful, Sal!" he snapped, his voice rising. "That's not funny. If they're just meat, why aren't they buried like regular folk? Why leave them like this?"

"Lily-livered liberalism," she spat, her disdain palpable. "People with too much power and less backbone than a jellyfish. Did anyone really believe this half-baked idea of being frozen and revived would ever work? That's why we're here now, sweeping the problem under the carpet."

He paused, glancing around as if to take in the enormity of their task. "Pretty big carpet," he mused, placing his gloved hand on the pod nearest to him. "Each one of these poor souls has a story." His curiosity piqued, he looked up at the small rectangular window of the cylinder, his gaze lingering. "I wonder what story lives inside this one?"

That container looked no different from the countless others surrounding it, yet it held a unique individual—me—Richard Green. And the man was right; I had a story to tell. I had looked to live another day, to defy the finality of death, and I'd paid the fee for a chance to shake hands with the future.

And my story was far from over. Because, despite this betrayal by our fellow humans, mine was a story that would begin again. Long after the people who had consigned me to this place had all met their makers.

At least I wasn't alone in this futuristic necropolis. Somewhere in this vast cavern, among the hundreds of thousands of other human containers, was Helen—my wife, my anchor to a world that had long since forgotten us.

My rigid body continued to be held to attention as the lights dimmed and went out, and the vast metal doors rolled shut. I'd been preserved like this for a century. But no one could know how much longer the capsule they'd encased me in could protect my physical being from nature's predilection for decay. How long it could safeguard the fragile body and hopeful dreams within.

So, Helen and I, along with the rest of this army of travelers in time, just as we had when we first entered this uncertain sleep, continued to wait... And wait......

Chapter 01 - Awake

When I died, I never expected to see the light everyone talked about—the one that was supposed to guide you gently to the other side, where loved ones awaited to embrace you. But there it was, a distant glow, like a solitary star in an endless void, pulling me toward it, toward an isolated pinprick of existence. It flickered softly, casting a warm, ethereal hue that contrasted sharply with the cold, dark expanse surrounding me, a beacon in the abyss.

As I drifted closer, two figures began to materialise from the fog that clouded my mind, their forms emerging like shadows from a dream. One loomed over me, a towering silhouette that seemed to absorb the light, while the other lingered in the background, a mere wisp of presence. My gaze shifted to the distant figure, and as its face sharpened into focus, a grimace twisted its features. It was a menacing familiarity that sent a chill down my spine, a fear I couldn't quite place. Just as I tried to grasp it, darkness enveloped me once more, swallowing me whole like a predator in the night.

When I next opened my eyes, the light was blinding, a harsh glare that pierced through my eyelids like a thousand needles. But at least the images were sharp. I found myself staring directly into the face of a bald Asian man—young, handsome, with deep brown eyes that held a shimmering softness. He wore a wide, toothy smile that seemed to radiate kindness, and though I could only see his lips moving at first, it was as if someone had cranked up the volume on my senses, and I began to hear his words.

"...try to stay calm. You're still slightly sedated. We're reviving you gradually."

My eyes struggled to adjust to the brightness, and I couldn't make sense of my surroundings. I was in a stark white room, sterile and clinical, with walls that seemed to pulse with an unsettling brightness. A panel on the far wall appeared darker than the rest, a shadowy anomaly that felt out of place. Was it a panel, or just a trick of the light? Or was my mind playing up on me.

The man continued speaking, but I couldn't focus. What was I being revived from? Then it hit me like a punch to the gut—a flash of Helen's face on her deathbed pierced through my thoughts, her frail form surrounded by the sterile smell of antiseptic and the muted beeping of machines.

'Aaagh!' I tried to scream, but my voice faltered, my limbs unresponsive. "AAAGH, AARRHH HH!" My body convulsed, panic surging as I felt pressure on my shoulders, a firm grip that anchored me to the present. I jerked from side to side, and the gaping chasm of darkness loomed again, pulling me in. As I fought against it, I heard the man's voice trailing off into the distance. "You're beginning to remember..." His words faded into nothingness, swallowed by the void.

Finally, I awoke again, desperate to stretch, but my arms and legs were still restrained, bound to the cot like a marionette. I could only move my head. I lifted it, and the man was still there, watching me with a kind expression that seemed to promise safety. Through his blue bodysuit, I could see the contours of a muscular torso, the fabric clinging to him like a second skin. He leaned closer, his voice low and soothing, a balm for my frayed nerves.

"I need to be sure you're calm enough to remove these restraints. They're for your safety. We didn't want you to panic or injure yourself."

The light still hurt my eyes, but a pleasant, familiar scent—like freshly ironed clothes—filled the air, wrapping around me like a comforting embrace. It was faint, but it soothed me, and I began to relax, the tension in my muscles slowly ebbing away.

"What can you remember?" he asked, his tone gentle yet probing. "It won't all come back at once, but do you know your name and why you're here?"

I let my head fall back, heavy with exhaustion. Yet, breathing in that comforting fragrance, I found the strength to speak. "Richard," I croaked, swallowing hard to clear my throat. "I died and was frozen. And now you've brought me back." Even as I said it, disbelief washed over me, a tidal wave of uncertainty. We had talked about this, but I never truly believed it would happen.

"'We,'—oh my god." I lifted my head again, desperation clawing at me like a wild animal. "Helen—is…is she here? Has she been revived?"

The man placed a calming hand on my shoulder, his grip firm yet reassuring. "Richard, you need to take things slowly. There's plenty of time, and so much to learn."

"But—"

"Right now," he interrupted, "I need to know if you're ready for me to take these restraints off. Once you're up and about, we can talk properly. Well?"

"Of course, I am." I nodded vigorously, determination surging through me like a jolt of electricity. "I prepared myself for this. I'm sure I'll be okay." As he began to unfasten the straps, I repeated, "Please, can you tell me if my wife Helen has been revived? That's all I care about."

"There'll be plenty of time for your questions later. You must understand that we need to take things slowly to avoid overwhelming you. All I can tell you right now is that very few records have survived the thousand years since you died. Which means," he paused, looking intently at me, "we're going to have to rely on your memories to fill in the gaps." He continued removing the restraints, his movements precise and careful.

"I'll take your wife's details before I go today and try to find out what I can."

A thousand years! The thought sent a shiver down my spine, a cold dread creeping deep into my body.

He stood beside the bed I was reclining on, which floated like a cot, higher than a dentist's chair, a surreal sensation that made my stomach churn. "My name is Ankit," he said, his voice steady. "I'll be your contact here until you're able to leave. That will be as soon as we're confident you can handle your new surroundings."

"What about the other man who was standing over there when I first came to?" I asked, nodding toward the opposite wall, where shadows danced ominously. "He didn't look very friendly."

A puzzled expression crossed Ankit's face, his brow furrowing slightly. "Richard, what's your last name?"

"Green," I whispered, gradually getting used to my faltering voice. As I spoke, I caught a flicker of concern cross his features before he masked it with a forced smile.

"Well, Richard Green," he said, his smile more genuine now, "I've been the only person here. Don't worry; it must have been a figment of your imagination. It's not unheard of for people to experience hallucinations just after being revived."

"Nothing would surprise me at the moment," I replied, rubbing my face with my freed hands, feeling the hardness of my smooth chin beneath my fingertips.

Now that my upper half was free, I shakily propped myself up on my elbows and assessed my body. I wore a blue bodysuit like Ankit's, and everything seemed in proportion to how I remembered, albeit slightly more muscular—a good thing, I thought. But without a mirror, I had no idea what my face looked like. All I knew was that I was as bald as Ankit, and that definitely wasn't a good thing.

Noticing Ankit's hairless head inches away, I blurted out the most ridiculous thing. "I thought they'd cured baldness." It seemed as good a conversation starter as any, a desperate attempt to lighten the heavy atmosphere.

Instead of a light-hearted response, he said casually, "I don't wear it in here. It's supposed to be a sterile environment, but is this what you mean?" He stepped back sharply, and I nearly knocked him over as I sat bolt upright, aghast at the sight before me. In seconds, a mass of pitch-black hair sprouted from his head, twisting and flowing like something alive, forming into a ponytail that swished around like a demented snake.

"That...that's got to be a joke," I stuttered, becoming very frightened.

He just smiled, a glint of mischief in his eyes. "As I told you, you've got a lot to learn. And anyway," he grinned, "this isn't my usual style."

Aghast at the transformation, I exclaimed, "My God, that's amazing! How are you able to do that?"

"I can't tell you at the moment; you'll begin to learn things soon enough. Right now, I need to ask you some more questions about what you remember."

For the next few hours, I recounted the story of my life with Helen, our hopes and fears about this strange new world I found myself in, the laughter we shared, and the tears we shed.

When we finished, I looked around the stark white room, the clinical walls closing in on me, and said, "So I actually made it. I am in the future."

"This is now, Richard. The future is a long way off. And it always will be..." He smiled as he said it.

I had to smile with him at the thought.

"And this is yours." He picked up a grey box from the floor and placed it on the table between us, the surface smooth and cool to the touch.

"What is it?" I asked, my curiosity piqued.

"It contains the possessions we found with you."

I reached out and placed a hand on the box, feeling the weight of my past pressing down on me. "Oh...thank you." I knew what was inside, the remnants of a life I thought I'd lost forever.

"I'll leave you to your memories for now, but I promise I'll find out anything I can about Helen," he said, his voice sincere.

"At least I should be grateful you're speaking English," I said, more to myself than him, a weak attempt at humour.

As he crossed the room, he glanced back. "No, I am not." Then he walked straight through the wall, disappearing into the unknown.

I considered his cryptic words for a moment before pulling the grey box toward me and lifting the lid. Inside, the two tiny green stones embedded in my wedding ring gleamed up at me, and I smiled as I slid it onto my finger. In that moment, I felt a connection to my past self, a sense of completeness that seemed to have been missing for so long. I picked up the broken pieces of the storage device that had once held precious images and recordings of my life. Aside from my wedding ring, only a few faded photos encased in plastic had survived, fragile echoes of a time long gone.

But then, as I sifted through the contents, I noticed something else at the bottom of the box—a small piece of plastic glowing dimly. When I picked it up, it began to unfold in my palm, brightening as five words scrolled across its surface: *"Be careful who you trust."*

What was this? A message for me? Who shouldn't I trust? Unease settled in my stomach, a heavy weight that threatened to crush me, especially after seeing that other man standing behind Ankit when I first awoke. I still wasn't convinced it was just my imagination. I stared at the message for a few more seconds before realising there was nothing I could do about it right now. I folded it back up and tucked it into a small pocket in my bodysuit, a secret I would carry with me.

Looking around the room, I realised I didn't know if it was night or day, and I still felt incredibly tired, the exhaustion creeping back in like a thick fog. So, I lay back on the sterile cot that was cradling me.

Before I knew it, I'd become so relaxed that I should have drifted into a restful sleep. But my mind wouldn't quit; it kept jumping back to Helen. Strangely, the one episode in our relationship that I'd purposely blocked out for so long rushed back to me, a vivid memory that clawed its way to the surface. As the light in the room slowly dimmed and faded away…

I began to recall the very last time I'd seen my wife.

Chapter 02 – First Goodbye

In a strange way, I'd been looking forward to her dying. It felt like the beginning of something new for us both. A release from the heavy chains of her recent suffering—and that made me feel incredibly guilty.

The meeting I'd just had with her doctor had left little room for doubt; neither Helen nor I had much longer to wait. We had both come to terms with the inevitability of her condition, which had nearly run its course. My guilty conscience whispered that I wanted it to be over, partly for my sake, but just as much for hers.

So, despite the aches and pains, my aging body was offering up, I'd leaned over the hospital bed and looked down into her familiar eyes. Even then, beneath the film of tears, they were still as clear and green as the emerald stones embedded in my wedding ring. Just as my own blue eyes mirrored the fresh, dazzling hue of the sapphires, which sparkled from the ring on her gnarled and frail hand.

I'd recalled how long it had been since we'd exchanged those rings. And how, in the intervening years, they'd served as a constant reminder of the bond between us. As early lovers, the contrasting colour of our eyes had been a frivolous topic of conversation. A gentle smile crossed my face as I remembered the private ditty we'd always shared. *"Blue and green should never be seen,"* one of us would begin, then go on to chant together, *"except in the eyes of R and H Green."*

Those bands of precious metal and stones, along with the love we had nurtured, had endured the years unscathed. Only our bodies had succumbed to the relentless march of time, leaving us in this moment— perhaps not at the end of our journey together, but certainly at the mercy of fate.

She was at the point where she could no longer speak. The little strength she had left was virtually beyond her control, as its focus was drawn to the pain, making its last push to overcome her failing body. Although she was able to hear my words of comfort, over the humming of the vigilant machines that stood guard around her bed, what little communication she had with me had dwindled to mere sight and touch. And even as those last faculties begun to ebb away, her eyes clung to me. Filling with tears, as if knowing they'd soon be still.

Yet they made a last effort to respond to what she called my 'charming smile,' which she'd said altered my whole face and never failed to lift her spirits.

Responding to her desperate effort to communicate I slowly mouthed the words I'd said countless times. "I love you, Helen." Then moving closer still I whispered, "I'll wake you in the future."

We'd often speculated about this moment, wondering if everyone becomes aware when death is near, if the finality of it eventually gains acceptance in the rejecting consciousness. Or was it just a physical process? When the last dregs of energy seep away, and there's nothing left to fight with? When the effort to remain in this world becomes too great, and the fear of the unknown becomes just a little more acceptable? This had certainly been our experience, as well as that of others we had known who had faced the dying. They spoke of feeling powerless in the presence of the inevitable, their anger directed at Time and its relentless march into the past, taking their loved ones with it into the fading realms of distant memories.

Whatever the truth, that time had arrived for Helen. The connection we shared through our eyes felt almost telepathic, an understanding passing between us. She knew... I knew... It was finally here.

A strained smile flickered across her face, then slowly faded. Despite her struggle to maintain eye contact, her gaze drifted, as if something beyond my shoulders was calling her. The warmth of her hands slipped away from mine, and in that moment, Death claimed another victory, chasing the final flicker of life from her sparkling eyes. A solitary tear escaped, falling onto the white cotton pillow, forming a tiny wet circle —a full stop at the end of her story. Or perhaps, if fate allowed, just the end of the first chapter.

We'd been alone in the small, quiet room of the Institute, just as we had planned. Suddenly, an overwhelming loneliness enveloped me, the likes of which I'd never felt before. It encouraged the tears that began to moisten my cheeks, and I lost the battle to control my emotions. With my forehead pressed against our entwined fingers, I surrendered to the sobs that wracked my shoulders, warm tears bursting free from where I'd stoically kept them locked away.

After a few moments, a strange calm washed over me. With great effort, I raised my head, sniffed back my tears, and shook my shoulders, regaining some semblance of control. Taking a deep breath, I spoke softly, as if she could still hear me. "Yeah, I know, I promised I wouldn't cry. I'll call them in now." With that, I leaned over and pressed the red call button on the wall above her bed.

It felt like an out-of-body experience, watching everything unfold through a milky lens. Within seconds, the room filled with people in green surgical gowns. They moved with practiced efficiency, removing the tubes from my wife and unplugging the wires that connected her to the wall. I knew they had to act quickly to give her the best chance possible, and this was obviously a well-rehearsed routine, yet it felt as if time had warped— everything happened both in slow motion and at super speed. Before I knew it, they were gone, and I found myself alone in the room, sitting in the same chair where just moments ago, I'd been speaking to my wife. I stared at the empty space where her bed had been, feeling as if Time had swooped down, snatched Helen from me, and marched inexorably on.

Neither of us had ever been religious. I'd reluctantly attended Midnight Mass on Christmas Eve because she thought it romantic, but our beliefs excluded any acknowledgment of an omnipotent intelligence overseeing our lives. Yet, in this moment of despair, I set aside my disbelief. I pressed my palms together and prayed. "Please God," I murmured, bowing my face down to my hands as if that would strengthen my plea, "let it work."

I knew what I was doing was futile. All I could do was cling to hope, hang on to it, and keep the faith—not the religious kind—that her journey would be successful. Her mind was now shut down, and when, or if, it awoke, only seconds would have passed for her. She would arrive at her destination in what would feel like the blink of an eye. But for me, I knew it would take the rest of my life—and a whole lot of luck—if I was ever going to join her.

And when my time finally arrived, I'd been lucky enough to join her on the journey, one that would hopefully lead us to a peaceful and civilised future.

Now all I had to do - was find her.

Chapter 03 – A Stranger Visits

The room was bathed in that eerie half-light that accompanied early morning. That pervasive radiance which promised the sun was just over the horizon and the day was on its way. As the light gradually increased, so did my awareness; slowly returning to me the realisation of my present situation.

Each morning, this artificial dawn had been my alarm, coaxing me awake before Ankit arrived. But today, before I could fully grasp my surroundings, I was jolted by the sound of footsteps approaching. My heart raced as I sat up, startled, my mind racing with the thought that I'd overslept and Ankit was already here. But as I blinked into the dimness, I saw a figure moving toward me, and recognition hit me like a cold wave. It was the man I'd glimpsed standing behind Ankit, a shadowy presence that had lingered in my mind. *So, I hadn't been imagining things after all!*

In those fleeting seconds of recognition, I took in his features. He was Asian, like Ankit, but taller and less defined, perhaps in his twenties. His hair, dark and glossy, fell in a way that felt almost traditional, a stark contrast to Ankit's wild, gravity-defying style. Yet, there was something unsettling about him as he approached, an aura of menace that sent a shiver down my spine.

Instinctively, I jerked back, my body reacting defensively as I swung my legs off the cot. But in my haste, I lost my balance and tumbled backward onto the floor with a loud thud, a strange sense of impending doom washing over me. As I scrambled to get up, the man raised his arm, a gesture meant to halt my movements. "Don't be concerned..." he began, his voice sharp and clipped. But before he could finish, Ankit's voice boomed from the doorway, slicing through the tension like a knife.

"Ramoon! What are you doing here?"

I watched as surprise flickered across the man's face, his eyes darting nervously. In a swift motion, he shoved something into the pocket of his cover-all, a furtive action that only deepened my unease. Then, with a smile that didn't quite reach his eyes, he turned to Ankit. "I'm sorry. I didn't realise this man hadn't begun his induction. I just wanted to ask some questions for my journal." Before Ankit could respond, Ramoon rushed toward the exit, glancing back over his shoulder as he murmured, "I'll check with you again later."

Ankit's gaze followed him, a mix of alarm and concern flickering across his features. I wanted to tell him that this was the man I'd seen standing behind him when I first regained consciousness, to share the irrational fear that had gripped me in that moment. But I hesitated, unsure of who I could trust in this strange new world.

I felt the piece of plastic in my pocket, its message echoing in my mind: *Be careful who you trust.* Vulnerability washed over me, and I chose silence, not wanting to complicate things further.

Despite the unsettling encounter, my thoughts were consumed by Helen. I needed to know if Ankit had discovered anything, as he'd promised. "What about Helen? Have you managed to find out anything yet?" I asked, my voice tinged with urgency. The apologetic look that crossed his face told me all I needed to know.

He gestured toward the empty wall, and to my astonishment, it began to morph as we approached. The surface bulged and shifted, like a living organism responding to an unspoken command, forming two easy chairs and a knee-high table between them. There were no seams or joints, just a seamless transition from wall to furniture, as if the room itself was alive.

"I've been granted permission to share some knowledge with you before you interact with the information system," Ankit explained, his tone serious. "As I mentioned before, Richard, over a thousand years have passed since you were preserved. For reasons unknown to us, everyone like you was stored deep underground on the far side of the Moon. It's only in the last hundred years that we've begun to revive those most suitable."

"All of these Cryogens, as they've become known, have integrated and settled into our various societies."

I listened, my heart heavy. "But what does this have to do with Helen?" I pressed, desperation creeping into my voice.

"Much of the data stored with the Cryogens has deteriorated beyond retrieval," he continued, his expression grave. "We've had to rely on people's memories for a lot of information. Only some of the possessions stored in their containers have survived."

I glanced down at my wedding ring, its familiar weight a bittersweet reminder of what I'd lost. "And Helen?" I asked, my voice barely above a whisper.

"In some cases, the Cryogen tanks themselves have been breached, leaving the bodies inside lost forever," he said, a sigh escaping his lips. "Our current records contain no successful revival of a Helen Green."

My heart plummeted at his words, the weight of despair settling heavily in my chest. I barely registered the rest of his explanation. "She could have been among the very first Cryogens to be revived, but if not, and her container remains intact, she could still be one of the many thousands awaiting revival. Don't worry, Richard; it doesn't mean you've lost Helen for good. After your induction, you can put yourself forward to be involved in the Cryogen work. That way, you can ensure you're there if she does get revived in the future."

"So, what do I do now?" I asked, my voice flat, the urgency draining away.

"Well, I've gained permission for your formal induction to start tomorrow. It'll be the beginning of the process to get you out of here and mixing with others. I'm sure you'll appreciate a bit more freedom and some company. But for now, you should get some sleep; you're still recovering, remember."

"I am not sure I'll sleep, Ankit. I can't stop thinking about Helen. If I don't find out what's happened to her soon, I'm going to go mad." I realised I was fidgeting, rubbing my knees anxiously, and Ankit was watching me intently, concern etched on his face.

I managed a smile as he prepared to leave, but it faded as I lay back on my cot, surrendering to the encroaching darkness. My mind drifted with the fading light, haunted by thoughts of the dangers that lay ahead.

And for that matter. What part did that mysterious man called Ramoon, play in it?

Chapter 04 – Which Society

It was my first night of uninterrupted sleep since being revived, a surprising twist given the chaos swirling in my mind. Yet, I wasn't complaining. The tranquillity wrapped around me like a warm blanket, leaving me feeling relaxed and calm—at least until Ankit arrived, his presence shattering the fragile peace I'd found.

"Come on, it's time to go," he said, his voice echoing slightly in the sterile room. I hesitated, and all my enthusiasm dwindled into a ball of uncertainty. And together, with the ball of nerves that had already made its home deep in the pit of my stomach, they bounced around and made me feel decidedly sick. The thought of stepping through that door filled me with dread; I couldn't shake the feeling that I might walk straight into a solid wall. But I knew that door represented more than just an exit—it was freedom, the first major step into my new life, and the beginning of my journey to find Helen.

Ankit stood just outside, his disembodied arm extending into the room, beckoning me to follow. "Don't worry," he assured me, his face reappearing through the wall. "Just pretend there's nothing here and follow me."

I felt nothing physically as I passed through the threshold, but emotionally, I felt like a coward for having to close my eyes. It was my first time, after all. I told myself it was bound to get easier.

As I opened my eyes, I found myself in a long, enclosed corridor, its smooth, glowing walls stretching endlessly in both directions. The bright finish was almost blinding, and I was surprised to see no visible exits—no sign of the doorway I'd just come through. It was as if I'd stepped into a surreal dreamscape, where reality was distorted and disorienting.

"Crikey, Ankit," I exclaimed, my voice echoing in the silence. "If all the doors in this place are like that one, I'm going to get really confused. How do you know where you're going?"

He tapped the side of his head with a grin. "It's all in here, Richard. Don't worry."

Halfway down the corridor, Ankit approached the wall and touched it at shoulder height. To my astonishment, the section immediately lost its solidity, becoming transparent as if it had vanished under his touch. Through the shimmering surface, I caught a glimpse of a mirror image of the corridor we were in, and then the low hum of an electric motor filled the air, bringing movement within it. I realised we were looking into some kind of tunnel, and my heart raced with excitement. *We must be standing on the platform of a futuristic tube system,* I thought.

My assumption was confirmed moments later when a cobalt blue, windowless shuttle glided past, filling the entire area of the tunnel. Its surface was flawlessly smooth, devoid of any imperfections. As it obscured the transparent section of the wall, I found myself questioning whether it was still moving at all.

Ankit's gaze shifted to another section of the wall, and he seemed to see something I couldn't. "Just follow me as you did before," he instructed, and then he disappeared through the wall.

The compartment we entered was empty, and without waiting for Ankit's guidance, I sank into one of the moulded seats attached to the walls. It was as white as everything else in this strange place, and I felt it adjust to my shape as I sat down. A shiver ran down my spine as I tried to dismiss the sensation of something alive groping my backside. Just one more thing to get used to, I thought.

I sat there, expecting the shuttle to lurch into motion, but it remained still. Doubts crept in, and I began to wonder if there was a problem, if we would have to walk to our destination instead. My mind raced with questions about what this 'induction' would entail. The thought of being intimately examined by an array of instruments sent a chill down my spine.

"Where is this information centre, anyway?" I asked, trying to mask my anxiety.

"It's on the edge of the city, about a hundred miles away."

"Wow, that's a big city. While we're on-route could you tell me exactly what to expect when we get there?"

"No," he replied sharply, catching me off guard. But as I opened my mouth to respond, Ankit smiled and raised a finger to silence me. "Because we've already arrived."

As we disembarked, I looked around in amazement. "I couldn't even tell we were moving," I whispered to no one in particular.

I attempted to calculate the speed we must have been traveling at, but my mind was too preoccupied with the impending experience to focus. Ankit must have sensed my nervousness because he turned to me, his expression reassuring. "I know you're worried about what you're about to encounter, Richard. It's only natural to feel a measure of trepidation. But you have nothing to fear, I assure you." I appreciated his words, but I wasn't sure they helped.

We passed through several more doorways, and to my relief, it did get easier. We even used a vertical version of the shuttle, which Ankit informed me had taken us one hundred levels up.

"I see why you smiled when I remarked on the size of this city. It's unbelievable. Are we underground, or are we in a super skyscraper?" I asked, my curiosity piqued.

"You'll find out soon enough," he replied, his tone teasingly vague.

At least I was going to get some answers soon. Any more of his procrastination would drive me mad. Not that I believed that could happen—not with the state of my new body. I felt healthier than I'd ever been, leaner and more muscular than I'd ever imagined. I had no imperfections that I was aware of; everything seemed to be in peak condition, and I felt alive—more alive than I ever had.

Finally, we entered a large room, at the centre of which stood a wooden oval table, about six feet across at its widest point, surrounded by matching high-backed moulded chairs. It resembled one of the posh boardrooms from my past life, and I was pleasantly surprised to see some colour amidst the sterile white.

As I looked closer, I noticed the table emitted a strange inner glow, which intensified as I approached. It was disconcerting, and Ankit seemed to sense my unease. "It serves as an interface to the information system. You'll see. Take a seat."

Once again, I felt the intimate—and slightly uncomfortable—movement of the chair as it adjusted to my form. Ankit settled in the chair beside me, and I watched as the top of the table began to move forward, almost touching us. It grew larger in our direction, and instinctively, I raised my arms as it contacted my midsection. The table formed around me, merging with the chair, which wrapped around my legs. As I became completely ensnared by this living furniture, I glanced over at Ankit for assurance.

"This is normal, don't worry, Richard. Although you can't feel it, the information system has bonded with your body and has already made connections with your brain."

"That's comforting," I replied meekly, trying unsuccessfully to sense anything moving inside me.

One by one, all my sensations ebbed away, leaving only an unsettling wave of nausea to wash over me. Then, just as that too subsided, my mind drifted into a dreamlike state, where colours and shapes fought to coalesce into meaningful thoughts. But even those clouds of unformed reality flickered and died. Just when I thought I would lose my grasp on reality completely, I became self-aware again, standing upright in pitch blackness.

Normally, I wouldn't have paid much attention to the dark, but now it felt as if it were closing in on me, wrapping me in its bitter cold embrace. Before it could fully envelop me, shadows began to form in the distance.

Gradually, the shadows morphed into windows, cut into the fabric of the darkness before me. Through these windows, images began to tune into focus, revealing a new world around me—humanity spanning the solar system. An inhabited Moon, a terraformed Mars, and a population now numbering in the hundreds of billions.

Like the resurrected memories of an amnesiac, knowledge flooded back to me, supported by the images through these strange dimensional windows. The exploitation of the solar system had reached spectacular heights, a testament to the superior intelligence of advanced technology, granting humanity the means to exploit all the resources within its reach.

The majority of the human race no longer supported the creation of wealth, nor were they influenced by those holding power. These two most corrupting constructs had been handed over to the information system, which now managed them. Power and wealth no longer shaped human society as they once had.

I observed a multi-society civilisation, diverse groupings on different continents and planets, where people lived content and happy within the laws of their particular societies. There were societies of different religions, naturists, separate sexes, modified humans, vegetarians —even a society where it was acceptable to insult and abuse others, where absolutely no law applied. That particular setup seemed like anarchy to me, and I wondered who would choose to live there.

Surrounding and binding all these diverse groups was the largest society, known as *Open Society*. Here, everyone who entered conformed to common rules of behaviour regarding privacy, modesty, and decency, leaving behind the extreme practices of their particular societies while communing with others.

I thought all of this sounded like something Helen would have dreamed up. Surely, the humanity I knew could never have been this selfless—at least not on such a grand scale.

Once again, I saw images of different habitats through the floating windows. There were cities hundreds of miles wide, buried deep underground. A new city, destined to be the largest on Earth, was being constructed beneath the Pacific Ocean. I wondered where all the people would come from to fill them.

In my first life, I'd once heard—though I wasn't sure how true it was—that if all the humans on Earth stood shoulder to shoulder, they would easily fit on the island of Corsica. I doubted that was true now. But if it ever was, I wondered what kind of numbers would be needed to populate these incredible cities.

I used to enjoy watching TV programs about large construction projects, but these images surpassed anything I'd ever seen.

Slowly, the scenes in the floating windows began to fade, retreating into the fog, signalling the end of the session. Not everything had come to me as clearly as I'd hoped, but somehow, I knew the basic information I'd just received was merely an introduction to this new time.

I couldn't help but think about how much Helen would love this life. As her name crossed my mind, I felt the darkness creeping back into my consciousness. But it retreated, along with the shadows surrounding me. As my sensations returned, I found myself back in the room, facing a smiling Ankit.

"I think it's amazing the way you organize your societies," I said, my voice filled with awe. "It's clearly a preferred way of living, promoted by most of your communities. What a pity we had to wait for machines to perfect it."

Ankit looked down, a shadow of shame crossing his features and said almost apologetically "Yes, it's a pity you didn't adopt it earlier."

His words struck me, but I was too busy grappling with the anxiety building within me about what might have happened to Helen. As I lay down to sleep, I tried to convince myself that now that I'd learned about the world around me, my journey was about to begin in earnest.

Yet, once again, I found myself unable to sleep. No matter how hard I tried, I couldn't connect with the darkness that had kept me company for so many years. Sitting up, I swung my legs out of the cot and onto the floor. Leaning forward, I rested my elbows on my legs, placed my chin on my thumbs, and pressed my face into my palms, breathing deeply into my cupped hands.

In an attempt to distract my mind from the horrible outcomes that kept running through it, I searched my memories, fortified by my previous life's experiences. I used them to open my own window through time, seeking refuge in a safer time when Helen and I were both young. It was there that I sought solace for the night.

To the very beginning of our story.

Chapter 05 - School

Helen had only been twelve when her father's government job uprooted them from their peaceful townhouse in rural Berkshire and plopped them close to us in the bustling city of Nottingham. Harold Croft, her father, had made the decision that would change everything for their family. Helen said her mother's face fell when she heard the news and her three older brothers grumbled and complained. But eventually, they settled into a comfortable four-bedroom detached house on the outskirts of the city, a far cry from the idyllic countryside they'd left behind.

Just a few miles away, a council estate sprawled out, where David Green, his wife Jean, their two daughters, and I— their son— lived in a rundown semi-detached house. "Renting" was a generous term; it implied my parents were paying for our home, but in reality, it was the state that paid the local council in the form of benefits. The flaking paint on its metal framed windows, and unkempt and overgrown garden it sat in, displayed a neglect that was typical of many houses that didn't have a tenant who owned them.

The stark contrast between our two neighbourhoods reflected the different expectations and aspirations of their inhabitants. Yet, both estates fell within the catchment area of the same state school, a melting pot for children whose families couldn't afford private education. It was the school that Helen and I attended throughout our teenage years, and for most of that time, I was blissfully unaware of her existence, let alone the quiet strength that lay beneath her surface.

Back then, Helen's demeanour was one of shyness, a quiet reflection of her inner world. She rarely spoke unless absolutely necessary, avoiding the spotlight like it was a scorching sun. These qualities matured her beyond her natural age and her unfashionable dresses that clung to her as if knowing they were coming to the end of their useful lives, re-enforced the image. In fact, they were so bad that some kids joked that they belonged to her mum or even her grandma. But Helen, with her young shoulders bearing the weight of maturity, shrugged off their jibes with an ease that belied her age.

Her shoulder-length brown hair framed her plain features, and her quiet, mouse-like ways sent a clear message: "Please leave me alone." If she was trying to blend into the background, she was succeeding. She kept to herself, never uttering a word more than necessary, and faded effortlessly into the throng of other "Plain Janes" around her. Little did anyone know the remarkable woman she would eventually become.

In stark contrast, my height and Mediterranean good looks had earned me a spot among the top boys in school, a group I'd foolishly convinced myself was the in-crowd. Only later would I realise they were just a bunch of bullies. I was at that stage in life where the need to impress and gain respect was paramount, whether it was genuine or not. We wore our bravado like a badge of honour, feeding the insatiable need of fathers, brothers, or uncles who sought vicarious validation through us.

Like many others, I jockeyed for the position of leader within our group. But in our world, leadership was dictated by aggression, dominance, and sheer size. Jason Wentworth had all those qualities in spades. He was massive, brutal, and undeniably good-looking, which only added to his arrogance, especially around girls. The gap in his front teeth—one lost in a fight with a rival gang—was the only flaw I could cling to, a small comfort in my envy.

Despite my reservations, I revelled in the benefits of being part of the gang. I felt a sense of belonging that was sorely lacking at home. The adoration from classmates, both girls and boys, filled a void, even if it was rooted in admiration, deference, or, as I suspected, outright fear.

And the rules of our little crew were as childish and cruel as you'd expect from teenagers straddling the line between childhood and adulthood. You stood up for each other, no matter what, and you never brought shame upon the gang. The consequences of breaking those rules were too grim to contemplate. At least I didn't want to think too much about them having observed them myself. Because, in addition to being thrown out of the gang and ostracised, which in itself brought untold shame, some very nasty things could happen to you involving Jason's dad's razor and a tin of black boot polish.

I still remember the day John Spear made a joke about Jason's mother to the wrong person. The humiliation that followed was compounded by the laughter of Jason's two shrieking sisters. It was a brutal reminder of Jason's sadistic side, and I learned quickly to keep my distance from it.

No, during those years, Helen might as well have been living in a different universe. It was amusing, really, considering how intertwined our destinies would eventually become.

It wasn't until our final year at school, when the girls began to fill out and the boys started to take notice, that I truly saw her. Until then, our interactions had been nothing more than posturing, practice for the real thing we all eagerly anticipated.

My best friend had pointed Helen out to me a year earlier, claiming she had "potential." I'd kept an eye on her since then, my youthful ego piqued by her utter disinterest in me.

Questions began to swirl in my mind about what I was truly gaining from being part of the gang. I had no independence, shackled by petty rules, and many of my actions were beginning to weigh heavily on my conscience. I was growing weary of it all, and it struck me as a shame that my first intimate experience hadn't been with someone special like Helen.

But at least I had found some success with girls, unlike my best friend Pete, a fellow gang member, who was a bit of a "jack the lad." He loved playing tricks on anyone he could. Academically bright, he often seemed to lack common sense, his big mouth and flaming ginger hair preventing him from engaging his brain. He had a knack for saying the wrong thing at the worst possible moment.

I often chuckled at the memory of him in class with Miss Clarkson, our rotund French teacher. As she bent over her desk to pick up a board rubber, Pete blurted out that it looked "just like two whales mating." The entire class erupted in laughter, but I could see the embarrassment wash over him. I remember thinking that if that was how he related to women, he was destined for a lonely life.

So that was Pete, he was a tall and awkward sort of boy and always had problems relating to the opposite sex. And if his lack of success in that area was one of the reasons he'd wanted to be part of the gang in the first place, it hadn't seemed to have done him any favours. Up to then, no one had ever actually seen him with a girl.

As I reached the end of my school days, relief washed over me. I was finally escaping the life I'd fallen into. The night of the last term disco approached, and I walked toward the old school hall, anxiety bubbling within me. It wasn't fear of the event itself but the realisation that I was about to carve my own path in life.

The electro-pop of the nineteen eighties boomed from the speakers, and the rotating glitter ball cast a kaleidoscope of colours across the room, making the heavy red drapes seem alive. Pete and I navigated through the throng of dancing bodies toward the stage, where soft drinks were being sold from an old trestle table. My digital watch blinked 7:45, the red numbers glowing like a countdown to something significant.

Then I saw her. Helen stood in the corner, leaning casually against the black Yamaha piano, a small group of friends gathered around her like courtiers attending a queen. As we approached, Pete pointed in their direction, joking, "I think I'm destined for one of that lot over there." His voice held a hint of hope as he asked, "Do you think any of them will turn into Derry Abby?"

'I wouldn't think so,' I replied, my gaze fixed on Helen. My eyes weren't focusing on anyone other than the standing girl. Then, perhaps subconsciously, the music, along with the continued conversation from Pete, seemed to fade into the distance, as I leaned against the stage looking directly across at Helen.

It was as if I was seeing her for the first time. Her natural beauty, untouched by makeup, radiated a confidence that drew me in. It wouldn't be long before the changes in her body, obvious even now, would draw a lot of attention from the opposite sex. Was I finally realising I could feel something deeper than mere lust? After all, she wasn't the type I usually went for.

I barely registered Pete's comments about scouting for *"real talent."* I was lost in the moment, battling the urge to approach her and to fight the mad compulsion to go and talk to her. I felt like I was under some kind of spell that held me captive.

Just as the reasons for approaching her started to outweigh the reasons that were preventing me Jason Wentworth's unmistakable drawl sent a shiver down my spine. "Don't even think about it, Richard. They're not in our league." He draped an arm around my shoulder, steering me away from the corner. "You won't get anything out of them. I've got some great girls lined up for us tonight. This way, my man." In that moment, all the courage I'd built up drained away, and I realised I was just another victim of this overbearing bully.

As we walked towards the entrance, I strained to take one last look over my shoulder at Helen. Who at that very moment had turned her head in my direction and smiled.

And somewhere during this recollection of a distant past, my new body had reluctantly relaxed and offered up a doorway, into the sleep I so desperately needed.

Chapter 06 – Things That Go Bump

But my journey into that elusive darkness was not destined to last. As I drifted in and out of sleep, a distant noise began to weave its way into my consciousness. Was it a fragment of a dream waiting to unfold, or was it something far more sinister, clawing its way into my reality.

Then the sound grew louder, a rhythmic *scratch, tap, scratch*, and I stirred from my slumber, propping myself up on my elbows. What was that? I swung my legs over the edge of my cot, the cold floor sending a shiver up my spine, and tilted my head, straining to hear more clearly. It wasn't a figment of my imagination; it was real, tangible, lurking just beyond the threshold of my door. But what—or who—was on the other side? My heart raced, a wild drumbeat echoing in my ears, as I felt the weight of dread settle over me.

With a resolve I didn't quite understand, I lowered myself onto my hands and knees, creeping toward the doorway like a thief in the night. The noise came again, *scratch, tap, scratch, TAP*! Someone—or something—was definitely there. Then, without warning, a thunderous BANG, BANG, BANG! reverberated through the room, sending a jolt of terror coursing through my veins.

"HELLO!" I shouted, the word bursting from my lips with a force that startled even me. My voice echoed in the silence that followed, and I quickly added, almost in a whisper, "Is that you, Ankit?'

The noise stopped abruptly, plunging the room into an oppressive silence. A chilling sense of isolation wrapped around me like a suffocating shroud, and I felt a cold shiver race down my spine. I crawled backward toward my cot, each movement slow and deliberate, as if I were caught in a nightmarish rewind. Reluctantly, I closed my eyes, desperate to escape the reality that had become so unsettling.

My mind was a chaotic whirlpool, swirling with the events of the past few days. I couldn't shake the feeling that the noise at the door was somehow connected to the stranger who had come to visit me. Ramoon. The very thought of him sent a fresh wave of unease crashing over me. The more I pondered his presence, the more sinister he appeared, a shadow lurking just beyond the edges of my awareness.

As my thoughts began to slow, detaching from reason, drowsiness pulled me deeper into the murky waters of half-dreams. I found myself being revived once more, but this time, my body felt alien, foreign. I opened my eyes to a bizarre scene: a crowd of people surrounded me, their faces twisted in laughter, pointing and jeering as if I were the punchline of a cruel joke. Why were they laughing? Panic surged within me, and I glanced down, bracing for the horror of discovering I was naked in public.

But instead of my own body, I saw the form of a monkey, dressed in ludicrous clothing, performing an absurd Irish jig! At my feet lay another monkey, lifeless and grotesque, and grafted onto its body the horrifying sight of Helen's lifeless head.

As I fell further into the full horror of my worst nightmare, my subconscious mind screamed.

Chapter 07 – Where's My Robot

"So, you're telling me, I still can't interact with other people?" I couldn't wrap my mind around the absurdity of it all. When Ankit had arrived that morning, I'd clung to the hope that I would finally escape the stifling confines of the white room. Instead, he stood before me, delivering the crushing news that my induction had only just begun.

I let out a heavy sigh, a sound of resignation that echoed in the sterile space around us. There was no point in protesting; I knew that. "Then at least let me have a robot to keep me company. You must have some of those lying around. You could program it not to reveal anything you don't want it to, so I'd at least have some company. Because, if I have to stay here much longer, Ankit, I swear I'm going to lose my mind."

"If by robot you mean an android—something that looks human," he replied, as I nodded my head, "there are no such things."

"What!" I exclaimed, disbelief flooding my veins. "You've got to be joking. You still haven't mastered that yet?" I recalled the fervent speculation and eager anticipation of my time, when everyone knew that human-like robots were just around the corner. I'd even seen some rudimentary models created by different governments and even private companies. Why weren't they everywhere?

"It's not that we couldn't create them, Richard." He continued, "Robots exist all over this environment. They're built for specific tasks, and those tasks dictate their shape. There's just no need for a human-shaped robot."

"But..." I began, my mind racing with a list of reasons why an android would be invaluable. But before I could unleash my thoughts, Ankit cut me off.

'Look, Richard, before you tell me you can think of plenty of reasons to create a robot in the image of a human, you need to analyse and question those reasons carefully. Take it from me there are fundamental ethical arguments surrounding the creation of something that resembles a human being, only to make it subservient.'

I frowned, feeling the weight of his words. "Oh, but I was—'

"And as for helping the less fortunate—the elderly and disabled—there are no such people in our societies. The need to assist those individuals back in your time speaks volumes about the failings of your society, and I doubt you want to argue with me about that." I shut up.

But Ankit continued, "And before you tell me that they'd provide companionship, let's refer to your own internet. Even in your day, you were making significant strides in social networks. Most people with access to your technology could find like-minded individuals to interact with, no matter how obscure their interests. We have far superior ways of connecting now—ones you'll master like the rest of us. Trust me, Richard; no one alive today is lonely."

I narrowed my eyes staring at the ground. 'I am Ankit.'

He offered a sympathetic smile, but it felt like a hollow gesture. "That's because you're missing Helen, Richard, and you're stuck here, as you put it. But this isn't the norm; it's only temporary. I admit this would probably be torture for someone from this time, but people like you should be capable of spending some time alone.'

His words deflated me like a punctured balloon. "I know that, Ankit, but you have to remember that I've only just discovered I'm in an underground world—buried deep beneath the surface of the planet.'

I realised there was no point in continuing this conversation. I'd get nowhere, even if I argued all day. So, I decided to yield for now and shifted the topic to the strange noises I'd heard at the door the previous night.

'It was probably someone forgetting where they were going," he said dismissively. His tone surprised me, especially considering how he'd reacted to Ramoon's intrusion. But the look in his eyes told a different story. Something was off; he'd lost his usual cheerful demeanour, replaced by an unsettling gloom. He definitely seemed depressed in some way. *Perhaps everyone has off days*. I thought. Whatever the reason, I wasn't in the mood to pry, so for now I let it pass.

As we travelled back to the information centre, a row of windows suddenly appeared along one wall of the shuttle. It must have stopped because when I looked out, I was met with an astonishing sight: we were in an enclosed transparent bridge spanning a vast open area. For all intents and purposes, we hovered above a bustling town centre. Had we come this way before, or were we redirected for some reason?

Peering down into the open space, I saw patches of greenery—small trees and bushes interspersed with clusters of chairs and tables. People sat outside cafes and bars, sipping drinks and enjoying meals. I noticed some of them carrying what looked like shopping bags. I couldn't make out their faces, but the overwhelming majority appeared to be Asian.

Ankit had mentioned we were in an underground city called India Prime. So, we must be beneath India, I thought, my mind racing to absorb the implications.

It was difficult to gauge the size of this place as everything was enclosed. Our 'tube' hovered between the ground and an all-encompassing illuminated ceiling. Patches of mist floated above us, creating a convincing illusion of clouds in a summer sky. Just as I was about to ask Ankit why we'd stopped, he spoke.

"Something for you to look forward to Richard." He said from behind me.

But I didn't respond; my attention was captured by a large screen dominating the central area to one side of the square. It had drawn a crowd, and I could see people gathering around it, their faces lit by the glow of the broadcast. The broadcast showing on the screen was that of a demonstration, and the image focused on a man holding a banner. It read, *"Don't let them kill us all off – protect the humans."*

Ankit followed my gaze as I lifted my arm to point out of the window. "I would have thought we'd be beyond demonstrating by now."

But before he could reply, the images outside the window blurred, as if someone had splashed water sideways onto a wet painting. I realised the train had accelerated to its normal speed.

As the windows disappeared, Ankit sighed. "I'm afraid there's always going to be a disruptive element in any free society. Just like in your day, we have ours."

"Yes, but what was all that about—protect the humans? What do we need protection from?"

"That was Jon Numan, the leader of a group of protesters who suffer from paranoid delusions. But don't worry about it right now, Richard. You have more important things to learn before you need to concern yourself with any of that."

His tone made it clear: *don't ask me about this again because you won't get any answers.*

Resigned to the fact that I had little control over the flow of knowledge I was receiving, I nodded, my mind swirling with questions. I hoped today would reveal more about the remarkable achievements I'd glimpsed the day before—the awe-inspiring construction of cities built by the descendants of my time.

But I'd only just begun to explore this new world. I was blissfully unaware that what I'd discovered so far would pale into insignificance compared to the revelations that were just around the corner.

Chapter 08 – The Goldilocks Zone

As I stepped into the *table room*, as I was now beginning to think of it, a familiar sense of anticipation washed over me. I settled into the same chair I'd occupied before, and soon, a warm, dreamlike haze enveloped me, pulling me into its depths. This time, instead of merely gazing through hovering windows, I felt as if I were suspended in the vastness of space, floating effortlessly, my gaze fixed on the Earth below. It was as if I were on the brink of uncovering the secrets of this strange new world I'd stumbled into.

One of many it seemed because my position changed so that I could now see a large group of Earth-like planets. Each with their own, dusty grey moon, fashioned to act like the original. Global sized pacemakers, sustaining the ebb and flow of the life-giving oceans on the planets beneath them.

But this was just the beginning. My perspective panned out to reveal more of the solar system, and suddenly, I was seeing all of these Earth-like planets, circling the Sun like a string of living pearls. The sight was mesmerising, the technology providing these views was incredible. Like a celestial version of *Google Earth*, but far more immersive, I thought. It really did feel like I was floating in space, *perhaps this was the latest version*?

I was captivated by the images flashing before me, the speed at which I moved through these scenes leaving me breathless. A disembodied voice provided an audio commentary, but it faded into the background, a mere whisper against the vivid tapestry of visuals. I had no control over what I was witnessing; it was as if the system was curating my experience, revealing only what it deemed necessary. Yet, the boy in me couldn't help but yearn for the day I could explore this universe on my own terms.

Then without warning, everything spun around me, a dizzying whirl that sent my senses reeling. Just as quickly, it subsided, and I found myself being drawn away from the Sun, past the inner planets and beyond Jupiter. I ventured further out, where Saturn and Uranus should have been, but instead, I was met with a sight that stole my breath away.

Neptune hovered before me, a shell of its former self. Its ethereal rings had vanished, and the once-vibrant blue of its atmosphere had morphed into a rancid green, a testament to its depleted mass. Its eight major satellites were gone, replaced by a grotesque collection of moon-sized machines, their monstrous tentacles reaching deep into what remained of the planet's atmosphere. Like celestial vampires, they were siphoning away its life force, and disgorging it sunward, presumably to aid in the creation of new Earths. I couldn't shake the thought that these machines would deliver the same fate to Neptune as they obviously had to its long-lost moons.

I traced the trail of material across space as it joined that being transported from the Kyper Belt and elsewhere in the outer solar system. Like a planet-wide meteor storm leading back toward the Sun and meticulously controlled by an army of shepherding spacecraft.

As I returned to the life-sustaining embrace of the Sun, I watched in awe as the material was manoeuvred to collide at a predetermined point, creating a gravity well that would serve as a launchpad for future celestial construction. The laws of physics would do the heavy lifting, while advanced macro and nano-machinery would accelerate the development of these new human habitats beyond my wildest imagination. Forming the ocean bearing planets I know saw hovering in space.

These descendants of humanity were manipulating nature on a grand scale, reshaping the solar system to suit their needs. I realised with a mix of admiration and dread that several outer planets, along with the Asteroid and Kuiper belts, had either been dismantled or were in the process of being consumed. The sheer scale of the technology required for such an endeavour was mind-boggling. How had they compensated for the gravitational upheaval caused by the movement of such colossal masses? Surely, it should have thrown the entire system into chaos.

The desire for familiarity among these people drove them to create cloned worlds, replicas of their mother planet and its moon. I gazed down at the Sun and the elliptical plane of the planets, witnessing the vast circle these 'Earths' formed around it. It resembled one of Saturn's rings, incomplete yet encompassing a star instead of a planet. The sight was so overwhelming that I struggled to grasp its true scale.

There must have been over fifty planets, and still, there was ample space before the Sun would be completely encircled. *But where had all this material come from? How many major planets, besides Neptune, had been dismantled or were in the process of being sacrificed?* I could only imagine the countless moons of rock and ice that had already been lost to this grand design.

Humanity must have expanded beyond my wildest dreams.

When this monumental task was complete, it would surely stand as humanity's greatest achievement. Yet, I knew many from my time who would condemn me for even considering it so. The obsessive hysteria that had emerged from the 'Green' movement in my previous life had bred a bitter hatred for humanity's exploitation of resources.

As I gazed upon this cosmic spectacle, I couldn't help but think of the Dyson Sphere I'd read about in my boyhood science fiction novels. But this was different—it was being constructed from planets, and its grandeur was staggering. The scale of it took my breath away; it felt like a dream come true.

But just as I began to revel in the wonder of it all, my old friend, fate, was poised to deal me a different card altogether. Because for me, things were about to get much, much worse.

Chapter 09 – Here's My Robot

The space around me vanished, snuffed out of existence in a heartbeat, plunging me into an abyss of darkness. I stood once more, confronted by the eerie glow of strange dimensional windows, each one a portal to a different time and place. A vivid montage of historical imagery unfolded before me, accompanied by a symphony of sounds that enveloped me like a shroud.

I watched, transfixed, as figures—both real and fictional—were mercilessly ridiculed for their audacious desire to escape the clutches of mortality. Alchemists, with wild eyes and frenzied gestures, toiled in their laboratories, desperate to concoct the elusive elixir of youth. Charlatans hawked dubious hair restorative potions at bustling fairs, their voices rising above the din of eager crowds. I could almost feel the heat of the hot baths where people flocked, seeking cures for ailments, while shadowy figures of vampires lurked in the corners, their thirst for blood a chilling reminder of the lengths some would go to sustain their immortality.

The scenes morphed through the ages, and suddenly, the stark headlines of the 20th century blared to life. Advertisements for youth-preserving products flashed before my eyes—potions promising to prolong life, vitamin regimes that claimed to be the key to vitality, and the allure of plastic surgery that beckoned with the promise of eternal youth. Then, a familiar face appeared: a man advertising cryogenics, the very company that Helen and I had once entrusted with our dreams. I felt a magnetic pull as one of the silver containment pods hovered before me, gleaming like a beacon of hope.

I was witnessing the relentless human quest for longevity; a history steeped in ambition and desperation. But then, the scenes shifted, and I was thrust into a future beyond my own. Headlines proclaimed genetic breakthroughs that had yet to materialise by the time of my death. "The first woman to reach 200," one headline declared, while another triumphantly announced, "Eternalists achieve their goal—aging removed from the human condition."

But then, a jarring contrast emerged. "Majority choose to die," a newsreader intoned, her voice echoing with a disquieting finality. "It seems that most people are turning their backs on the opportunity to live forever." My heart sank as another scientific paper flashed across the screen, its headline reading, "Eternalists treat their children at birth." A massive screen on the wall lit up with the stark message: "The Darwin effect—evolution wins out, Eternalists outnumber general population for the first time in history."

I was captivated, entranced by the very future Helen and I had yearned for—a world filled with souls who craved immortality as fiercely as we did. But the montage continued, and images of death began to invade my thoughts. A natural disaster unfolded before me, accompanied by the chilling headline, "Eternalists not immortal after all—56 die in earthquake, oldest 210." Reports of murders and suicides flashed like lightning, each one a stark reminder of the fragility of existence. "Fear of death heightened—have we got more to lose? A world of recluses—cautious to the point of phobia—too scared to take any risk at all."

"Where to next on Immortality, as scientists suggest discarding the human body?" The question hung in the air like a dark cloud, heavy with implications.

Then, a clip from a news report captured my attention—a mass protest in what appeared to be St. Peter's Square in Rome. People waved banners that screamed, "*Don't turn us into robots!*" Where was this going? I began to wonder, as my subconscious began to ponder its significance.

I found myself peering into an auditorium that resembled a university lecture hall. The racial makeup of the audience made me think it must be somewhere in India. The student's faces were fixated on the stage, and sunlight streamed through the windows, casting a warm glow on their youthful features. A man stood confidently at the podium, and behind him, a large electronic screen displayed the provocative words, "*Shedding the corporeal shell—What's to be afraid of?*" As he began to speak, his voice resonated with conviction.

"Not since we immortals became the only type of humans have we had to fear any change in our physical condition. But we don't have anything to fear. This change is just another evolutionary step for our race. The new bodies feel the same as our biological ones. And as I am about to demonstrate, you can't tell the difference."

Then, he uttered something that sent a chill down my spine: "Could all the non-biologs stand up?" A gasp rippled through the auditorium as nearly every other person rose to their feet.

"These people have interacted with you most of the day, and no one has been able to tell any difference. That's the whole point of this transition. From the outside, and even to the person inside, there is no difference."

My heart raced, pounding against my ribcage as my subconscious reached a terrifying conclusion, one it was reluctant to voice. The images before me faded, replaced by another headline, and a commentator read it aloud, confirming the dread that had settled in my gut. "The Darwin effect—evolution wins out, artificial humanity outnumbers the general biological population for the first time in history."

My body jerked as the realisation crashed over me like a tidal wave. "Hang on!" I shouted, my voice echoing in the void. "What are you on about?" My heart thundered in my chest, and a spasm of uncontrollable trembling seized me. "You're trying to tell me I am a robot!" I screamed, the words tearing from my throat. "No, that can't be right! No..." I couldn't tell if I was shouting aloud or if it was merely a frantic echo in my mind. The world around me began to blur, the dizziness creeping in like a thief in the night, inviting the darkness to reclaim me once again.

Then, a scream pierced the air — a primal cry of terror. "Noooooooo!" Was that my own voice, fading into the distance as I slipped away?

Chapter 10 – State of Being

It took me a moment to grasp that I'd awakened once more in the stark, sterile confines of the white room. The one I'd originally been revived in. My eyes darted around, landing on Ankit, whose face was etched with concern, a furrowed brow betraying his unease.

"Richard," he began, his voice steady yet tinged with urgency, "there was no other way we could tell you. We hoped you wouldn't react like this, considering your interest in science and your preparations for whatever you might encounter in the future. Perhaps it was just too much of a culture shock."

I raised my arm, staring at it in disbelief, as if it belonged to someone else entirely. "But this looks real. It feels real. How can it not be?" My voice trembled, disbelief lacing my words. "I mean, I still feel all the same needs as I used to. Why do I have to go to the toilet if I'm a robot?"

Ankit seemed to find this question amusing because he smiled then gestured toward the chairs opposite us, his expression softening. "I've been allowed to discuss this with you, Richard. Let's sit down and have a drink. I'll explain everything."

As we settled into the chairs, I continued to scrutinise my arms and hands, as if expecting them to reveal some miraculous truth. "It's amazing. What am I made of?"

He didn't answer immediately, instead launching into a narrative about humanity's evolution from fragile biological beings to the resilient, artificial bodies we now inhabited. "When the idea was first proposed, there was an uproar, a vehement backlash against the change. It was not unlike your reaction just now. No one wanted to be turned into a robot—though that's not a term we use anymore," he added, a hint of disdain in his voice. "But as the fear of death grew unbearable, so did the reluctant acceptance of this transformation."

"That's why there are no androids, isn't it?" I blurted out, recalling our earlier conversation. "Because effectively, that's what we are."

"No, Richard, we're not," he replied, his tone firm yet reluctant. "But yes, that is a contributing factor."

"Is there nothing biological left anymore?" I pressed, my heart racing.

"There are no biologs, or completely biological humans left. Since Indian scientists first created these artificial bodies, there have been upgrades. Nothing biological remains—only simulations of biological features. A layer of synthetic skin, indistinguishable from the real thing, covers an artificial skeleton that primarily houses energy cells to power the body. To ease the fears of those reluctant to embrace this change, most internal structures, such as the heart and digestive system, were simulated."

He paused, letting the weight of his words sink in. "Everything the human body did that you were consciously aware of, and all the feelings it ever had, it still does. It hungers, desires sex, experiences feelings and emotions. You sense your heart racing and spine tingling. Richard, unless someone told you otherwise, you'd never know you weren't a biolog. You'd have to sever an arm to realise there was anything different."

"The body is merely a vessel for your true self," he continued, his voice growing more passionate. "Your essence—the consciousness that once resided in the grey matter of your brain—is now supported by a neural network far more complex than the human brain ever was. It's encased in an inch-thick shell of evantium, an almost indestructible metal that can be manipulated at a molecular level."

"We call it the brain pod," he explained, his eyes gleaming with fervour. "Even if something were to destroy the rest of your body, that evantium shell can be placed into another body. You are virtually immortal, Richard. Only extreme heat, like the plasma found in the Sun, or certain weapons," he said with a hint of disgust, "could obliterate you entirely."

Virtually immortal. The thought sent a shiver down my spine. "If that's the case, there must be some incredibly old people around. How old are you, Ankit?"

The question seemed to catch him off guard. He hesitated, searching for the right words. "Age has only ever been a measure of how long someone has lived, not their condition. In the past, many people incorrectly assessed their fellow citizens based on age, but no one asks that question anymore, Richard."

"Oh! I'm sorry, Ankit. I didn't mean to offend you. I guess I have a lot to learn about what is and isn't acceptable anymore."

"That's alright; I'm not offended. It's part of my responsibility to help you learn." Yet, beneath his calm exterior, I sensed a deeper truth he was reluctant to share, not just about his age. There was something more he wasn't saying, something he wanted to conceal.

Before I could delve deeper, he continued. "What you need to understand is that you're not a robot or an android. You're an evolved human. This was always on the cards. Consciousness and the desire to survive—it's a natural evolutionary step for intelligence to seek ways to escape the chronological limits of its biological genesis."

"I suppose so," I replied, feeling a strange calm wash over me. "I can't apologise enough, Ankit. I don't know why I reacted the way I did. I should have expected something like this. Helen and I always thought they would clone a biological body from one of our own cells, grow it to maturity without a brain, and then revive ours, treating any damage before transplanting it into the new body."

"Well, now you know what really happens."

A brief silence enveloped us as I struggled to collect my thoughts. Acceptance was my only option. I turned back to Ankit, my curiosity piqued. "You know, with all this, I almost forgot about the ring of planets I saw. They're so impressive—how many are there?"

"The sixty-fourth one is under construction, but eventually, there will be eighty such home worlds." His enthusiasm barely concealed the relief that washed over him at my apparent acceptance of my new reality.

"It's an incredible achievement Ankit. I can't imagine how it's managed."

"It might seem like a vastly complex exercise to you, Richard, but the information system manages all human affairs now. From the orbits of the new worlds to satisfying the myriad diverse living environments needed by the people who inhabit them."

I ran my hands over my face, searching for any sign that it wasn't biological skin. I couldn't tell, and then I asked, "I was nearly ninety when I died. How was it possible to create a body that looks exactly like me when I was in my twenties?"

"As long as there's the tiniest fragment of genetic material for the information system to use, it can extrapolate your exact physical characteristics, even down to your looks. It only ensures it gets the face right, as that seems to be the only thing that bothers people. Most can't remember their younger bodies in great detail, so they're satisfied with what we provide, as long as it's in the correct proportions."

"Your new body won't age unless you want it to?" he added, and just like that, he began to change. The right side of his face morphed before my eyes. Within seconds, half his hair lost its colour, his ear grew larger, wrinkles spread across his skin, and a jowl formed. He turned to his left, and I watched in awe as he transformed into an old man right before me!

"No!" I exclaimed as the older part of Ankit's face began to revert back to youth. "I'm quite happy with this, thanks." Still marvelling at my hands, I couldn't help but reference one of my favourite fictional characters. "God, I've turned into Data."

Ankit chuckled, amusement dancing in his eyes, but he waved it off. "You don't know it yet, Richard, but you're a bit more advanced than that. You'll feel better when you interact with others in the same situation. But you understand that we need to expose you gradually to this new life?'

"Of course," I replied, incredulous at Ankit's youthful return. "You know, I have a feeling this is going to be one heck of an adventure. And I'm going to start by looking for Helen."

I locked eyes with Ankit, and a realisation struck me. This man would likely become one of my closest friends in this life, whatever length it might be. Yet, I couldn't shake the underlying sadness I'd sensed since yesterday. "Can I ask you a personal question?"

"Of course," he replied cautiously.

"I've noticed you haven't been yourself lately, as if you're depressed in some way. Is there anything wrong?" I added, knowing I had no way to act on my next words, "Is there anything I can do?"

He hesitated, weighing his response. Finally, he sighed, "Unfortunately, Richard, we still face problems like those in your time. My wife and I have decided to separate, and it wasn't my decision. That's why I'm not myself."

"Oh, I am sorry." I said feeling horrified that I'd raised the subject. "Can't you take a break or something?"

"No," he said, forcing a smile. "My work gives me something else to focus on. I prefer to be here. And I'd rather not discuss it anymore, if that's alright."

A wave of sympathy washed over me. He had been so kind, so supportive. I wanted to comfort him, to embrace him, but I hesitated. In my time, such gestures between men were rare, yet by the time I'd died, they had become commonplace. But now, I was unsure of the norms in this new world.

He began to rise. "I have to go now, Richard, but I'll be back in the morning."

"Thank you, Ankit. I truly appreciate everything you're doing for me. I just hope I can return the favour in the future."

"I'm glad to help you reconnect with the world, Richard."

I smiled back at him, relief flooding my senses. "At least I've gotten the worst of it out of the way—the biggest shock to my system, I mean. There can't be anything more shocking than finding out I'm living in an artificial body, can there?"

He offered a forced grin but worry flickered in his eyes as he didn't reply.

'Can *there*?' I pressed, the gravity of my words sinking in.

As he walked toward the exit, he turned back to me, sadness pooling in his big brown eyes. He sighed deeply before saying, "Yes—the answer is yes. There is something else, and I really hope you can cope with it, Richard. Because it's much more significant than what you've learned today."

And with that, he was gone.

Chapter 11 – The Biggest Shock

Well, that frightened me. The words Ankit had spoken echoed in my mind, a relentless drumbeat of dread. I spent the rest of that evening replaying our conversation, each iteration more unsettling than the last. Was it possible that anything could be more shocking than what I'd already learned? I racked my brain, but nothing came close to the chaos swirling within me.

As I drifted into that twilight state between wakefulness and sleep, spectres from my past began to invade my thoughts, as if summoned by the turmoil in my heart. A cacophony of familiar faces tumbled through my mind, each one a ghost from a life I thought I'd left behind. My beloved mother, her warm smile radiating pride, and my father, a towering figure of strength and expectation, loomed large in my memories. They had always been so proud of my achievements, and I'd revelled in their admiration. And then there was Pete, my best mate, his cheeky grin framed by a riot of bright red hair, reaching across the years to say hello. I longed to share my experiences in this strange new world with them, to tell them everything.

I missed them all terribly, but the ache in my heart—or whatever was inside there—was most profound for Helen. The longing was almost physical, a weight pressing down on my chest, making me feel uncomfortably weary.

Some memories were like daggers, sharp and painful, especially those from my school days. I found myself trapped in a recollection of Jason Wentworth, my so-called friend, bullying and stealing from a pair of first-years in the school dining room. The air was thick with tension; everyone around us knew what was happening, yet no one dared to intervene. One of the boys, the stronger of the two, looked up defiantly, only to have his courage shattered by the brutal slap of Jason's hand against his cheek. The boy crumpled to the floor, trembling with shock and fear, and I felt a wave of shame wash over me, overwhelming and suffocating.

It had been ages since I'd confronted these dark memories, and I couldn't help but feel the hot sting of tears welling in my eyes. I touched my face to make sure this body was capable of reflecting my feelings, half-expecting to find it dry, but my fingers came away damp. They'd done a good job with this body, I thought, as I surrendered to the depths of sleep. The faces from my past lingered, watching over me, and as they faded into the shadows, all I could think was, I miss you all. They left me to grapple with my dreams, which felt less haunted now by the uncertainties of tomorrow.

When I awoke, I felt surprisingly refreshed, given the tumultuous images that had visited me during the night. Despite the soothing memories, I'd also been jolted awake several times by nightmares that replayed the torment my former self had endured. At least no one had tried to enter the room; I suspected it had been sealed tight against anyone but Ankit.

As I sipped my coffee and finished my cereal, I steeled myself for whatever awaited me that day. *Whatever it was,* I reminded myself, don't react. *Give yourself time to process it and discuss it later with Ankit.*

By the time my friend arrived, I was a bundle of nerves, taut and ready to snap. I'd given up trying to guess what the next shock could be; all I felt was an overwhelming desire for it to be over.

The journey to the information centre did nothing to calm my frayed nerves. Instead, it dredged up memories of the protesters I'd seen on the screen in the township. But before I could voice my concerns, we'd arrived.

As soon as I relinquished control to the system, a barrage of sound and vision assaulted my senses. I was plunged into a vivid portrayal of history, reminiscent of the one I'd seen the day before about the quest for immortality. This time, however, I was engulfed in a series of vignettes showcasing humanity's technological advancements.

I watched the dawn of mathematics unfold, the birth of inventions like explosives and the printing press. Old British newspapers heralded the onset of the Industrial Revolution, while American headlines boasted of the first manned flight. I saw people conversing on telephones, and then the screen erupted into a nuclear mushroom cloud, fading to the sound of Neil Armstrong's iconic words from Apollo 11. The double helix morphed into a Japanese woman seated at a computer, and then another donned a pair of glasses that revealed a heads-up display, a fusion of communication and media.

Humanity's technological triumphs played out before me, and so far, it was all as I remembered. But then, images shifted to the terraforming of Venus and Mars, and a media announcer introduced the first domed city on the Moon. I watched in awe as Saturn loomed, surrounded by moon-sized machines, and a group of Asians began to morph their bodies. I assumed these were the new artificial bodies. A headline flashed: "Next stop – the stars," over an image of colossal space arks hovering in Earth's orbit.

Then the focus shifted to a studio debate. A presenter challenged one guest, asking why they believed they were qualified to dictate how others should live. The man's arguments were steeped in religious fervour, while another guest proposed an extreme, anything-goes society, where nudity, violence, and chaos reigned. The presenter interjected, "Isn't it true that these extremes fail to meet our needs for coexistence?" He turned to the religious man, asserting, "You can't dictate behaviour in private homes; even the devout have human needs." Then he faced the tattooed man, saying, "And you can't force others to accept your lifestyle of being naked and having sex in front of their children. Doesn't *'Open Society'* offer the best compromise? A common set of rules when interacting with general society, based on decency and respect. As the Indian government has adopted, where there are no restrictions on what you do in the privacy of your home. As long as it's consensual and within the law?"

The religious man's disgust was palpable. "Do you think I'd live in a country where creatures like him can corrupt my children?" he spat.

The tattooed man shot back, "I won't be told what to do in my own country. We live in a free society, and I'll do whatever I want in it."

"But" said the presenter, "India has now started to create separate communities to cater for certain needs and beliefs." And looking at the tattooed young man said. "For example, a society where everything you want is allowed because everyone in it has opted to be part of it.

Surely where these fundamental ways of living are concerned, we've got to live separately, and when we do come together it should be somewhere we conduct ourselves in a manner that most people accept. When you're both in *'Open Society'* neither of you will be offended, because *you*," he said looking at the religious man. "Won't make comments about sex and debauchery, and *you*." He looked at the other man, "Won't take your clothes off and make offensive remarks about other people's beliefs.

And if you can't modify your behaviour for a short period in order to interact with people who have different beliefs, then you'd be free to stay in your own society. After all, both of you just share this society with the rest of us. Neither of you owns it. And neither of your beliefs are right for everyone."

The tattooed man retorted, "Like I said, I'll do whatever I want. It's a free country."

Ironically, the religious man found common ground with his opponent, declaring, "I won't stop fighting until your kind is wiped from the face of the Earth."

The presenter sighed and turned to the screen, and with an air of resignation said. "Will we ever learn?"

The scene shifted to a montage of human history's horrors: oppression, dictators, massacres. Images of World War II death camps twisted my stomach, and I watched in horror as bombs exploded, and the Twin Towers fell. A nuclear mushroom cloud loomed in the distance, and a newsreader's voice echoed, "Are we too weak to survive?"

Suddenly I was floating in Earth's orbit, gazing down at a forest of nuclear mushrooms blanketing the American continent. As the Earth spun beneath me, I realised this devastation was global. *How could we have let this happen?*

A window appeared, displaying the front page of the 'Moon Times' with the headline: 'Earth lost – no survivors.' Another window confronted me: 'Venus and Mars uninhabitable – Moon creeks with refugees.' I watched as the domes above the cavern cities on the Moon began to blow out, lost to the void of space. No one could have survived. Three planetary bodies and the Moon had become barren wastelands.

But there must have been survivors, I thought. How else could this vast population exist? Thank God some of humanity had survived that catastrophe.

Yet the worlds floating before me appeared lifeless and sterile. As the surface fires flickered and faded, the images turned black for a moment. Then, everything shifted outward, and when the scene returned, I found myself deep in space, hovering above an alien world.

The planet before me drifted at a great distance from its sun, a gas giant dominating its system like Jupiter did ours. But unlike Jupiter, this world was inhabited. Massive, amorphous creatures floated in the sky, their surfaces shifting with brown and grey patches, semi-transparent like ethereal cousins of the clouds.

I heard sounds, like a distant fax machine, fading in and out in a rhythmic pattern. The beings were communicating, and suddenly, their language transformed into English in my mind.

One of the floating creatures, surrounded by others, called out in a haunting, whale-like shriek. "We cannot continue our existence on this planet; it is a dead end for our civilisation. We've relied too long on our relationship with the creatures on our nearest moon. They help us create and use our artifacts, but we need to interact with our surroundings independently. We must leave Manoora and search for another planet where we can transform and be free."

The crowd of creatures around the speaker grew restless, their alien sounds a mix of agreement and dissent.

"The moon creatures have built ships under our guidance, and they're ready to take us to our destiny. Once we find a suitable planet, we can transform ourselves and gain the freedom we've long awaited."

I watched as the planet became surrounded by colossal starships, the aliens floating purposefully within, embarking on a journey to find their fate, escaping the futile existence they'd known.

My mind raced with the possibilities of what I was seeing, but I struggled to suppress the absurdity of it all. Yet, strangely, I felt calmer than before, and I continued to follow the unfolding story.

What happened next confirmed the conclusion my subconscious had already reached. The alien ships entered our solar system, and inside the first one to breach Earth's orbit, one of the creatures spoke again, surrounded by its fellow Manoorans. A deep sadness tinged its voice.

"We've travelled so far to meet these creatures, following the transmissions of their remarkable culture and achievements. And now we find they've destroyed themselves. How can it be? They had so much, and now they've thrown it away, as if terrified of reaching their potential. We must carry the lessons from this tragedy into our own future."

Then the scene shifted to a future time. A group of gas creatures floated in one of their ships, gazing down at something below. The image panned down to reveal a human man and woman standing on a platform. One of the floating creatures addressed them.

"What does it feel like?" it said to its fellow Manoorans.

Chapter 12 – Coming to Terms

I felt as if I'd clawed my way out of a surreal fugue, my senses dulled, and my mind bemused by an unsettling calmness that wrapped around me like a heavy fog. Was it possible to sedate a body like this? Or was I simply in shock? The thought lingered, but it hardly mattered. No amount of contemplation could have prepared me for the staggering revelation I'd just stumbled upon. I'd awakened in a future teeming with aliens, all of them living in artificial human bodies! Surely, that was enough to drive even the sanest person to the brink of madness. Was I mad? I couldn't tell.

A chill seeped into my bones, a profound loneliness settling in as if an ethereal tether had snapped, severing my connection to humanity. I sighed deeply, the sound echoing through my new form, a reminder of my isolation. Yet, a flicker of solace ignited within me—I wasn't entirely alone. I wasn't the last true human. My fellow Cryogens, though a million miles away from what anyone in my time would recognise as real, still existed. Their mere existence offered me a fragile sense of belonging in this alien world.

But for now, I was adrift, alone in a strange place. The comforting safety of the white room was a distant memory, having awoken somewhere entirely different. How had I even arrived here from the information centre? *Had I fainted from shock?*

The room I found myself in was anything but clinical. It was oddly normal, filled with stand-alone furniture that seemed to breathe life into the space. As I lay on my cot, the vibrant colours swirling around me made my head spin. Yet, despite the chaos of my thoughts, this place felt inviting, warm, and strangely comforting.

Even in my disoriented state, the racing thoughts in my mind began to weigh heavily on me. That peculiar physical exhaustion that comes when mental strain comes creeping in. I needed to escape, to shut it all out, so I closed my eyes and surrendered to the welcoming embrace of sleep.

But sleep was fleeting. I jolted awake, heart racing, my mind still tangled in a nightmare where I was trapped in a real-life version of the 'Invasion of the Body Snatchers.' A horde of pod people had cornered me, their outstretched arms reaching for me, vacant expressions twisted into grotesque masks of desire. I shivered, then smiled at the absurdity of it all, relieved to find no pods lurking in the shadows, no one slowly morphing into me.

As the memories of my awakening flooded back, panic surged through me until I noticed I wasn't alone. Ankit sat across the room in a bright blue easy chair, engrossed in an info-tablet. He looked up as I rose slowly from my cot, my legs shaky beneath me.

"Are you one of those aliens?" I asked, my voice barely above a whisper.

He nodded, his expression sombre.

"And we really did wipe ourselves out?"

"I'm afraid so, Richard. It happened so quickly that we could only watch as we travelled here to make contact. It was like witnessing our dreams die. We had hoped to trade with you for your technology, to create our own artificial bodies. Even though the design we'd chosen for our bodies were vastly different from yours we envisioned a future where our two races could coexist in harmony."

"But when you arrived, we'd already annihilated ourselves. You didn't need to create new bodies; you had a ready supply just waiting." A hint of accusation crept into my voice, and I couldn't suppress it.

"Everything left behind was designed to serve the human form. All we needed to do was cleanse the environments of radioactivity, and we could begin anew. We were so captivated by your culture and achievements that we saw no reason not to pick up where you left off."

"And try not to repeat the same mistakes?" I added, my scepticism palpable.

Ankit offered a resigned smile. "The information system we found was damaged by the war. Many records were lost, including any mention of you and your fellow Cryogens. It's been a dilemma for us since discovering you hidden away on the far side of the Moon. The last hundred years of reviving people have been the most challenging. Some of us feel guilty, as if we've stolen something from you. Others believe we're doing the right thing by reviving you, giving the original human race a second chance."

"What do you mean, *Original Human Race*?" I challenged, my fists clenching involuntarily.

"You must understand, Richard. We Manoorans were so eager to shed our past that most of us now identify as human. We adopted human life out of respect for your legacy. Our greatest desire is to revive as many of you as possible and to live together as one race."

"So, will you eventually abandon the terms '*Cryogen*' and '*Original Human Race*'?" I pressed.

"There'll always be a reference to the original human race as long as our history includes its story."

"Our history!" I felt anger bubbling within me, the weight of my fists a reminder of my frustration.

"I know it's difficult," Ankit said, glancing at my clenched hands. "But all of us—Cryogens and Manoorans alike—will constitute the future human race. We had no concept of history on our home planet, so everything that ever happened in this solar system will become our shared history."

"Do you really think we can merge into a single race, Ankit? What happens when we Cryogens start to breed? Aren't you afraid there will be those who want it all back?"

Ankit's expression shifted, as if he'd forgotten something crucial. "Oh, Richard," he said slowly, as if delivering tragic news. "I'm sorry, but because these bodies are immortal, they can't replicate. Creating one from scratch would mean making an Android, not a true sentient being as we define it."

Yet another revelation, I thought and asked. "So, when there are no more Cryogens to revive, that's it? The end of what's left of humanity?"

He nodded. "Of the original race, yes. But hopefully, in time, we can all consider ourselves human. We pose no threat to your culture, Richard. We've embraced it and wish to preserve it. I can assure you, unless someone reveals their origins, you'd never know the difference between us."

Yet that assurance did little to ease my unease. The term *"Original Human Race"* felt like a label marking us as a species on the brink of extinction.

I had to accept that I couldn't change anything that happened during my suspension. All I could muster was a quiet, "Oh," as I glanced around. Desperate to change the conversation before I said something I would regret, I asked, "Where am I now, anyway?"

"This is your allocated home. I chose it for you, so I hope it's acceptable. It's still in India Prime, so it should suffice until you decide what you want to do with your life."

"You already know what I want to do, Ankit," I said, a hint of aggression creeping back into my voice. *Calm down*, Richard, I reminded myself. "I won't rest until I find Helen, or until there are no more Cryogens to revive."

Ankit's defensiveness was palpable, aware of my frustration with the situation. "I'm sorry; I didn't explain properly. I meant after you've found Helen or discovered what's happened to her. I chose this place because of its proximity to the Institute, so you can be involved in the Cryogen project."

"Oh," I said, guilt washing over me.

He moved toward the door, pausing to turn back. "On that note, I've arranged for you to meet a few people this evening. One of them is a high official whose permission you'll need to seek to join the project."

"Thank you," I replied, my voice softer.

"I'll let you explore your new home for now." He nodded at the time display on the wall. "Expect us at seven."

I twisted my head in the direction he'd looked, feeling a strange sensation on my scalp.

"Oh, and you might not have noticed yet, but the system has provided you with that hair you wanted. You can learn how to change it later."

I couldn't tell which happened first—my hand reaching up to feel the new mane of hair or my anger dissipating like mist in the morning sun. I couldn't let my friend leave with a negative impression of me. I'd only been reacting on instinct. "Ankit," I said, my voice earnest, "I'm sorry for how I reacted. I didn't mean to come across as ungrateful or angry. I'm just... confused."

"I know that, Richard. I can see the kind of person you are deep down. Don't worry; it'll all be okay. I promise I'll do everything in my power to help you find Helen."

"Thank you, Ankit. I appreciate everything you're doing for me." I forced a smile, though it felt heavy on my lips.

"Before you go, who are these other people you're bringing later?" I asked out of curiosity.

"They're Cryogens like you, Richard," he replied. "You're going to meet some other humans from your own time."

Chapter 13 – Fellow Travellers

At last, I was about to meet other people—real people, like me, or as close to real as one could get in this bizarre place. I approached the panel on the wall, ready to check if I needed to prepare anything for my guests, but Ankit had already beaten me to it. He'd already issued instructions for later.

With nothing else to occupy my mind, I sank into one of the chairs and took a moment to absorb my new apartment. It was a cozy room, not overly spacious, yet not so small that it triggered my claustrophobia. I realised I still carried the fears that had shaped the person I once was.

A scattering of blue and cream cushions softened the harsh lines of the box-like seating, creating a welcoming focal point in the room. The green flooring felt more like plush carpet than anything else I'd encountered, and it enveloped my slippered feet in warmth, a comforting embrace in this strange new world.

The walls, painted a soft cream, were adorned with vid screens that simulated windows, offering a view of an idyllic countryside beyond. Lush bushes and shrubs carpeted the landscape, framing a stream that wound its way along the contours of a gentle hillock. From hidden speakers, the soothing sound of water rushing over rocks filled the air, a frenzied journey to a destination that didn't exist.

Suddenly, as I gazed into this manufactured reality, a wave of homesickness washed over me. Yet, paradoxically, it lifted my spirits, reminding me that there was still something familiar anchoring me to reality. I had no doubt that meeting other humans would help me adjust to my new surroundings.

With nothing to do but wait, I tried to relax, and soon I began to realise that I could, in fact, come to terms with this peculiar setup. I was starting to look forward to participating in this strange society. I only wished Helen were here with me to share in this adventure.

The flood of new information had left me feeling absent-minded, and I began to forget things. The thought crept into my mind just as I stood before the entrance to my new home, which seemed to scream, *"You're Free!!"*

The realisation hit me like a sledgehammer. Of course, I could go out. But as I stood before the doorway, a wave of reluctance and fear washed over me, and I clung to the warmth and security of this apartment. All the anxieties I'd built up about the door in the white room came surging back.

"Don't be a scaredy-cat," I could almost hear Helen's voice teasing me from the recesses of my mind. So, with a deep breath, I stepped through the door and into the grey corridor beyond.

The air was still, yet it smelled fresh and sweet, a testament to the air conditioning that must be at work. In the distance, I could hear birdsong, and I decided to follow it, hoping to find some people. The corridors I navigated all looked strikingly similar, and perhaps due to the overload of information, I began to worry that I might have difficulty finding my way back.

I thought I heard movement ahead and caught a faint whiff of coffee, but still, there were no voices. Then, without warning, the corridor opened into a square filled with small groups of people sitting around tables. The scene could have been plucked from any quaint city square of my time, but the sound—or lack of it—was utterly surreal. I'd found myself right in the middle of the twilight zone.

The people in the square were animated, their mouths moving in lively conversation, yet not a single sound escaped their lips. It was disconcerting. I knew I wasn't deaf; I could hear everything else—the rustling of glasses, the chirping of birds, the soft clinking of cups against tables. But the silence of their chatter was unnerving. *How were they communicating? Was it telepathy? If so, why were they moving their mouths?*

Panic gripped me as a young man turned to me, mouthing silent words. It jolted me from my stupor. I spun on my heel and ran, desperate to return to the safety of my apartment. It felt like a nightmare, and it was about to get worse—I realised I was lost. I'd sprinted down a corridor, but they all looked the same, and if the markings on the wall were for anything other than decoration, I couldn't decipher them.

I paused at a corner, surprised that I wasn't gasping for breath after my frantic dash. Reluctantly, I considered that I might have to find those silent people again to ask for help. But what if they couldn't hear me either?

"Damn," I shouted, frustration bubbling over. "How the hell do I find my way back home?"

"Do you require assistance?" a voice replied from behind me.

Finally, someone I could hear! I turned around, relief flooding through me as I said, "Hello..." But to my dismay, the corridor was empty.

"Hello!" I shouted again, my voice echoing down the hall. "Is someone there?"

The voice came from nowhere again, and I quickly realised it was the information system. I needed to ask Ankit if this mental fog was only temporary.

"Yes, I need to get back to my apartment, please," I said, my voice steadying as I waited.

"Follow the green markings on the wall," the voice instructed me.

I looked at the jumble of markings at the corner of the corridor, and some of them illuminated. Out of the chaotic mess of symbols, a green arrow emerged, guiding me. At each corner, another arrow pointed me in what I hoped was the right direction. Eventually, I found myself at a door-sized section of wall glowing green. Without hesitation, I stepped through it, and sure enough, I was back in my apartment.

A shiver ran down my spine as I let out a sigh of relief, reflecting on the bizarre experience. But as I settled down to recover, the system informed me that I had mere minutes to prepare for my guests.

At precisely seven o'clock, the familiar sound of a door buzzer echoed through the room. The entrance became transparent, revealing Ankit, flanked by a group of people.

As he stepped inside and moved toward me, he gestured to the guests behind him. I inhaled sharply. The first man, extending his hand for a shake, was the same man who had entered the white room. But before I could recall his name, Ankit introduced him.

"Richard, this is Ramoon. He's the official responsible for the Cryogen project."

The man took my hand, his jovial demeanour clashing with the disingenuous smile that crossed his face. "We were never introduced when we first encountered each other, Richard, but Ankit has told me a great deal about you."

The words, laced with an unsettling undertone, made me uneasy. There was no reason not to like him; his manners were pleasant enough, but the supercilious twist of his expression set off alarm bells in my mind. I'd never been one to judge people before getting to know them, but there was something about this man that I just didn't like.

"I'd also like to introduce you to three of your fellow Cryogens," Ankit continued, sweeping his arm toward the other visitors who began to approach. Two men and a woman moved toward me, all smiling. For a fleeting moment, a flashback to my Body Snatchers nightmare gripped me, but I blinked it away and returned their smiles. They appeared to be in their early thirties, dressed in crisp suits reminiscent of the business attire from my time. The two men wore light tan suits accented with red, while the woman's suit was a striking combination of lime green and chocolate brown.

Earl Jeffries, a handsome black man with noble features and a soothing voice, reminded me of Britain's first mixed-race King Leroy, who had reigned at the time of my death. Then there was Jennifer Lee, a petite and attractive Chinese woman with shoulder-length black hair. Her dazzling smile revealed teeth so white they seemed almost unreal. Finally, there was Simon West, an unassuming yet handsome redhead who avoided eye contact when I shook his hand, looking down in a way that reminded me of Helen. I thought I detected a hint of an Australian accent.

As we chatted, Ankit asked the information system to provide the drinks and snacks he had previously selected, and I gradually began to relax.

Earl was grave and sombre, his voice holding a serious and calming tone. In his previous life, he had been a lottery winner who invested and made his fortune in the American media. None of his several ex-wives had wanted to join him in the *Great Adventure*, as he put it. However, one of his sons had, but tragically, he had been unable to be revived successfully.

"It was like losing James all over again," he said in his low baritone voice. "I'd already said goodbye to him once because he died of cancer when he was only twenty-one."

Jennifer came from a wealthy family that owned a successful chain of restaurants worldwide. She leaned forward, elbows on the table, chin resting on her intertwined fingers, smiling at me with an air of self-assuredness.

"They all thought I was mad for wanting to be frozen and almost disinherited me. So, I pretended to give up the idea until I got my hands on the money. I was a very wealthy woman when I died. Not that any of that matters now, because there's no longer any such thing as personal wealth. You see, you can have just about anything you want. And anyway, even if I were poor, I am alive and look at me! I died in my nineties, but I am in my prime again." Her infectious smile drew smiles from all of us.

Simon had been a world champion tennis player, having won everything except the Australian Open. "That didn't please my fellow Australians," he said, confirming my suspicion about his nationality. "I joined the movement when I lost the use of my legs in a riding accident. I couldn't bear the thought of never playing again, so it was either commit suicide or take a chance on this. So, I chose this as a possible way to recapture my youth, and in the meantime, I set up a successful surveillance company. Of course, it's sod's law that this society considers that later profession illegal, and even though I am young and healthy, I don't seem to be particularly good at tennis anymore."

"You've got a long time to get better," Jennifer chimed in, rubbing his arm in mock sympathy.

I turned to Ramoon and asked, "What do I need to do to become involved in the Cryogen project? Ankit may have told you that I am desperate to find out the fate of my wife." And in an attempt to conceal my desperation, I added, "And I want to be involved in reviving what's left of the human race anyway."

For a moment, I thought I saw a shadow cross Ramoon's face, accompanied by a strained smile. He replied in a clipped tone, "We all consider ourselves part of the human race now, Richard."

I'd forgotten that. "Yes, sorry, Ramoon. I just need to get used to all this. What I meant to say was that I'd like to help retrieve as much as possible of what seems to be considered by…" I hesitated, wanting to say Manoorans, "the general population, a great treasure."

"We generally allow several months for Cryogens to settle into whichever society they've chosen before asking them to contribute," he said, staring deep into my eyes, unnerving me. "But I can see that you're adjusting quite quickly, so I'll put in a word for you. Just understand that I can't make the final decision on this; so, don't get your hopes up just yet."

Almost as an afterthought, and with slightly too much enthusiasm for my liking, he added, "You have been made aware that a very high percentage of Cryogens aren't able to be revived, haven't you?"

"Yes. Ankit has told me," I replied, my dislike for this man growing by the minute. I wanted to ask how long it would be before I got an answer, but I decided to wait until I was alone with Ankit and try to work through him.

All I wanted to do was talk about Helen, but I was acutely aware that I couldn't let any of them think I was obsessed. Overdoing it might put them off helping me, and worse still, they could think I was absolutely batty and in need of treatment. I couldn't risk that, so despite my irritation, I had to steer the conversation elsewhere.

I glanced over at Ankit and said, "I had a very strange experience earlier." I began to recount the bizarre encounter with the silent people in the square.

By the time I finished, they were all looking at me with amusement. Ankit placed his drink on the table between us and began to explain. "Sorry, Richard, I didn't think you'd risk going out on your own today. With your senses not being fully activated, I would have warned you about the barriers you might face."

"I'm not sure I understand, Ankit. Apart from not being able to hear those people talking earlier, all my senses seem to be working fine," I said, adding, "or even better."

"You're right; you don't understand," he replied. "Your new body has more capabilities than your biological one ever had. Some of those extra senses haven't been turned on yet. Communication will be a little like learning to talk all over again. Can you remember when you said you were glad I was speaking English, and I said I wasn't?"

I'd completely forgotten that. There had been so much swirling in my head. It was one of the things I meant to ask.

"Yes, I forgot to ask you about that. What exactly did you mean?"

"Well, most of us speak Hindi. But you hear English, and vice versa; there's instantaneous translation."

"But what about earlier, when I couldn't hear anyone?"

"That's the most complex ability you'll have to learn to use. It will require a conscious effort when it's first turned on, but like walking, it will become automatic. You see, in this society, no one—not even the authorities—has the right to invade your privacy. That includes overhearing your conversations. We have the ability to turn on the transmission of our voices only to those we want to hear us. This can include individuals, groups, or if you don't mind everyone overhearing you, a general transmission. I know it sounds complex, but it will become second nature to you."

"So, I couldn't hear anything earlier because none of those people were transmitting on a general frequency?"

"Not exactly. It's because your communication abilities haven't been fully turned on. Apart from allowing you access to transmissions from a few key people you've already met," he gestured to the others, "most of your other advanced senses haven't been activated at all. Had they been, what you would have heard was random conversation created by the system, aimed at your level of tolerance. But not the actual words the people were saying. It's very advanced. It even convinces your eyes that their lips are moving in sync with the false conversation."

My mouth fell open at what I was hearing. I slowly shook my head and said, "I wish I could say that's amazing, Ankit, but to be honest, it's just one bizarre surprise after another lately. This world is completely balmy." Before I could contemplate the extremity of these revelations, I asked, "When will I get all these advanced senses turned on, and what exactly are they?"

"I'm hoping that's one of the things your new friends are going to help you explore," he said, glancing at the three other Cryogens. "I've arranged for you to have all your senses activated."

"Yes," Jennifer said, moving forward. "We thought we'd take a trip to the library tomorrow, Richard, and get you *turned on*, so to speak."

"Library!" I laughed. "Why would you need one of those when you've got access to everything through the information system in your own homes? Libraries disappeared in my time."

"It's just one of many things that aren't necessary anymore, but they've been retained to satisfy the underlying psychological need for human activity and contact. There are cinemas, clubs, sports centres, and just about every social activity we used to have back in our time. You'll come across a lot of things that you'd think wouldn't be needed anymore and indeed aren't. They're just retained to maintain our culture and sense of belonging."

The mention of most people speaking Hindi got me thinking again about why the institute was in India.

"There's something that's been nagging at me," I said. "I haven't heard any mention of other countries or cultures. I know we're in the middle of India, but I would have thought there would be more of a mix of races after all this time…"

Earl answered, "Richard, it's because the Manoorans wanted to replicate the distribution of races at the point when humanity became extinct. Approximately ninety-five percent of humans were of Indian descent by the time the race was wiped out."

My brow furrowed, confusion washing over me. I knew India had a large population, but ninety-five percent!

"I suppose I'm going to regret asking how that came about, aren't I?" I said to the group.

"Have you learned anything about India's contribution to human society at all?" Jennifer asked.

"Only that they developed the first artificial bodies and were responsible for laying the foundations of the Open Society principle."

They all exchanged glances, and Jennifer said, "Well, that settles it then. The first thing we'll do tomorrow when we get to the library is to show you…" She paused, looking accusingly at Ramoon.

"What?" I asked.

"Just how India saved the Earth from an invasion from space."

Chapter 14 – Why most of us are Indian

As I approached India Prime's city library, I couldn't help but feel a sense of awe wash over me. This place was not just impressive; it was monumental, a colossal titan that loomed over the other structures nestled beneath the artificial sky. Its vast panes of gold-tinted glass shimmered like a beacon, shouting its existence to the underground world while keeping its secrets hidden from view. I navigated my way toward it, relying on the same instinctual path I'd used to find my new home.

The city streets were eerily deserted, and as I walked, I felt as though I'd stepped into a scene from a disaster movie. The absence of bustling crowds made the enormity of the city feel even more pronounced, and I couldn't help but wonder why they continued to build more planets when there were so few people to inhabit them. After several blocks, I had only encountered a handful of souls, and the surreal atmosphere weighed heavily on me. But the thought of my friends waiting for me at the library entrance brought a flicker of comfort to my soul.

As we entered the library through a section of tinted glass, I paused, inhaling deeply. The air was infused with a familiar scent that transported me back in time—a smell I hadn't expected to encounter in this futuristic world. It was the unmistakable aroma of new carpet, and it instantly conjured memories of the day Helen, and I had chosen the carpet for our first home. I could almost feel the excitement of that day, the way the scent lingered for weeks, wrapping us in a cocoon of new beginnings.

Yet, that comforting smell was the only familiar thing in this vast building. The stark blocks that adorned the walls were a chaotic blend of primary colours; each embedded with small screens that flickered with video clips as we strolled past.

"You don't see the same things that I do," Simon remarked, noticing my gaze fixated on one of the screens. "We all perceive different things based on what the system knows about our preferences. Until your senses are fully activated, you'll only see random images on these screens. But our advanced eyesight reveals what the system wants us to see." He grinned, adding, "So you wouldn't have noticed the video I've just seen advertising *tennis for beginners*."

We ventured deeper into the library, where alcoves branched off the main corridor, leading to small study rooms. I followed my friends into the first empty one we encountered. Simon gestured for me to take a seat near the wall, at one end of a table that resembled a miniature version of the one at the information centre. I guessed it provided an interface with the library's vast information store.

"I suppose this thing is going to merge with me, is it?" I asked, half-joking.

Jennifer leaned closer, her eyes sparkling with excitement. "Absolutely! And the first thing you're going to learn about is the first invasion from space and India's response. Are you ready?"

"Yes," I replied, my mind racing at her emphasis on the word "first." It was clearly a reference to the Manoorans, but before I could ponder its implications, I felt myself being drawn into that familiar half-sleep, a dreamlike state that preceded communication with the information system.

Suddenly, a vision of Earth from the night side filled my mind, and I felt as if I were floating in space once again. But this time, the proximity to the planet sent a jolt of acrophobia through me, threatening to make my stomach churn. Just as quickly, the nausea subsided, sparing my breakfast from an untimely exit.

The image panned around me, revealing hundreds of moonlit metallic objects the size of apartment blocks, suspended in stationary orbit. Their centre sections revolved, making them sparkle like diamonds scattered across the night sky. As I drew closer, I noticed thousands of smaller ships emerging from the larger ones, each the size of a washing machine, resembling futuristic computer mice from my past. Illuminated tubes of white and orange liquid spiralled around their exteriors as they rained down upon the planet below.

The scene shifted abruptly, and I found myself zooming over New York harbour, where the iconic statue lay shattered, broken in half like a child's toy. Along 42nd street the sounds of screams and crashing vehicles filled my ears as panicked hordes scrambled for escape. A deep, low buzzing accompanied the glint of the small, almost half-spherical invaders as they darted in all directions, seeking out human targets to unleash their dark green energy upon. Pulses of this energy, as small as golf balls, shot forth with terrifying velocity, ready to tear through flesh and fabric alike.

People were running for cover, their screams echoing in the chaos, pleading for their lives as flames engulfed the scene. I felt a strange relief that this experience didn't come with the sense of smell, as I glanced around at the piles of smoking remains scattered across the ground. This was nothing short of a systematic genocide of humanity.

In a sudden shift, I found myself soaring high above the Earth once more, gazing down at the familiar shape of the Indian continent. I began a rapid descent, the land growing larger beneath me. As I looked down, I noticed entire swathes of the continent changing colour! An orange hue spread over the brown landscape, followed by white, and finally, specks of green emerged. It resembled a sea of dust motes disturbed by a raging wind, but whatever it was, it had a purpose, dispersing evenly in all directions. As I drew closer, the tiny specs resolved into individual entities, and my heart raced as I realised they were people—flying people!

I was mesmerised by the sight of this vast army of Indian supermen and women, clad in coveralls of orange, white, and green, effortlessly soaring through the sky with sleek contraptions strapped to their backs. *What could this mean?*

My fall halted just above this human tide, and questions flooded my mind. Were these people escaping? Had the rest of humanity been annihilated, leaving these brave souls as the last survivors, destined to repopulate the world? Just as I began to entertain this grim possibility, I was yanked back to the chaos of 42nd Street.

A man lay sprawled on the sidewalk, surrounded by a cacophony of screaming, frantic people caught in the throes of panic. He had been knocked over in the crush, arms raised defensively against a swarm of the small alien ships speeding toward him.

As he looked up, a shadow crossed his face, and he closed his eyes, bracing for the inevitable. But instead of the blinding flash he anticipated, he was met with the sound of explosions erupting around him. Slowly, he opened one eye, fearfully curious about what he might see. *Was he not going to be killed, but rather captured for experimentation?*

To his astonishment, something hurtling through the air at incredible speed was striking the alien ships. It was difficult to discern what it was, but the orange, white, and green streaks must have been some secret weapon from the government. And it was working—the small spaceships were exploding!

The man and his fellow Americans halted their panic, captivated by the unfolding spectacle. At last, he thought, the cavalry had arrived—thank God! He knew the U.S. government must have had something up its sleeve.

He sat up, a smile breaking across his face, but then fell back as the crowd around him recoiled in shock from something that had plummeted from the sky. Oh no, he thought, this is it. But the figure that landed beside him wasn't an alien ship; it was a large Indian man in a green jumpsuit, smiling down at him.

"We're here to help you. You have nothing to fear anymore," he said, his Indian accent perfectly masking the polite English words. He grasped the man's elbow, helping him to his feet.

Before the American could express his gratitude or even ask who he was, the Indian man leaped into the air, joining his fellow countrymen. The American watched in disbelief as the man flew with incredible speed, like a kamikaze pilot, straight into a disoriented spaceship, causing it to explode.

The crowd around him erupted in cheers, jumping for joy and punching the air in support of these brave souls sacrificing their lives to protect theirs.

I became acutely aware that this was happening all over the globe, as similar scenes unfolded in major cities across Earth. The explosions that erupted when members of this Indian Army made contact suggested they were armed with a type of explosive I'd never encountered. It wasn't long before the threat on the ground dissipated, and the remnants of this heroic swarm took to the skies, presumably to join another battle elsewhere.

Suddenly, I found myself floating back in orbit, watching as the building-sized spaceships came under attack from the flying Indians. The large ships struggled to manoeuvre, and the tide of brave souls pouring into space reminded me of a swarm of bees on the offensive. The sheer volume of explosions overwhelmed the alien vessels, causing them to break apart under the relentless assault. I couldn't believe my eyes.

When the last of the ships had exploded, the remaining members of this army turned as one and flew back to Earth, heading toward the continent that had birthed them. What a spectacular scene! But just as I began to savour the moment, the familiar sensation of being drawn back to reality pulled me into consciousness.

When I emerged from my trance, I looked up at my friends, my heart racing. "That was incredible—what an unbelievable sacrifice for the rest of humanity! But now I'm even more confused. How did that affect the makeup of humanity? If most of the Indian population sacrificed themselves as human bombs, how did they account for such a large percentage of the survivors?"

"Well, that's because you didn't see the entire story, Richard," Jennifer replied, her tone serious. "By the time that scene played out, most of humanity had already been killed by the invaders."

"And" she continued, "those human bombs, as you called them, weren't human. What you witnessed were the first versions of artificial bodies designed for human habitation. India had secretly developed them due to their paranoia over potential threats from China. As you saw, they were far more advanced than the cyber-suits we had in our time." She referred to the all-encompassing body suits that had been the norm for entering cyberspace in the 21st century. The virtual reality successor to the 20th century's television.

"The Indian leaders had hoped to convince their people to embrace the security these artificial bodies would provide. Initially, they intended to use them as a remote robotic army against any aggressive acts from their powerful neighbour, and ultimately, to ensure the survival of their race as an alternative to their biological bodies."

"How did they manage to keep so many hidden?" I asked, my curiosity piqued.

"They were developed in vast underground hangars, unknown to the general population. When the threat from space became apparent, the Indian government relocated its population there. They allowed their central computer system to take control of the artificial bodies and move them to the surface, where the invaders overlooked them, mistaking them for mere artifacts of the dominant species. It was a decisive moment in the survival of the human race."

"Why did they wait so long to help the rest of the world?" I pressed.

"Their leaders assumed other countries had secret weapons as well, so they only acted to protect their own interests. But the invasion shattered Earth's homocentric notion of the universe and forced all nations to unite, including, some say too late, India. Even then, it was only the overwhelming outcry from their own population that compelled their government to take the action you just witnessed. Unfortunately, there wasn't much of the Earth's population left to save apart from their own. The rest had been decimated, reduced to just a few tens of millions. That's why, from then on, most of the Earth was repopulated from the Indian continent."

"That's such a shame," I said, my heart heavy. "We must have lost so much from all those other cultures. But at least it was the Indian race that survived. I can't think of many other cultures I'd trust with the future of humanity." *Except for the French*, I thought, the Francophile in me surfacing.

"I know what you mean," Earl chimed in. "But we do owe the Indian race a debt of gratitude for creating the multi-society system, including Open Society. Their ideas of a decent and respectful social order, along with their willingness to accommodate the diversity of human lifestyles, helped shape what we have today. It laid the foundation for the social model that began to stabilise humanity."

"A little too late," I muttered, and everyone nodded in agreement.

"And don't forget, the Indians invented these fabulous new bodies," Jennifer said, attempting to lighten the mood by twirling around as if showcasing a new dress.

Her playful gesture lifted the heaviness in the air, and I took a moment to absorb the entirety of this new world. "You know, Helen will think she's gone to Heaven. This place isn't anything like we expected, but it's better than anything we could have ever imagined."

The others exchanged glances when I mentioned Helen's name. Placing her hands over mine, Jennifer spoke in a more serious tone. "Don't get your hopes up too high, Richard. Remember what Ramoon said. Most Cryogens aren't viable; something about ice crystals forming in their cells. People like us, preserved using later techniques, have a better chance."

"I can't give up until I know for sure!" I almost snapped, but I took a deep breath, chastising myself for the outburst of frustration.

"In that case," Simon suggested, trying to ease the tension, "I propose we call it a day and come back tomorrow to get your other senses activated. You've got a nice surprise coming." He smiled at me, and I couldn't help but feel a flicker of anticipation.

I wanted to protest that I'd had enough surprises to last several lifetimes, but instead, as I began to follow them toward the exit, I muttered, not very enthusiastically, "I can't wait."

Chapter 15 – Turning Me On

"So let me get this right," I said, my voice echoing slightly in the vast corridor as the four of us made our way back to the library the following day. "I'm going to be remotely hooked up to the central information system so I can access most of its data?"

Earl nodded, his expression a mix of excitement and reassurance as we approached the grand entrance of the library, its towering walls looming like ancient sentinels.

"It's like Wi-Fi," I declared, a grin spreading across my face. "I'm a walking internet machine!" My spirits had lifted significantly since yesterday, and my newfound joviality seemed to lighten the atmosphere for my relieved companions.

"It's the main way the system learns your preferences," Simon explained, his tone earnest. "Without it, it wouldn't be able to manage society the way it does. The link lets it know if you're being enticed or cajoled into doing something you don't want to do. For instance, if a group of friends tried to drag you to a casino to gamble, but deep down you were against it, the system would recognise that and deny you entry. It wouldn't matter how much you wanted to please your friends."

"But thank goodness that kind of peer pressure is a thing of the past," Jennifer chimed in, her voice warm and reassuring. "Most people accept you for who you are. Whatever your dislikes or minor phobias, it makes you... well, you."

"What if I didn't agree with gambling but still wanted to try it to see if it was as bad as I thought?" I asked, curiosity piqued.

Earl chuckled softly. "Well, that would be possible. You'd just have to access the system and arrange to experience it on your own at a future date, with an assigned companion to gauge your reactions. You can even override the system in extreme cases if you want to feel uncomfortable. Surprisingly, quite a few people exercise that right. In fact, there's a society dedicated to it."

"I can see how that might ensure no one finds themselves in an uncomfortable environment," I mused, "but it does seem like a lot of trouble."

"Like the trouble of an entire race annihilating itself, you mean?" Jennifer shot back, her eyes narrowing slightly.

"Errm... yes," I conceded, acknowledging her reference to humanity's failed attempts at survival. "When you put it like that, I suppose no trouble is too much."

We continued down the corridor in contemplative silence, each of us lost in our thoughts about the fate of the human race. It was Simon who broke the spell, glancing over at me with a hint of mischief in his eyes.

"Anyway, we're meeting with the administrator who oversees this section of the library. We jokingly call her the librarian, but I doubt she has any duties we'd recognise as fitting that description. Ankit has already arranged for her to activate all your senses, Richard, so we shouldn't have to wait."

"And don't worry," Earl added, his tone reassuring. "The system can't read your mind unless you initiate a link, and even then, no other human has access to that information. The system only detects your feelings to ensure you avoid unnecessary situations. It's a pity we didn't develop something as sophisticated as this before the eventual collapse of our race. One simple thing, it seems, could have saved us."

"One of the things I find most fascinating about these new senses," Simon interjected, his enthusiasm palpable, "is how they can help people connect with each other. It's incredible! If you're looking for a particular type of person, you can initiate a scan of your immediate area, and it matches you up with people nearby who share similar tastes, interests... and," he added with a playful wink, "even comparable libidos. No need for a smartphone!"

"A bit like the apps we used to use, Richard, and a sight better than my disastrous attempts at internet dating," Jennifer chimed in, supressing a laugh. "I'll never forget that *'sixty-nine-year-old public speaker'* I got matched with after my ad was translated into Chinese!"

We all erupted into laughter, the sound echoing off the polished walls as we continued down the impressively long corridor. Jennifer, who had to quicken her pace to keep up with us, said, "You'll find it great fun accessing all the information, Richard; it's so impressive. All you have to do is concentrate on what you want to know, and pretty soon, you'll have an answer. It kind of appears in your head—sometimes as a visual, sometimes as a thought. It's strange, but... you just know."

We arrived at what I assumed was the reception area, a bulky red seat with large, indented armrests stood like a beacon in the otherwise empty corridor. A panel of controls was embedded in the cabinet next to it, and a less impressive grey chair sat in front of that. Just as we approached, an attractive, official-looking Caucasian woman emerged from the room on our left, her demeanour business-like. "Mister Green, please take a seat and place your arms firmly down into the armrests," she instructed, her voice smooth and authoritative.

She settled her elegant frame into the other seat near the controls, carefully smoothing her black skirt under her slim legs. Looking at me over the glasses perched on her prominent nose, she suddenly said, "That's it, Mister Green."

That's it! I thought, momentarily distracted by the absurdity of her needing glasses. I'd been so engrossed in wondering why she needed them that I hadn't noticed anything happen. Honestly, these people were so obsessed with our past that it bordered on the manic. I mean, glasses! She must have better eyesight than anyone had ever had in my time.

Dismissing me, she turned to my friends. "Perhaps you'd better start with something simple, like person location. It'll come easier if the subject is someone he's familiar with, for example, his contact at the Cryogen lab?" she suggested.

"Thank you," Jennifer said, pulling me away gently. "Come on, Richard."

I followed her into one of the study rooms, still convinced that nothing had actually happened. I didn't feel any different at all.

"Right, Richard, sit down here, and we'll give it a go to see if everything's working as it should."

I sat down, and Jennifer continued with her instructions. "Close your eyes and think of a map of the Earth, and a date—say, nineteen twenty. Then imagine that date at the top of the map and try to superimpose the names of all the capital cities you already know onto it."

I focused on Washington, Paris, Beijing, and a few other capitals I was familiar with. Soon, the names began to appear by themselves as I concentrated on different parts of the map.

"Is it working?" I heard Earl ask, his voice tinged with anticipation.

"Yes," I replied, excitement bubbling within me as the resolution of the image improved, and different markers began to appear on the map, independent of my thoughts. These were capital cities I didn't know. I found that I could look at any part of the map and zoom in to see the information. The system had clearly picked up on my initial efforts and was now completing the picture. I smiled, feeling a rush of exhilaration before opening my eyes and breaking the spell.

"I take it I don't have to keep my eyes closed for this to work?"

"No, and it's not the only thing you can do either," Simon said, his enthusiasm infectious. "What the librarian said about person location is a simple task, as long as the subject is someone you know and allows you to track them. All you have to do is think of the person. Close your eyes again and try thinking of Ankit and where he is. It should come to you instinctively after a while, so you can do it with your eyes open."

As I let my eyelids fall, a fleeting thought crossed my mind: what if I was presented with an image of Ankit in the bath or on the toilet? I quickly shook the image away; somehow, I thought it unlikely in this society. With my eyes firmly shut, I focused on my friend's face—the strong jawline, hawkish nose, dazzling smile, and, of course, his incongruous hairstyle. I pushed everything else aside and concentrated solely on Ankit trying to conjure up an image on the inside of my eyelids.

But just as I thought I was going to be successful, the face I'd constructed in my mind began to change. The hair receded back into the scalp like a nest of retreating snakes; the skin lightened, the features softened. The mouth was moving, but no words were coming out, just like the people in the square. As the image cleared, I realised this new face looked familiar, and then I began to hear the words.

The sound gradually increased as I concentrated on his lips and then it came to me. It was the man I'd seen waving the banner and protesting on the vid screen the other day.

"Richard, listen to me, this is important," he said urgently. "Don't believe everything the Manoorans tell you; some of them are different. Some of them want to—"

But the voice suddenly trailed off, and I leaned forward as if that would make the words clearer. But they ceased abruptly as another voice interrupted.

"Richard, Richard... are you alright?"

The man's face began to break up, gradually replaced by Simon's, who was leaning over me with concern etched on his features. Still shaking my shoulder, he said, "Wake up, Richard! Are you alright?"

"Is everything okay?" Jennifer echoed, her voice laced with worry. "You looked out of it for a while. Did you find Ankit?"

I explained what I'd just seen and heard, and Jennifer frowned. "That shouldn't have happened. I think you ought to tell Ankit about this and ask him to check it out. Something just went seriously wrong somewhere."

But my intuition nagged at me, whispering that I shouldn't share this episode with my Manooran friends. After all, the warning message could be about them. "Do you think I should, though?" I responded, uncertainty creeping into my voice. "I mean, why on earth would the leader of the protesters attempt to contact me? And what if there's something to it?"

As we travelled back to Earl's apartment, they filled me in on everything they knew about the protesters. Apparently, they were Cryogens who had been successfully revived, only to discover fundamental defects in their core personalities. The initial manifestation of those defects was severe paranoia, causing them to flee what they perceived as a society of hostile aliens trying to kill them.

"But in reality," Simon explained, "the Manoorans only want to help these people. They could all have healthy lives or at least be reborn."

"Well, part of my reluctance comes from this," I said, holding out the warning that was unfolding in my hand. "I don't believe this relates to any of you; I think it means the Manoorans, just as the message I've just received does."

Confusion flickered across their faces until Earl pointed to the scrolling message. "Where did that come from?"

After explaining where I'd found it, I expressed my belief that it didn't refer to Ankit either. "But I don't want to say anything about this to him, either, just in case. I don't know how close he is to Ramoon, and I certainly don't trust that man."

"Okay," Jennifer assured me, her voice steady. "We won't say anything until you feel ready."

Looking around at the contents and décor of Earl's apartment, I realised my fellow Cryogens were trying to capture a sense of their own time. The room felt so familiar to me, and a striking similarity to the home I'd shared with Helen washed over me like a sudden wave of déjà vu. While Simon's rooms had been simplistic and very masculine, with brown and beige colours covering the stark angles of the simple furniture, Earl's was decorated with flowers, purple vases, and cushions. It looked inviting and comfortable, but also quite feminine, and I wondered if it was an attempt to recreate something he'd shared with someone special.

I couldn't help thinking that Helen would like this room.

Simon's reference to being reborn reminded me of a question I'd been meaning to ask them for some time. "I keep hearing this term 'reborn' being used all over the place," I said, curiosity bubbling up. "What does it actually mean?"

Earl passed me the coffee he'd just retrieved from the panel on his overly decorated wall. "Even though these artificial bodies are immortal, they're barren, so they can't reproduce, which means there are no natural children." I nodded, recalling what Ankit had told me. "However, in some circumstances, people can choose to have most of their memories removed, leaving only the core personality behind. It sometimes happens when people feel they've lived too long and want to start afresh. They also do this to any Cryogen that's not suitable for revival but still retains a degree of their core personality. It's also a form of punishment for certain criminal activities.

Anyone undergoing rebirth is transferred to a child-like body so they can enjoy growing up again and experience the joys of childhood once more. Criminals who undergo this are closely monitored and only exposed to experiences designed to influence them positively."

"It also helps those who want it to have children," Jennifer added. "But with so few reborns, there's a very long waiting list. Luckily, time is something these people have plenty of, so they can afford to wait."

"What about all the memories from their previous lives? Do they just leave it all behind, then? It sounds like dying to me."

"That's pretty much the case with the criminals, Richard," Simon contributed. "But most of the others reintegrate their old memories when they've grown up and matured. It doesn't matter how many times they do this; the previous memories just keep building up and become part of that individual's development as a person. Most people take advantage of rebirth to relieve the lethargy that inevitably comes with immortality."

"Of course," Jennifer interrupted, her tone teasing. "Like most things in this crazy future, it's a bit weird because it means everyone could eventually parent everyone else. Your own children could adopt you if you're reborn, and when you reintegrate your memories, you'd remember being brought up by your kids!"

"That's just not right," I said, struggling to comprehend the bizarre combinations of family structure this procedure could create. "They don't allow that, do they?" But I could already sense from Jennifer's tone that she wasn't joking.

"In practice, they don't," Simon said, smiling at my horrified expression. "Generally, people aren't placed with anyone they've parented or been parented by, just like the system prevents child/parent bonding by inhibiting anyone's attraction to people with whom they've shared that relationship. I think what Jennifer is referring to is the eventual need to allow it. I mean, there's a finite number of people, and if they all live forever... well, they'll have to let it happen."

"We've all discussed this before, Richard," Earl said, his voice serious. "I don't think it will ever occur because the number of memories accumulated by the time it would need to be allowed would necessitate having to have some of those memories permanently stored or selectively erased."

I took a drink of my coffee, enthralled by what I was hearing. "So, this is what happens to Cryogens when they're not viable for revival?" I asked.

"If it's possible to salvage the core personality, yes, and it seems like there are more, and more of them nowadays. We've heard that it's because the majority underwent cryogenic suspension using the old procedure that allowed ice crystals to form, causing irreparable damage to their brain cells."

My heart sank, and I could feel the weight of despair settling in. Jennifer reached over and touched my shoulder.

'Helen?" she asked, not really a question but a confirmation that she understood.

I nodded, recalling the explanation of the new techniques the technicians were going to use on me when the time came. "She was preserved before me using those earlier techniques."

Simon placed his hand on my other shoulder, his expression serious. "The problem is that there's often no previous memory to save from these Cryogens. If Helen has been reborn and you find her, she may have no recollection of you or your previous life together."

"I only want to find her, or at least discover what's happened to her, Simon. If she's one of these reborns and has no memories, I can try to make her fall in love with me again. I could recreate everything we did together so she could rebuild the memories. She could access her previous life through me." With my head bowed in submission, I said, "I've got to do something to find her, or at least convince myself I'm trying; this is really starting to get to me."

It was impossible to hide my desperation from my friends, and it showed on their concerned yet supportive smiles.

"Speak to Ramoon tomorrow, Richard. Ask him to get you onto the Cryogen project as soon as possible. It's the only place to be if you're ever going to find out what's happened to her."

"Yes," I nodded, the rigid, hard face of the administrator flashing in my mind. "I'll contact him tomorrow; it'll give me something to focus on."

"You can speak to him after we get back, then," Earl said, his excitement palpable. "I've arranged something special for tomorrow. Something I think you're going to rather like."

"Oh, and what's that?"

"You'll have to wait until tomorrow. I want it to be a surprise."

The degree of change I was encountering, and the speed at which I had to absorb it all, was having a marked effect on me. I was becoming desensitised to all the strangeness around me. So, I showed little enthusiasm at my friend's promise of a 'surprise.' I doubted anything could truly surprise me now. But I couldn't ignore Earl's uncharacteristic excitement, so I tried to muster as much enthusiasm as I could in my reply. "I'll look forward to it, then," I said, forcing a smile.

As I walked back to my apartment, my mind was a whirlwind of thoughts. I couldn't shake the dislike I'd instinctively developed for Ramoon, nor could I forget the man who had appeared in my mind to deliver a warning. Was this connected somehow to the message I'd received before?

What was he trying to tell me about the Manoorans? Should I be wary of all of them, or was the warning just about Ramoon? The man had said, "Some of them are trying to…" But trying to - what?

Chapter 16 – A Visit to the Past

The following day, I awoke to the sweet symphony of birdsong, their melodies weaving through the warm sunlight that filtered down through a dense canopy of towering trees just beyond the walls of my room. It wasn't a real forest, of course—just a simulation, courtesy of the vidilic-covered walls that surrounded me. Vidilic, that plastic-like substance that enveloped surfaces and carried the virtual reality of this age, made it all possible. Anyone unfamiliar with the technology would have sworn my room had only one wall, the one at the back of the now conventional bed where I'd slept. I felt as though the forest was wrapping around me, and aside from the absence of rain, the environmental controls of the room replicated nearly everything else in this virtual paradise. A gentle breeze and dappled sunlight caressed my face as I greeted the day with a satisfying stretch. After finishing a yawn that felt like it echoed through the trees, I smiled and said, "I never thought I'd have an alarm clock as good as you."

It might not have been as precise as the shrill timepieces of my past, but it still roused me early enough to meet my friends. I had no idea what this place was going to throw at me next, and I had to admit to myself that the notion Helen and I had shared about fitting in quickly was a drastic overestimation. It was going to take years to learn everything about this future and its strange, new ways.

I was grateful that my apartment was close to the main square, as it gave me the chance to walk instead of relying on one of the tubes that crisscrossed the city. Jennifer was right about certain things being psychologically important. I relished the comfort that the exercise brought me, even though my new body didn't technically need it.

Arriving early, I settled at a table outside a quaint little bar, watching three women at the next table savouring their breakfast while discussing the latest fashions. A smile crept across my face as I recalled what I'd learned. I wondered if their conversation was genuine or merely a product of the system's programming. If their conversation's 'intimate mode' was activated, they could have been sharing their latest romantic escapades for all I knew, which underscored just how useful the technology was. The last thing I wanted was to overhear total strangers discussing their bedroom habits.

Before long, the others joined me at the table, and we all enjoyed breakfast while speculating about what the day ahead had in store. "So, what exactly are we going to be doing today?" I asked Earl, who was practically vibrating with excitement, eager to reveal his 'surprise.'

When he answered, his tone was charged with enthusiasm, as if he were sharing a secret that would thrill me. "We're taking a trip to your old city, Nottingham."

My heart raced at the mention of my home. "But that's back in the UK; won't it take a long time?"

"Methods of travel are far more advanced nowadays, Richard. We'll be traveling to Midland City and then going on from there. It lies underground between the old surface cities of Nottingham, Leicester, Derby, and Birmingham."

"So, are you telling me there are areas of Midland City that replicate the old cities above?" I asked, my curiosity piqued.

"Well, yes, there are," he said, pausing dramatically before adding, "but we're going to the surface, Richard, to the real Nottingham. Ramoon arranged it for us; it's a great privilege because unless you work up there or have a holiday approved, access is pretty much restricted."

I must have looked taken aback. "You mean it still exists!"

"Of course, and it's populated too, but very sparsely, mainly by people involved in preserving the way it was before humanity became extinct. A lot of Cryogens work in the cities on the surface because they never used to live in confined spaces, even ones as advanced as this."

"Well, you were right, Earl; this is definitely going to be a treat." Excitement bubbled within me. "Let's go.'

I didn't even want to contemplate the speed at which the underground tube travelled as it whisked us across the continents to my home. Like all cities in this world, Midland City was enormous, dwarfed only by its northern neighbour, Yorkshire City. But these paled in comparison to the super cities I'd heard about—Channel City, sprawling beneath the English Channel, with areas extending beneath parts of London and Paris; NorthAm City, encompassing vast swathes of the eastern American seaboard, second only in size on this planet to the largest city of all, India Prime. Some cities on other planets were even larger, the largest being India Central City on Earth-Three. These cities were so vast that even with their enormous populations, there was no sense of being crowded. In fact, it was possible to wander for days without encountering another soul. The need to socialize was now satisfied by the conscious effort to meet others, rather than being driven together by commercial necessity.

We reached the surface using one of the vertical travel tubes, and when the doorway indicated we'd arrived, we stepped into a small antechamber. Beneath the pervasive fungal odour emanating from the cold, grey concrete walls, I could just detect the musty scent of dampness, forced into the air by patches of sunlight crossing the floor. Like still spotlights on a West End stage, these shafts of light poured into the room through large picture windows, offering a tantalising preview of what lay beyond.

The light was so different from the uniform brightness that surrounded us underground. When we finally stepped into the full sunshine, I found it more mellow and gentle, reminiscent of the bright, hazy days of my youth. The white, cotton-candy clouds drifted across the late summer sky, and the almost imperceptible sound of the wind whispered of the magnitude and power of Mother Nature, dwarfing the artificial habitats created within the cities. I took a deep breath and spun around, taking in this new environment and its welcome onslaught on my senses.

We'd emerged into a wooded area next to a sloping hill, and apart from the small grey bunker that surrounded the tube we'd just arrived on, there were no other buildings. A gentle breeze wafted the mid-morning heat over my face, as if greeting an old friend. The warmth brought back vivid memories of stepping off a plane into the stifling heat of a well-earned holiday, accompanied by the forgotten smells of a distant summer. And though I couldn't pinpoint its source, I swore I could smell freshly cut grass mingling with the heady fragrance of wildflowers that surrounded us.

Somewhere, I could hear real birds singing. But otherwise, it was quiet, reminiscent of the times I used to lie in the middle of the cornfields behind my parents' house, gazing up at the sky and forgetting the world existed. "This is great, but it doesn't look like any part of the city I remember," I remarked. "Do we need the tube again, or will we be walking into the city?"

"Neither" Simon said. "We're going to take a hover pod the rest of the way. It'll give you a chance to see how the surface has changed."

"And what exactly is one of those?" I asked, already bracing myself for another new experience.

Jennifer laughed as I began to realise what response was coming.

And Simon didn't let me down, stating the obvious as if I were someone who struggled to grasp anything. "It's like a pod that you sit in," he said slowly, "...and it... hovers." Then, with a huge smile on his face, he pointed to the sloping hill and said, "And we'll be getting one from over there."

As we strolled over to the hill, Jennifer said, "The travel tubes and other methods of getting around are all okay for long distances, but there's still the matter of traveling on the surface to places that are just too far to walk." She added, probably referencing the psychological needs she often spoke about, "And while we're on the surface, it gives us an element of freedom, reminding us of our beloved cars."

We reached a clearing at the bottom of the hill, and Earl raised his arm straight, showing his palm. "Hover pod to Nottingham, Earl Jeffrey." At that moment, an entrance appeared on the side of the hill, and what looked like a giant egg cup moved toward us from the inside. It was ebony black and shiny, and inside, two beige seats faced each other. To one side, there was a flat panel that resembled a control console.

"Shall we get in?" Earl asked.

"But there are only two seats," I began to protest, before realising I should keep quiet. Earl had already touched one of the controls, and the pod was transforming into a more elongated elliptical shape, with two more seats emerging inside.

While this transformation occurred, four steps emerged from the outer side of the pod, allowing us to board. As we settled in, I leaned over to see the bottom part of the egg cup and the steps melt away, absorbed into the section we were sitting in. By rights, we should have toppled over, I thought. But the exterior was covered in a thin blue film of light, which must have been stabilising us somehow.

"Please stay inside the vehicle to enable the barrier field to be activated," came a voice from somewhere inside the pod.

Distracted by the workings of this pod, Jennifer had to pull me away from the side before a gentle swish brought a reduction of sound and stillness. It was the only indication of the vehicle's cover activating. The force field, if that's what it was, fascinated me, and I touched it. It resembled glass but must have been much stronger. When I lifted my hands from it, they left no marks.

"Wouldn't you have just loved to have one of these, back in our time?" Simon asked.

"It's better than my old Porsche," I replied, "but I'd love to know what's keeping us upright."

"Well," Earl offered, "the blue light surrounding the base is an anti-gravity field that, depending on the level it's set at, allows us to climb out of or descend into Earth's gravity well. At the same time, we're moved horizontally by the magnetic attraction of a grid embedded beneath most of the landmass of the planet. And what you've just touched, as you've probably guessed, is a force field."

With his hand placed on the control console, Earl said, "Robin Hood statue - M1 - normal." With that, we lifted a few hundred feet from the ground before starting to glide across the landscape.

"We don't normally have to verbalise these instructions. Most people use the mind link, but I wanted you to be able to see and hear exactly how we're controlling our surroundings."

"So, what does '*normal*' mean?" I asked.

"That's just how fast you want to travel; if you're in no rush and want to enjoy your surroundings, then this speed is sufficient. Of course, during your journey, you can alter this setting to whatever's required. And these things can go incredibly fast."

I didn't doubt it and looked down for the road that Earl had just referenced. "Why would there still be motorways if you don't need cars?"

"There are no motorways."

"But you just mentioned the M1."

"Oh, I see. No, we just use the reference if there are landmarks close by." He paused, then added, "And there's a particular landmark, where junction 26 of the M1 motorway was, that you won't have seen before."

The only thing I could see was a vast sea of greens and rusty reds covering the forest below. It was a fantastic sight in itself. The Earth, or at least much of it, must have been reclaimed by nature—an environmentalist's dream. A solitary hawk soared above us, banking on a gust of wind before hovering for a moment and then plummeting down, likely to an abundance of scurrying prey.

Then, on the horizon, towering above the trees, I began to make out the figure of a kneeling archer. I recognised it immediately. It was a duplicate of the statue of Robin Hood that guarded the foot of the castle in the city. Only this version was much larger and more colourful; the boots, tunic, quiver, and arrow were all different hues, as the kneeling bowman aimed his arrow into the sky.

It was hundreds of feet tall as we hovered beside it, and the arrow bore the words *"The Future"* etched into it.

Before I could ask about it, Simon said, "Apparently, a wealthy eccentric had it built in 2110 because he was so proud of his home city. And this is what he left behind.'

Noticing I was scrutinising the arrow, Earl added, "It illuminates in the dark; it's the only part of the statue visible from a distance at night."

The hover pod then started to move off in what I recognised as the direction of the city. I couldn't help but think of the landmarks I might have recognised had they still existed—my old gym at Cinderhill, Bobbers Mill Bridge, and the pubs that lined Alfreton Road into the city, where I'd stopped for a drink on my way to a night out. I couldn't see any of them. "I don't suppose much has survived from our time, has it?" I asked, the obvious question hanging in the air.

"You'll be surprised when you get into the city," Earl replied. "Most of the architecturally interesting and historical buildings have been preserved, even after all this time. The rest have gone, and as you can see, nature has taken its course and reclaimed what it used to own. However, it is possible to ascend higher into the air and instruct the hover pod to overlay the scene with the view at whatever point in time you choose. The force field acts as a lens through which you'd see the ground as it was then."

I thought of the Broxtowe Estate I'd been raised on and said, "Well, I don't suppose anyone would miss some of the buildings constructed in our time. Especially the houses on those large council estates."

"No, they're not needed anymore. Only a few of the workers actually live in the surface buildings; most of them reside in local townships underground. The biggest population above ground is in the hotels dotted around. As you can imagine, the cities on the surface are quite a magnet for tourists."

A large smile crossed my face as I saw what was appearing on the skyline. I looked at Simon as if someone were playing a practical joke. "What on earth is that?" I exclaimed, pointing to the massive castle coming into view on the hill above the city. "That is not Nottingham Castle. What happened?"

All of them were smiling now, and Jennifer explained the existence of what looked like a medieval castle perched upon Castle Rock. "The building you remember was destroyed by the invaders from space. The surviving residents had always been disappointed that it never actually looked like a castle, so they decided to '*improve*' the new building. What you see now is the result."

"If you're impressed with this, Richard, wait until you see what they've done to Buckingham Palace," joked Jennifer.

I just shook my head, amazed at the scale of the metamorphosis. The castle was now a formidable fortress with battlements, arrow slits, and a massive drawbridge spanning the newly created moat. It reminded me of something out of the Harry Potter movies.

The image of the old castle had been somewhat of a joke to the city's visitors in my day because, where they'd expected to see what I was now looking at, they found a museum and art gallery. But they would have definitely been impressed with this—the latest incarnation of the first castle on this site which was built for William the Conqueror.

We shifted position and hovered over the Old Market Square, and I felt a rush of nostalgia wash over me. To my astonishment, it seemed that apart from the absence of tram lines, nothing had changed in the city centre. It was as if I'd stepped back in time, the familiar sights and sounds wrapping around me like a warm embrace. The stone lions, majestic and stoic, reclined outside the council house, their presence a testament to the city's history. They were the most iconic landmarks, where countless souls had gathered to meet, and they stirred memories of my first proper date with Helen. If only those lions could speak; their stories would fill volumes, rich with laughter, love, and the bittersweet pangs of youth. What a book that would be.

Before me, the square was alive with the vibrant energy of the annual medieval market, a kaleidoscope of colours and sounds that ignited a sense of belonging deep within me. The air was thick with the scent of roasted meats, spiced pastries, and the sweet aroma of candied fruits, mingling with laughter and the chatter of excited vendors. "This is a great attraction for tourists, Richard," Simon remarked, his eyes wide with wonder. "I've never been to Nottingham before, but I looked it up last night when Earl told us we were coming. Does it look like it did in your day?"

"It certainly does," I replied, my voice barely above a whisper, overwhelmed by the flood of memories. This market had thrived in the square for generations, and all I could offer Simon was a nod, afraid that words would betray the emotions swelling within me.

As the hours slipped by, I revelled in the joy of revisiting the familiar haunts of my past. I introduced my friends to the places where I'd laughed, danced, and courted Helen, each location a chapter in the story of my life. They listened intently as I recounted tales of drinking in *'Ye Old Trip to Jerusalem'*, the oldest inn in England, nestled against the base of Castle Rock, now overshadowed by the impressive new castle. Established in 1189, its historical ties to Richard the Lionheart's crusades, notorious highwaymen and the Luddites of the Industrial Revolution, echoed through its ancient walls, each brick steeped in history.

The current inhabitants of this time seemed to have embraced the rich tapestry of human culture, weaving together celebrations from every corner of the globe while creating new traditions of their own. The desire to honour the past and commemorate significant events served as a vital thread, binding them to their humanity. Today, the medieval market coincided with the vibrant festival of Diwali, the festival of lights—a celebration that resonated deeply with me, as Helen and I had often travelled to the neighbouring city of Leicester to partake in the lively festivities.

As we descended on Maid Marion Way and made our way down Friar Lane into the bustling market square, the atmosphere enveloped us like a warm blanket. The crowds surged around us, reminiscent of the Goose Fair, another cherished annual event that my city had hosted. I marvelled at how the cycles of the seasons had shifted; normally, these celebrations were held in the latter part of the year, yet today felt like the height of summer, the sun casting a golden glow over everything.

With our backs to the council house, we stood transfixed, watching the myriad of colourful floating lights that danced in the air, twinkling like stars against the backdrop of the blue sky. The carnival parade wound its way around the square, a riot of colour and sound that made my head spin with delight. I felt the familiar ache of loss for Helen, a bittersweet reminder of the love we'd shared.

Then, as the central part of the parade passed us, I noticed a man in the crowd who seemed to be shedding his clothes! My heart raced at the sight, surprised that such a display could occur in Open Society where nudity was prohibited. As I watched him quickly undress, I realised that beneath his outer garments, he wore a flesh-coloured jumpsuit.

Just as I was about to look away, content to dismiss this as part of the festivities, I was stunned to see him expanding. In mere seconds, the suit swelled to an enormous size, threatening to burst. The man began to float into the air, panic rippling through the crowd as people scattered in all directions. I squinted, trying to make sense of the chaos, and then I saw the words emblazoned across the fabric: "Cryogens unite. Don't let them kill us all off – protect the humans." *That message again.*

A flurry of activity erupted as a group of what I later learned were police, known as Upholders, rushed toward the man. They were taller than the average citizen, their muscular frames reminiscent of Sumo wrestlers, clad in green uniforms with striking blue stripes. As they approached the floating man, he suddenly grasped a pole that had extended from a nearby window, pulling himself back in. He deflated as he disappeared through the window of a nearby building. I turned to Earl, my heart pounding. "What's going on? That was the same message I saw on the vid-screen when Ankit was taking me to the information centre."

"It's the protesters again," Simon said, urgency lacing his voice. "Come on, I think it's time we left before we get caught up in this chaos."

As we travelled back in the hover pod, I couldn't shake the unsettling feeling that had settled in my gut. I turned to Earl, curiosity gnawing at me. "Do you know any Manoorans who live on the surface?"

"No, Richard. When they first arrived on Earth, almost all of them sought refuge in the enclosed cities. After their constant exposure to the open skies, I suppose they prefer the security of confinement. It's unlikely many would want to make a permanent home on the surface, but they do make up the bulk of tourists. It's primarily Cryogens who live and work up here, yearning for a connection to their past. Many feel it's their responsibility to protect and preserve what remains.

That said, the Manoorans hold human history in high regard, and you've probably learned that they aspire to claim it as their own. It's akin to how some Americans once viewed British history before 1492—a sense of belonging. I think that's what the Manoorans are striving for."

"It would be nice if we could all reach that stage, Earl."

"We can only live in hope Richard."

As we gazed down from the hover pod, it was surreal to think that Helen and I had once driven along the same route in my Porsche, now obscured by an overgrown forest.

Upon entering the bunker to begin our journey back, I took one last look at the setting sun, its life-giving rays warming my face. I thought to myself, *I wish you could come with me.*

When we returned to India Prime, we met Ankit and Ramoon in the main square. They were seated, sipping drinks and watching the people around them. Seizing the opportunity to catch them in a relaxed mood, I approached Ramoon once more about joining the Cryogen project.

"I'd very much like to be involved with it Ramoon."

"Even after your trip to the surface?" he asked, surprise flickering in his eyes. "Didn't it make you even a little envious of those Cryogens living up there, surrounded by familiar landscapes? I thought it might make you consider working up there yourself."

"No," I replied firmly. "It was a great experience, but I still want to be involved with the Cryogen project."

I sensed Ramoon's hesitation, as if he were trying to steer me away from my goal. I wondered if today's trip had been a deliberate attempt to present me with an alternative to the Cryogen project. But he had no chance; my priority was clear, and it was finding my wife.

"Perhaps I should explain," he continued, his tone shifting. "Under normal circumstances, we'd accept you without question, but the current uncertainty regarding your wife means we must ensure your motivation isn't driven by that particular obsession. Remember, the majority of those being revived are only suitable to be reborn. You were one of the few exceptions. If we discover that you've lost Helen, will you be able to cope with it, Richard?"

"I can assure you the answer to that question is yes, Ramoon. I can also assure you that my main allegiance would be to the Cryogen project. I am confident I can control my personal feelings in this matter."

This statement was a lie, my fingers crossed behind my back, but I refused to jeopardize my chances of being accepted into the project.

"Then I'll put your name forward to the board."

A wave of elation surged through me. I stifled the urge to press for details about when I might start. No matter how desperately I wanted to scream at Ramoon and demand immediate access to the institute to begin my search for Helen, I couldn't afford to show my impatience.

Ramoon regarded me thoughtfully, then changed the subject. "Don't worry about those protesters, Richard. We're close to finding them and getting them the help they need."

"Why?" I asked, curiosity piqued. "What's actually wrong with them?" I knew what my friends had told me, but I wanted to hear it from Ramoon.

"They can't accept the fact that we're struggling to revive more of their kind. They suffer from a psychosis that convinces them we're trying to kill them." He laughed, but it lacked sincerity. "Of course, we're not."

"One thing you'll learn on the Cryogen project is that some of the revived subjects display severe defects. This usually manifests as serious paranoid psychosis shortly after reintegration."

I wondered if they had considered that this might be happening to me, but I was too afraid to ask. Ramoon continued, "They avoid social contact and gradually fade from Open Society into one of the peripheral groups—usually those with a high degree of paranoia. They convince themselves that everyone," he paused, looking at the floor before meeting my gaze again, "well, we Manoorans anyway, are out to kill them all."

"That's just not true, Richard," Ankit interjected. "There's no evidence and no reason for that belief. Why would we want to extinguish the original human race when we were the ones who began reviving you survivors in the first place? Our biggest regret now is that we're unable to successfully revive most of the Cryogens who remain."

I appreciated Ankit's contribution, as I found it increasingly difficult to trust anything that came out of Ramoon's mouth.

Ramoon pressed on, eager to convince anyone who would listen how misguided the protesters were. "These individuals have serious issues, Richard, and their paranoia makes them potentially dangerous. But rest assured, we are tracking them down to help them fully integrate into a new society. We'll treat them with behavioural modifications, and if all else fails…" He trailed off, leaving the implication hanging in the air.

I couldn't help but voice my thoughts. "I'd best ignore any further attempts they make to contact me in the future, then," I said, relishing the prospect of seeing his reaction.

I wasn't disappointed. Ramoon nearly choked on his drink. "Puuuh! What do you mean?" he spat, anger flashing in his eyes. "Have you been in contact with the protesters?" For a brief moment, I glimpsed beneath the thin veneer of friendliness that masked the true animosity beneath.

"Not really," I replied, taken aback, then recounted the vision I'd had in the library.

"If anything like that happens to you again, you need to will the image away as strongly as you can. Then, when it's gone, contact me immediately."

"I will," I promised, trying to sound convincing, though I couldn't shake the uneasy feeling that passed between Ramoon and Ankit. Was I beginning to sense a hint of collusion between these two Manooran officials?

That night, as I drifted off to sleep, I couldn't help but replay my trip to the surface in my mind. The memories it had triggered were vivid and intoxicating, and as I slipped into slumber, the dreams that unfolded were dictated by the experience. The frustration over my search for Helen intertwined with the echoes of our past, taking me on a haunting voyage through the remnants of our previous life.

Chapter 17 – Something to Live For

During that last year at school, I felt like I was under a relentless spotlight, a stage where every adult in my life seemed to play the role of a nagging director. My parents, my teachers, and just about every adult I encountered pestered me with the same question: *What did I want to do with my future*? It was as if they believed my life was a script waiting to be written, and I was the reluctant actor who'd forgotten his lines. But honestly, I was at that age when the future felt like a distant planet, light-years away. I was more concerned with surviving the week than mapping out my life's trajectory. The future would sort itself out, I told myself, as I navigated the chaos of adolescence. All I knew was that I'd made a silent vow to escape the fate that had ensnared my father—a defeatist mindset that clung to so many souls in our neighbourhood like a persistent fog.

The Estate, with its crumbling houses and abandoned cars that looked like they'd been through a war, was a stark reminder of what I didn't want to become. It was a place where dreams went to die, where lethargy and dependence wrapped around people like a suffocating blanket. The streets were littered with the remnants of broken aspirations, and the air was thick with a sense of hopelessness. It was easier to fall into that trap than to claw your way out. The system was rigged, crushing aspirations before they could even take root, slowly locking people into a cycle of poverty. No, I was determined to break free from that fate. But unlike most young adults of my generation, I wasn't going to do it by chasing fame as a movie star, footballer, or pop sensation. Those paths seemed like shortcuts to wealth, and I'd never craved the spotlight. I knew I would have to put in the hard work, the kind that would leave me exhausted but fulfilled.

I had my mother to thank for my drive. Her unwavering determination and constant encouragement instilled in me a fierce sense of self-belief. She was my rock, the one who always reminded me that I was capable of more than I could imagine. It was that belief that propelled me toward independence. I was tired of others making decisions for me; I wanted to carve my own path. I had a natural intelligence, even if I hadn't fully applied it in school, and I was ready to use it.

Those attributes carried me through college. With sheer grit and determination, I earned the qualifications I needed to land the job I'd always dreamed of. But every step of the way was a challenge. I watched my friends land well-paying jobs, buying trendy clothes and enjoying nights out without a care in the world, while I buried myself in my studies. The contrast was stark, and it often felt like I was running a marathon while they were cruising in luxury cars. One lesson from my sociology classes stuck with me: the principle of deferred gratification. Sacrificing now for greater rewards later. That's how I viewed my struggle through college—an investment in a brighter future, a future that I was determined to seize.

Eventually, my hard work paid off. I landed a job in the IT department of a high street bank, and everyone thought I'd made it. The money started rolling in, and I rented a room in the city close to work. I even splurged on a second-hand sports car that made my heart race with pride. The sleek lines and roaring engine felt like a symbol of my success, a tangible representation of my escape from the confines of the Estate.

Yet, memories of Helen haunted me. What might have been. I'd resigned myself to the idea that she had probably moved on, swept away by someone better, while I'd been too focused on my ambitions to pursue anything serious. My romantic encounters had been fleeting and devoid of emotion, fitting neatly into the limited time I had to spare. But as the years passed, I found myself yearning for a more stable relationship, and Helen kept creeping back into my thoughts. Surely, she'd found someone else by now, I mused. How many times had I cursed myself for being a coward, for not standing up to Jason and the gang culture that had dominated our school? It could have been so different.

Fate, however, had other plans. Several years later, I received an invitation to a school reunion. I'd kept in touch with a few old friends and was surprisingly excited at the prospect of seeing familiar faces again. I didn't hesitate to accept the invite, secretly hoping to catch a glimpse of one face in particular. If she was there, I promised myself, no one would stand in my way this time. I tried to convince myself that there were other reasons to attend—impressing everyone with my job and the drive through the school gates in my Porsche. The thought of pulling up in that car made me feel invincible, like I was finally stepping into the role I'd always wanted.

But, as with many good plans, things didn't go as expected.

On the day of the reunion, I was at the small semi-detached house I'd recently bought and was in the midst of renovating. It was close to the school, and once it was ready, my best friend and housemate, Pete, and I planned to move in, giving up our city rooms. Sure, it would mean a longer commute to work, but I'd finally have my own little sanctuary, complete with a tiny garage for my car. The house was a project, a canvas for my aspirations, and I poured my heart into it, hoping it would reflect the life I was building.

Pete and I had grown closer after school, and I would later admit that our relationship had blossomed into a lifelong bromance. Such a funny term, I thought, but it fit perfectly. I loved him, just not in a romantic way. And when I considered some of his quirks—like his obsession with collecting vintage video games—I couldn't help but wonder how difficult it would be for him to find someone who would love him in that way. But he was my anchor, the one person who understood my journey and supported me through thick and thin.

On the day of the reunion, I'd planned to finish early and drive back to the city to change and pick him up. We were both looking forward to making a grand entrance in the Porsche. But, of course, the heap of junk refused to start. Unlike my stomach, the engine wouldn't turn over. "Bloody hell," I muttered, pounding the steering wheel in frustration. "Just great." The car reflected my life at that moment—stuck, unable to move forward.

"Pete," I said into the public telephone, trying to keep my voice steady, "you'll have to get there yourself, mate. The car won't start, and don't laugh. I'll see you at school. Oh, and can you bring me some clothes? I'm stuck in these tatty old jeans and a t-shirt under these overalls." I could almost hear the laughter on the other end of the line, but I didn't care. I was determined to make it to the reunion, no matter what.

As I walked off the main Strelley Road onto the gently sloping Denewood Crescent that led to the school, memories flooded back. I recalled winter days of heavy snow, when my friends and I had made slides along the pavement, nearly careering into passing cars on Fircroft Avenue. That walk was etched in my mind—from the first day my mother had dragged me along it, to the last enthusiastic sprint home after I'd finally left. Time is such a funny thing, I mused; it felt like just yesterday that I'd last made that journey. The familiar sights and sounds wrapped around me like a warm blanket, igniting a sense of nostalgia that was both comforting and bittersweet.

I approached the wrought iron gates that led to the circular raised flowerbed in front of the school entrance. Occasionally, I was overtaken by surprisingly new cars, carrying familiar faces from the past. Some of my old friends had obviously done well for themselves, and I couldn't wait to catch up. But more than anything, in the back of my mind, I wanted to see Helen. The thought of her sent a thrill through me, a mix of excitement and anxiety that I couldn't shake.

As I neared the tall oak doors, half-open and inviting, I spotted the unmistakable profile of Jason Wentworth stepping out of a gleaming Mercedes-Benz. He was the perfect picture of success, helping a stunning blonde out of the car. He wore what had to be a tailored suit, and his shoes looked like they belonged on a runway. The woman beside him was breathtaking, draped in a low-cut, figure-hugging satin green dress that likely cost more than a teacher's monthly salary. So much for my grand entrance! I felt a pang of envy as I watched them, a reminder of the social hierarchy that had always existed at school.

I didn't want to seem petty, so I approached Jason, arms outstretched, smiling like a father welcoming home a long-lost son.

"Ugh!" Jason recoiled, nearly stumbling over his girlfriend. The shock on his face was palpable. In that moment, I realised I must have looked like a complete mess. My designer stubble had morphed into a wild beard, and my hair was in desperate need of a trim. I was dressed in scruffy, torn jeans and a paint-splattered t-shirt featuring the impish face of Marc Bolan, the lead singer of T.Rex. The emulsion splatters even adorned my Doc Martens, painting a picture of someone who should have been sleeping under a cardboard box.

"Jason, it's me—Richard. It's been a long time, mate."

He didn't respond, his eyes scanning my appearance with blatant disgust. I felt a hot wave of jealousy wash over me as I realised how different we'd become. Jason, with his polished exterior and perfect smile—complete with a false tooth—seemed to have it all.

"Yeah," he finally replied, his tone dripping with condescension. "It's been a long time... mate. We'll have to catch up sometime." He roughly wrapped his arm around his girlfriend and turned away, their laughter echoing in my ears as they walked off, leaving me standing there, feeling like a ghost from the past.

I stood there, frozen in disbelief. They were actually laughing at me, and the anger bubbling inside me was almost unbearable. I realised then the extent of my school-day foolishness and shallowness. What a fool I'd been, and how I regretted not approaching Helen when I had the chance. I was determined to make things right if she was here.

But what if she reacted the same way Jason had? Should I wait for Pete to arrive with my clothes? At least I'd look respectable then. I stood there, wrestling with my thoughts, until my simmering anger made the decision for me. No, I thought. If she was as shallow as they were, I needed to know. I wasn't going to change for anyone, and I wanted to see who truly cared about me as a person, not as a mannequin with a credit card.

I squared my shoulders and pushed through the large wooden doors into the school. Several faces turned to me, their expressions a mix of vague recognition and confusion, but no one approached. The atmosphere was thick with nostalgia, and I could feel the weight of memories pressing down on me.

As I walked down the corridors, I was struck by how much some of my former classmates had changed. Some hadn't changed at all, while others had morphed into their parents. Regardless of their shape, they had all made an effort to dress well for the evening, and I began to wonder if my lack of effort was an affront to their collective pride. I felt like an outsider in a place that had once felt like home.

I couldn't dwell on that thought for long, though, because a finger poked into my spine. "I always knew you'd end up as a tramp, Rich," Pete said, holding up a suit bag and a training bag. "I think you'll be needing these, matey."

"No, I won't," I replied, raising my hands in protest. "I'm not dressing up to impress anybody tonight, Pete. But I will tidy myself up a bit and put on whatever shirt you've brought. I'll leave the rest in the cloakroom."

As a compromise, I cleaned the worst of the paint from my boots and slipped on the cream dress shirt that hung loosely over my worn jeans. I no longer looked like a complete mess, but I didn't appear aloof or unapproachable either. After brushing my fingers through my hair, I stepped back into the corridor, determined to find Helen.

The same old glitter ball was casting familiar shadows around the hall, and the scent of the polished wooden parquet flooring transported me back in time. I felt as if I'd fallen through a warp in space. I walked around the edges of the hall, peering into the shadows that cloaked the corners. Unless Helen had magically transformed into a diva like Olivia Newton-John at the end of Grease, that was where I'd find her.

In the corner to the right of the stage, a group of women stood, scanning the crowd for the grown-up versions of the boys they'd once had crushes on. And there she was—Helen! She was sitting down, deep in conversation with her best friend, Jean. She hadn't turned into a diva, but she had blossomed. A simple blue summer dress and an expensive haircut complemented her classic features, making her stand out among the overly made-up women surrounding her. She radiated a warmth that drew me in, and I felt my heart race at the sight of her.

Not that the other women weren't attractive; under different circumstances, they might have caught my eye. But on that night, they didn't exist. I'd worked myself into such a state that, to me, there was only Helen. But as I contemplated approaching her, my confidence plummeted, and shame washed over me for my past behaviour. *Stop being a coward*, I urged myself, pushing forward. Why was it so difficult to approach her?

As I drew closer, she looked up at me with that coy, Princess Diana-like expression that so many young women had tried to imitate. She had mastered it, and it looked stunning on her. My heart raced as I struggled to find the right words. The air around us seemed to crackle with unspoken tension, and I felt as if the world had narrowed down to just the two of us.

"Er... Hi, Helen," I stumbled, my mouth opening and closing as I fumbled for the right thing to say. Finally, I managed, "How are you?"

"I'm okay, thanks," she replied, pointing at my open dress shirt. "Still into T.Rex, then?"

"Oh," I said, realising I'd left a few more buttons undone than I intended. "Yeah, I'm starting to replace all my old vinyl with CDs now. It's like hearing them for the first time." I laughed nervously, hoping to break the ice.

"I'm doing the same with my old records. Nice to see you again, anyway," she said, her tone curt and dismissive. I felt a pang of disappointment, but I wasn't ready to give up just yet.

I reacted quickly, eager not to lose her attention. "I don't think it's how I thought it'd be. A lot of the people I used to hang around with are just shallow idiots. They don't seem to have grown up emotionally." I could feel the weight of my words hanging in the air, and I hoped she'd understand.

She looked straight into my eyes, and I felt as if she'd touched my soul. "Have you?"

A hot flush rushed through me, and I blushed more than I ever had before. "Yes, I have. I know I was a stupid idiot in the past, but I've grown up a lot." My voice was steadier now, fuelled by a newfound determination.

'That's good to hear," she said, her genuine smile lighting up her face. It was like a ray of sunshine breaking through the clouds, and I felt my heart lift.

I returned her smile, and almost immediately undermined my last statement by adopting a fake upper-class accent. "Would one like to dance, madam?" I held out my elbow, attempting an elegant bow that I knew looked utterly ridiculous. But somehow, I didn't care. The moment felt electric, and I was ready to embrace whatever came next.

As "In the Year 2525" by Visage filled the dance floor, I felt my overly conscious movements remind me why dancing had never been my favourite pastime. I felt awkward trying to keep up with the crowd as they moved effortlessly to the beat. The rhythm pulsed through the room, and I could feel the energy of the night wrapping around us.

I'd never been a great mover, so over the fading notes of the track, I shouted, "You don't fancy getting out of here and going for a quiet drink, do you? There's something I want to ask you." My heart raced at the thought of what I was about to do.

She looked at me suspiciously. "Err… Okay, but you're not trying to play a prank, are you?"

"No," I said, shaking my head. "Those days are gone, I promise." *And my name's not Pete*, I thought to myself, a smile creeping onto my face.

It was a warm summer evening, and the traffic was sparse as we walked back along Strelley Road toward the pub. A light breeze cooled the air as we crossed Bilborough Road and strolled up the country lane leading to the old Strelley Hall mansion house. The noise of traffic faded, replaced by the cooing of wood pigeons serenading us on our way. I couldn't help but notice the effortless grace with which she walked beside me. Was it something taught to posh people? Had I just never noticed it before?

Away from the main roads of the estate, the little noise that remained had almost vanished. All that was left was the sound of birds and the distant hum of the motorway. An unexpected nervousness washed over me, and the almost overwhelming urge to fill the silence compelled me to make my move.

As we approached the red telephone box, which stood hidden in the overgrown hedge and served more as a romantic shelter for teenage couples than a point of communication, I said, "I've been thinking about you a lot lately, Helen. I wanted to ask you out at school, but I was an idiot. I cared more about what that moron Jason Wentworth thought than what I actually felt." I stopped and turned to her, my heart pounding. "Please tell me you're not with anyone at the moment, because I'd like to ask if you'd go out with me." I stood there, hands clasped in front of me, fingers crossed, praying for a positive response.

She laughed coyly and said, "No," and as disappointment washed over me, she quickly added, "I meant no, I'm not with anyone." Accompanied by a radiant smile, she continued, "And I'd love to go out with you, Richard. I always liked you at school."

My heart soared at her words, and I felt a rush of relief and excitement. It was as if a weight had been lifted off my shoulders, and I could finally breathe again.

As we approached the Broad Oak pub, which sat back from the lane, enticing customers in from its hiding place behind a sprawling oak tree, Helen squeezed my hand. "You might want to reserve your judgment until you get to know me, though. I've got some pretty strong opinions about certain things, and they might put you off completely."

I squeezed back, grinning from ear to ear. "I don't think so somehow. I can't wait to hear them." The night was just beginning, and I felt a sense of hope blooming within me, a feeling that perhaps this was the start of something beautiful.

Chapter 18 – This is me

The pub was unusually quiet that night, a stark contrast to the usual cacophony of laughter and chatter that filled the air. The absence of the acrid smell of tobacco smoke, which typically clung to the walls like an unwelcome guest, was almost eerie. But I suppose I shouldn't have been surprised; after all, the main patrons were the very same people we'd just left dancing back in the school hall. As we slipped into a small back room, I felt a wave of relief wash over me. The polished horse brass gleamed on the exposed stone walls, and I thought, *Good, we won't be disturbed here.*

The overly varnished oak table in front of the large open fireplace offered us a ringside view of the flames that danced around the burning logs, their flickering light casting a warm golden glow that enveloped us like a comforting embrace. It couldn't have been more perfect.

"Have you got any other family besides John and David?" I asked, returning from the bar with our drinks. Those two younger brothers were at Player school at the same time we'd attended, but I was curious about the rest of her family.

"Yes," she replied, taking a sip of the white wine spritzer that I'd placed in front of her. "I've got three older brothers, and all five of them have tried out for one or another of the local football clubs." She winked at me, a playful glint in her eye. "That's why I'm one of those rare women who actually like football."

Tick one against my wish list for the perfect woman, I thought, my heart racing. It turned out that Helen had a plethora of interests typically considered "men's pursuits," and she attributed it to being surrounded by them at home. I didn't care where she'd acquired her passions; all I knew was that she was rapidly ticking off every box on my, until now, unrealistic list. She loved Science Fiction, my own personal obsession, often joking that I wouldn't watch anything unless it had a spaceship in it. She was also into gadgets, boasting the latest CD player and even a home computer! I began to wonder if she was pulling my leg. What man wouldn't want this? I glanced up at the oak beams supporting the ceiling and silently mouthed a prayer of gratitude. *Thank you, God.*

'So, what was it that you thought would put me off? The fact that you enjoy a lot of things that men do?" I asked, genuinely curious.

"Oh no!" she shifted in her seat, her enthusiasm palpable. "In fact, those things get me a lot of attention from men."

That deflated me a bit; *I bet they do*, I thought, a twinge of jealousy creeping in.

"No, it's my strong feelings about the way society is changing and the impact it has on all of us. A lot of people prefer not to think about it or believe there's a problem at all."

"What do you mean?" I asked, intrigued.

And just like that, for the next two hours, Helen unleashed a torrent of thoughts and feelings about how services and basic human decency were being eroded because they didn't generate profit.

"Society is slowly being destroyed by the markets, Richard. The values of fundamental aspects of our lives are becoming irrelevant simply because they don't have a monetary value. Only making or saving money seems to matter nowadays."

I didn't find her views particularly shocking; coming from a modest background, these concerns were familiar to most people I knew. I imagined that in the wealthier circles Helen's family inhabited, she probably sounded like a raving socialist.

"What sort of things do you mean?" I pressed.

"Well, look at how we're losing the services we used to take for granted. They're just withdrawn to save money or charged for to make more. Everything's done on the cheap, and the market people employ tactics to promote any change that benefits themselves. They make it seem like everyone agrees with it, which puts peer pressure on those who don't agree to keep their concerns to themselves. Money is power, Richard, and they have enough of it to change our world completely. Nothing will stand in their way—not public decency, children's innocence, or basic human values."

She leaned closer, lowering her voice conspiratorially. "I've even heard that in America, they're developing urinals for women. I mean, how disgusting! Why? Because it's cheaper than providing the privacy of a proper toilet."

"Men have always used urinals," I added, desperately trying to contribute to the conversation.

"That's because you can stand up and relieve yourself," she countered, her eyes flashing with passion. "But even those have changed, Richard. Men used to have porcelain partitions between them for privacy and hygiene. Do you have them now?"

"Well... not always," I admitted, feeling the heat rise in my cheeks.

"Exactly! And you'll get even less as the years go on. Do you think it costs more to remove them or less?" She answered for me. "No, there are no partitions between men's urinals for privacy or hygiene anymore because it saves money. And those are the exact things that men's pride won't let them demand. Can you imagine any man publicly admitting that he'd like those things? No, your natural arrogance—sorry, Richard—is being played on. They know damn well that no man in his right mind would ever open himself up to ridicule by asking for that type of thing."

"Why would any real man want those sorts of things, though?" I blurted out, regretting it the moment the words left my mouth.

"The same reason all the men in the past wanted and expected them. A little thing called dignity, Richard. Or do you think that all the men who came before this generation were inferior in some way?"

Quickly, I thought, I don't want this to turn into an argument. I didn't have any strong feelings on the matter either way, so I decided to go with the flow.

"No, you're right; it's just that it's what we've become used to."

"And that's where you've hit the nail on the head," she said, her voice rising with excitement. "If exposed to something enough, and the pressure is right, we can all get used to anything. We're losing sight of what's important. At this rate, there'll be no partitions in the sit-down loos soon. If you think about it logically, when savings or making money is concerned, it's beneficial to remove all aspects of our privacy and decency because catering to them costs money.

The next thing they'll want to bring in will be communal toilets, which they'll probably portray to us as something modern, good, and liberating—something we should embrace. They'll pressure us to accept them as a wonderfully modern concept. It's so easy to fool younger people like us, Richard. All you have to do is portray the thing you want to change as something that belongs to the older generation, and you can guarantee that most people our age will accept it. We never consider that what we're giving up is something that generations of young people like us fought so hard to gain in the first place."

"Don't you think this is all a bit extreme?" I said, trying to calm her down. "I'll go and get another drink, shall I?" I wanted to escape the uncomfortable topic of toilets.

When I returned from the bar, I sat down and looked at her. "Wow, you really are bothered about this stuff, aren't you?"

"I'm sorry for that. I've frightened you off now, getting on my soapbox and ranting away."

"No, no," I interjected, "it's interesting. I never thought of life that way. I just go along with things, and to be honest, I'm easily led. One of life's sheep, I suppose. Of course, what you're saying is obvious, and we have lost a lot of things that should be important to us. But what can we do? I'm not the sort of person who joins rallies and goes out protesting."

"I wouldn't ask you to do that. I don't myself. I'm just as guilty as everyone else of inaction. I suppose I'm waiting for someone to take the lead, and I'll follow, just like one of the sheep you think you are. I mean, I wouldn't want a revolution or anything; I don't like violence. I prefer evolution. But in this case, I feel so strongly that I'm sure I would go out on the street if others did."

"Have you never thought of being a politician?" I asked, setting her off on another tirade.

"They don't represent us, Richard. Just because some of them come from similar backgrounds to us doesn't mean they stay grounded. I really wish we had the power to reveal, in exact detail, just how wealthy every single politician is. Then we'd know who they represent from the general population. The most important thing that defines us in our modern world now isn't our colour, religion, or sex, or any of those other groups that they tell us are under-represented in parliament. No, it's our financial status that defines us all now. And if we want politicians to reflect us, they have to reflect us economically. Our parliament doesn't represent the people anymore, Richard, if it ever did. Every single one of them, whatever minority they belong to and however poor a background they originally came from, is wealthy enough to buffer themselves from the main problems that the majority of us have to deal with every single day."

At this point, I really thought that Helen needed to calm down. All this was exhausting me, and these weren't even my views. I thought this would be a good time to contribute a little more. But just as I was about to tell her about an article I'd read on the expenses paid to politicians, she revved up yet again.

"The problem now is that people are becoming desensitised to everything that can be used to make money. Sex, violence, nudity, crudity, disrespect, vulgarity—all these things have become money-making. I tell you, Richard, it won't be long before it's acceptable for little kids to see all sorts of sex and violence. That'll really mess with their minds, stealing their childhood, and then God knows how they'll grow up."

"I don't think that will ever be allowed, Helen. I mean, kids get protected from that type of thing on TV, and movies have ratings so parents can make sensible choices. They'd never allow kids to have access to that sort of stuff. It would be like allowing child abuse."

"I'm not so sure," she said contemplatively, looking into her glass. "I saw something on TV this afternoon that they would never have shown a few years ago. They said it was 'educational', but I'd bet money that ninety percent of the audience wasn't watching it for educational purposes. I mean, how long before they can broadcast any and every sexually explicit image you can imagine? And every violent act and personal tragedy is scrutinised by everyone under the guise of public interest and education?"

I couldn't think of what to say to this as she continued.

"Murders, executions, operations, autopsies—the list goes on. They don't care about the suffering it causes anyone, as long as they can make money out of it. We've just got it all wrong, Richard. No wonder so much of the world hates our Western ideals and values. I don't even think we have any anymore when greed is our God. It's not surprising that so many of us are attracted to other cultures, where common decency and respect come before fame and fortune. It feels like we're shedding all the civilised aspects of our society, and eventually, you won't be able to tell us from the basest animals that we evolved from."

I thought that was a bit harsh, and I was unaware that my mouth was gaping wide open at this outpouring of frustration at what Helen saw as unacceptable change.

"I know what you think, Richard. That I'm just a 'sensitive' woman and what I'm going on about won't ever come to pass. But because I'm conscious of these things, I'm more aware of them happening around me. And I'm convinced we're going to end up with a dysfunctional generation of citizens terrorising the rest of society. Then how will they bring their kids up? God, it's just one horrible spiral, to who knows where?"

She took a sip of her drink and sighed. "I'd love children one day, but what sort of life would they have? It's an absolute nightmare for someone like me who values privacy but gets exposed to all this intrusion and social experimentation. I just want us all to have some respect for each other and conduct ourselves with some decency in public. Do you think that's too much to wish for?"

"No," was all I could manage to say as I thought of the dirty books I had at home and blushed. Perhaps this wasn't going to turn out as I'd hoped after all.

"Do you know I refuse to go swimming now as a protest because the local authorities have taken away the private changing cubicles? It's just one communal room now, and no doubt once they can get away with it, we'll have mixed sex changing."

She hadn't noticed my red face, so I decided to participate in the conversation before she did. "You know, you can really wind yourself up thinking about this too much, Helen. You've admitted it yourself; there's nothing you can do about it."

"I know that, Richard," she sounded deflated. "But it just makes me angry when I think about it. It seems like some people want to break up everything that represents our modern civilisation. All those centuries of sacrifice and fighting by countless generations of young people to get these rights, and they're now being trashed by a few power-hungry, greedy businessmen who only really represent a rich minority."

She looked silently into her glass before saying, "I sometimes wish I could do what Little God tells me."

"Little God?" Oh wow, I was seriously getting worried now, and I jokingly looked around for the door.

She laughed, "Don't worry, I'm not going completely mad. It's just the name I've given to that voice in everyone's head. The one that tells them how they'd change the world if they had the power to enforce their own views. You know—the one that starts with 'if it was up to me...'"

I smiled back. "Does that mean that all those dictators and tyrants around the world are the ones who actually get the chance to act out what their Little Gods tell them then?"

She didn't answer but looked at me as if realising for the first time how she must be coming across. Probably because of my red face, she blurted, "Blimey, Richard, I can't believe I've just said all those things. They've been swirling around in my head for ages, but I've never been able to express them before. To be honest, I never really felt like I could say those things to anyone. Somehow, I feel comfortable enough with you to vent it all. But I must have blown my chances now. You must think I'm a right nutter."

"Yep," I smiled again, reaching for her hand across the dark wooden table. "But a very lovable one."

Her smile brightened her face, illuminating the shadows of our conversation. "I promise I won't rant and rave all the time; I just needed to get that out of my system. And don't get me wrong, I'm no puritan crusader. I'd never let my Little God control me. I don't believe in banning people from doing whatever they want in the privacy of their homes or in groups with like-minded people. I'd just like people to behave in a decent manner when out in public and respect their fellow citizens."

"You can rant and rave as much as you like," I said, feeling a lot better about my adult magazines after that last statement. "I agree with everything you said. I just haven't thought about it before. Like I said, I'm just a sheep and never question anything." I added, "Perhaps that's something you can teach me to do? I'd really like to see you again, Helen; you haven't changed your mind about going out with me, have you?"

"I should be asking you that," she whispered, staring pensively into the flickering flames. "After what I've just said."

But I knew right then that all the weird and wacky views she'd just shared with me were just a scratch on the surface of this complex woman. And it was exactly those unique things that would make her the love of my life. As I reached to hold her hands across the table, our eyes locked in a connection that told us both we had met the person we were going to be with for a very long time.

Chapter 19 – Celebrity Day

I stood there, aghast, as the message flickered on the vid-screen mounted on the wall. Even after the fourth replay, the words felt like a punch to the gut, a cruel twist of fate I couldn't quite grasp. It was unfair; it had to be a mistake. My heart raced, anger bubbling up inside me as the implications of what I was hearing began to sink in. I felt an overwhelming urge to lash out, to punch the smarmy 3D avatar that hovered mockingly in front of me. Frustration coursed through me, and I ran my fingers through my hair, sensing it shift colours in response to my agitation. By the time the full weight of the message settled in, I must have looked like I was wearing a chaotic, multi-coloured beret.

The message was from the Cryogen project, delivered in the most condescending tone possible, informing me that my help was not needed. The words *"no longer require additional input to the project"* echoed in my mind, each repetition stoking the flames of my fury. I swiped at the ghostly image, my clenched fist passing right through it, offering no physical relief, only amplifying my pent-up frustration. The avatar blurred momentarily, then continued as if mocking my inability to change it, or the message it delivered.

It didn't make sense. Ramoon had led me to believe that applying was merely a formality. There had been no hint, no suggestion that my application would be rejected. What was I going to do now? My anger surged again, a tidal wave of indignation. I was certainly not going to waste my time reviewing their ridiculous historical records to "identify gaps," as the patronising message had suggested. No, there had to be something I could do to overturn this decision. Nothing was going to stop me from finding Helen.

I tried to reach out to Ankit and Ramoon, desperate for answers, but my attempts were met with silence. Both their systems echoed the same automated message: they were away on business, and I should *"leave a message."* But neither had mentioned they would be gone, especially not on the day I received this devastating news. It felt like a cruel coincidence, a twist of fate that left me feeling even more isolated.

"Damn," I barked, frustration spilling over as I tried Ankit's home, only to be met with yet another automated response. "Some things never change."

At least I had better luck with Jennifer. If I'd found anyone else missing, I would have really started to panic. After I explained the situation, she insisted, "Come over to my apartment. The others are here. We need to figure out what this means."

By the time I arrived, my anger had begun to ebb, replaced by a creeping sense of paranoia. *Oh no*, I thought. Was I heading down the same path as the protesters?

My friends were just as bewildered as I was.

"I can't believe this," Jennifer shook her head, her brow furrowed in disbelief. "It just doesn't add up, Richard. We were all invited to join soon after being revived, but we found other interests and turned the offer down. They certainly gave us the impression it was an open invitation. There was never any indication of a limit to the number of people they needed. What could have changed."

"That's a good question, Jen," I replied, frustration creeping into my voice. "But we have no one to ask. The only people who could shed light on this have mysteriously vanished."

"It's too much of a coincidence that they both went away at the same time, just as you received that message," Simon chimed in, his voice laced with concern. "I've tried reaching them again, and I keep getting the same response from their systems." He shook his head, bewildered. "There surely can't be anywhere left in this system that we can't contact. Even trying to locate them with my senses hasn't worked."

"I forgot about that," I said, realisation dawning on me.

"You can prevent yourself from being located, so I assume that's what they've done. But why?" Simon's question hung in the air, heavy with implications.

"It's all a bit scary if you ask me," Jennifer added, her voice trembling slightly.

"Okay, okay," Earl interrupted sharply, attempting to dispel the gathering gloom that threatened to envelop us. "It's obvious we can't do anything about this right now, so I propose we keep our minds occupied until Ramoon or Ankit show up."

"And how do you suggest we do that?" Jennifer asked, crossing her arms.

Turning to me, Earl said, "There's still a lot you haven't learned yet. How about going back to the library to continue your education? It might take your mind off this until we get some answers."

I let out a breath of defeat. "All right, Earl. Lingering on this isn't doing me any good." I nodded at him. "What do you suggest I learn about then?"

"Well, up to now, you've had things dictated to you, so why not choose something yourself? Is there anything you'd particularly like to know about?"

I thought for a moment, my mind racing. "I've always wondered what happened to some of the famous people from our day. For example, what happened to Daniel Mountain? I always thought he'd have himself frozen," I mused.

"Killed," Earl replied flatly.

"Oh," I said "Okay, what about Emma Holmes then?"

"Killed."

"Amy Beeroff? She had a fantastic voice."

"Killed."

"Jenson Treacle?"

"Killed."

I stopped dead in my tracks, turning to Earl, disbelief etched on my face. "Hang on, that can't be right. Either by some fluke, I've just randomly picked famous murder victims, or something bigger went on. And my guess is that it was something bigger. So, what happened?"

"*See-me hear-me* happened," Simon answered, his tone grave. "Well, that and a few other social networking sites on the internet." As I opened my mouth to ask yet another question, Simon raised his hand. "Let the system show you. It'll explain a lot better than I can."

Before long, I found myself slipping into that familiar dreamlike state, the system preparing to unveil the events of Sunday, February 3, 2075.

I stood in my dark space again, and one of the dimensional windows began to open before me. The scene unfolded, revealing sprawling manicured grounds, imposing yew trees, and evergreen bushes, before panning up a wide gravel drive to a grand white mansion. Vans emblazoned with the logo of the mega media corporation CON/PPC were parked outside, and people in overalls rushed about, carrying equipment into the house. A man, presumably the owner, stood at the door, his face a mask of disbelief and anger.

Smaller windows opened in the darkness, following the workers as they scurried from room to room. They installed miniature cameras and microphones, fixing them in every conceivable location—over beds, baths, inside closets, and even waterproof ones stuck to toilet bowls!

Back at the doorstep, a man in the same overalls, "*CON/PPC live feed*" plastered on his back, held a clipboard and spoke to the owner. "Any attempt to tamper with or remove these devices is an imprisonable offense. Also, no one sleeping in the house should wear nightclothes, and only use the bedding we've provided."

"You mean the ones your cameras can see through?" the owner shot back; his voice laced with indignation.

"The price of fame, sir," the engineer replied cheerfully.

"Even for my children?"

An almost imperceptible wave of guilt washed over the man's face, and he swallowed hard before continuing. "I don't make the laws; I'm only following orders, sir. Now, before I go, I just need to remind you that you must get your agent to update your diary at least once a day on one of our preferred social networking sites." He grinned, adding, "Our subscribers do like to know as much as possible about their favourite celebs." He gestured to the edge of his clipboard. "Now, if I could just get your signature." He waited for the man to press his forefinger and thumb onto the scanner strip, completing the electrical circuit that confirmed his DNA and verified he was a live person before the screen confirmed his retinal image.

The engineers packed away their equipment and climbed back into their vehicles. As the doors of the last van closed, the familiar logo was emblazoned across them, the bright orange wording spelling out the strapline, "Our eyes on your world."

The scene shifted, and I found myself watching a news bulletin.

"News is coming in from all around the globe of international celebrities being killed by suicide bombers. Figures so far indicate over two thousand international celebrities and an additional five thousand members of their staff and members of the public are dead. No group has yet admitted responsibility for this terrorist attack, but many are blaming the laws allowing the media to force well-known individuals to reveal so much about their lives. The global campaign for privacy and respect has condemned the media corporations, calling for a review of their exemption from privacy laws."

Then, the newsreader's demeanour shifted from sombre to upbeat as he continued. "Stay with us, as we're joined later by both the British Prime Minister, whose government is currently introducing the new mind mapping technology, and the regional director of CON/PPC, who will both be explaining to you why privacy is a bad thing."

As the names of the famous victims scrolled up the news screen, the windows began to fade to black, and I found myself back in the cubicle surrounded by my friends, all waiting for me to respond to what I'd just witnessed.

I managed to take a deep breath before saying, 'that was the future where we most definitely didn't want to wake up. It would have been my worst nightmare, and the frightening thing is, it wasn't too long after I died. I mean, why didn't those people just move somewhere else to avoid all those bugs?"

"Because they were targets of the media, and there was nowhere else to go," Simon explained, his voice heavy with understanding. "They became social lepers. By that time, there was no hiding place. Everywhere they went fell under the same law. No one wanted to entertain them and risk having the same fate befall their home. Even hotels had to have special rooms already wired up to accommodate these celebrities."

"That sounds awful. I would have preferred to stay dead than be revived into a society like that," I said, shuddering at the thought.

"I don't think many of the celebrities liked it either, Richard. But they relied on the power of the media for their careers, so most of them reluctantly went along with anything it wanted them to do. The time when celebrities had any power over their private lives, or even their own bodies, was long gone. Many convinced themselves they didn't mind doing whatever they were asked to do, that it was their choice, and they still had self-control. In reality, they had lost the ability to restrict what they were selling to just their talent. The media demanded everything."

"Most did the bare minimum they could get away with to pursue what they loved. But these people couldn't refuse to do anything that was asked of them, no matter how intimate or private, without incurring the wrath of the media. By that time, it had become so powerful that it could erase people from history more efficiently than any Soviet dictator."

"I wonder how many great talents went undiscovered because they refused to put themselves in that position?" Jenifer added, her voice heavy with realisation.

"More importantly how could we have blindly walked into that?" I asked, incredulity lacing my tone.

"They say you have to experience extremes before there's a fundamental shift," Jennifer replied, her voice softening. "The death of so many well-known and loved people highlighted just how dangerous the media had become. It had brainwashed the public into believing anything it did was acceptable."

"Show someone burning to death, being murdered, begging for their lives; it was news, so they showed it. Show the famous through hidden cameras doing the most intimate things; they owed it to their fans, so show it. Show someone being raped; it was news, and the public had the right to see, so show it. Show any sexual act, the more explicit, the better; it was educational, so they showed it. Use mind mapping technology to read your thoughts; it was acceptable because if you had nothing to hide, you had nothing to fear."

"These were the arguments that pushed aside any consideration of public decency or respect for the individual involved, or any citizen's privacy. Those things were just barriers to making money. Society didn't matter to it because it had positioned itself completely outside the law. It had become as feared as any ungoverned institution in the world's many policed states. It had taken on a life of its own, wielding the power of life and death."

Jennifer glanced at Earl, who looked uncomfortable discussing the industry he had worked in for much of his first life. Noticing her attention, he said, "I'm not perfect, far from it. I fell under the same greedy spell as everyone else." He lowered his eyes, reflecting on the past. "I know I failed to retain some of my humanity back then or take any action to prevent those things from coming about."

"You died before those extremes became a reality, Earl," Jennifer added gently. "I don't believe you would have actively participated in it, just like I'm sure Simon would never have gotten involved with the misuse of the surveillance equipment he supplied."

Simon bit his bottom lip, the weight of the conversation hanging heavily in the air.

"Anyway," I said, attempting to break the tension, "are you telling me that this event changed everything?"

"That, and their own tools finally showing them for what they were," Earl replied.

"What do you mean?"

"The Campaign for Privacy and Respect had been fought into a corner and finally employed the very things they detested. They captured hundreds of hours of footage of countless media bosses...," she glanced at Earl, "obsessing over viewing figures and profits. The only thing that mattered was money, and the greed that fuelled the desire for it had no respect for even the most basic human needs. To these people, their fellow citizens were just objects to be used to make a profit. And that was finally proved when it came out that a group of global media owners had instigated and funded the terrorists who committed the murders of the celebrities. To them, it was just another acceptable tool to boost their ever-rising profits and pave the way for a whole new set of 'cheaper' celebrities."

"The public had been duped, and it was there for all to see. It was a wake-up call that put an end to the perception that *"freedom of the press"* meant freedom from the law. It instigated a charter for privacy and respect that all media companies had to abide by. It was restricted to only applying its practices where there was corruption or where they discovered a crime. The rights of the citizen finally won out over commercial interests, and the media took its rightful place in society."

"It's a shame all those celebrities had to lay down their lives before the world came to its senses, though," I said, my voice heavy with sorrow.

"This is depressing," Simon said, shaking his head. "We can't do anything about it. And the Manoorans have finally realised the dreams of personal control over private information that began to take shape back then. Can't we change the subject?"

"Sorry," Jennifer said, then smiled. "We do celebrate the lives of those who died in that atrocity, though, Richard. Every February 20th, we call it Celebrity Day. It's like a big costume or fancy-dress party, and you can attend as any one of the victims."

"Was Mac Zeffer a victim?" I asked, a spark of curiosity igniting within me.

"Yes, he was," Jennifer replied. "Why?"

"Because I'll be able to go as him," I said, a smile breaking through the heaviness of the moment. "Helen always said he reminded her of me when I was young."

Simon grabbed my chin, turning my face from side to side as he scrutinised my features. He shrugged his shoulders. "Nah, can't see it myself," he said, a teasing grin on his face.

Once again, Earl's serious tone brought us back to the present situation. "You know, I'm not sure we've accomplished what we set out to achieve by coming here. It certainly hasn't done me any good. I thought we were going to cheer you up, Richard, but I don't think we've been very successful at that, do you?"

Jennifer nodded in agreement. "I think, to completely take our minds off this, we all need a little light relief." She looked at the two others with a cheeky grin on her face. "I think we should take Richard to the Mumbai Temple tonight."

Before I could ask what, the Mumbai Temple was, Simon explained, "You'll love it, Richard. It's one of the best clubs in India Prime."

"I can't dance," I protested, a hint of apprehension creeping into my voice.

Jennifer winked at me, and said "Oh, you've got so much to learn."

Chapter 20 – I Found Something

Simon and Earl were waiting for me outside the café bar on the corner that faced the main square. As I approached, I felt a mix of anticipation and trepidation. I pulled up a black plastic chair opposite them, the coolness of the surface contrasting with the warmth of the evening air. I ordered a drink from the terminal point at the centre of the table, my fingers brushing against the smooth screen, and within seconds, a trolley waiter rolled to my side, delivering my choice with a flourish.

This was the first alcohol I'd experienced with my new body, and I couldn't help but feel a thrill of excitement. As I took my first sip of the ancient whiskey, a comforting heat travelled through me, igniting a warmth that spread from my throat to my chest. I marvelled at the lengths these people had gone to in order to replicate the biological experiences of the past. The rich, smoky flavour enveloped my senses, and I knew, with a certainty that felt almost nostalgic, that I was going to get drunk tonight. And for the first time in a long while, I was actually looking forward to it.

As we waited for Jennifer to arrive, before embarking on what she'd jokingly referred to as our "night on the town," I couldn't help but notice how different my clothing was from the other two men. I tugged at the figure-hugging beige and green t-shirt, feeling the fabric cling uncomfortably to my skin. "I can't get used to these clothes," I said, my voice tinged with frustration. "I'd rather choose something myself than let the system decide what's suitable. I feel like something out of Saturday Night Fever in these baggy flared trousers. I mean, look how high this waistband is!"

Earl and Simon were both dressed in more conventional trousers and Nehru-style shirts in sombre shades of grey and black. Simon chuckled, shaking his head. "You're not doing it right, Richard. Next time, I'll have to come over to your apartment and show you how to dress."

When Jennifer finally arrived, she took my breath away. She was wearing a figure-hugging off-the-shoulder aqua blue dress that tapered elegantly at her knees, accentuating her curves. A midnight blue silk belt cinched her waist, and her nails and stiletto shoes matched perfectly. Her short black hair was pulled back on each side by butterfly combs that mirrored the colour of her dress, and the drop earrings and single stone around her neck hung from invisible threads, completing the look with an air of effortless elegance.

Earl let out a drawn-out, "Veeeery nice," as he looked her up and down, admiration evident in his gaze. "You look amazing."

She smiled, basking in the compliment, her eyes sparkling. "And you lot brush up pretty well yourselves."

She ordered her drink, we finished ours and walked across the square, the cobblestones cool beneath my feet. We headed down the alleyway opposite, anticipation buzzing in the air. Ten minutes later, we entered another open space, and my gaze was drawn upward to the Mumbai Temple. The distinctive Mauryan-style arches dominated the outside of the buildings, their intricate carvings telling stories of a time long past. As we approached the entrance to the club, Simon's cheeky grin reappeared, hinting that mischief was afoot.

"Just a word of advice, Richard," he said, leaning in conspiratorially. "You need to suspend disbelief until you get used to this, and under no circumstances—laugh..."

I shot him a quizzical look, my brow furrowing in confusion. "You'll see," he replied, a glint of mischief in his eyes.

Once through the main entrance, we found ourselves in a wide corridor, the air thick with anticipation. At the end of the passage was the door to the club itself, and the absence of music or sounds of partying didn't surprise me; this society valued its privacy above all else. We passed a reception area halfway down the passage and joined an orderly queue moving toward the entrance.

"This is the largest group of people I've seen since we went to the surface," I remarked, feeling a little better about my attire now that I noticed some of the other men wore clothing just as ridiculous as mine.

As I stepped through the door, I was immediately enveloped by the pulsating energy of the club. The transition from the almost eerie silence of the corridor to the thumping bass of the music behind me made me instinctively bring my hands up to my ears. The frequency was so low that I could feel it vibrating through my feet, a primal rhythm that resonated deep within me. A remix of "Tear It Apart" by Whale blasted through the speakers, and I was astonished to hear something from my era, even if it felt like it was shaking me to pieces.

As I lowered my hands, I took in the scene before me. The bar area was alive with young, attractive people milling about, laughter and conversation blending into a symphony of sound. I couldn't help but smile at the sight of the barmen serving eager club-goers, their movements fluid and practiced. One barman, in particular, was being ogled by a group of women leaning over the bar, their skirts short and their bikini bottoms barely there. I slapped myself on the right cheek, muttering, "Stop it," trying to shake off the inappropriate thoughts racing through my mind.

Simon, who was behind me, noticed my reaction and leaned in closer, his voice low and conspiratorial. "Some things are a little more relaxed in these clubs, but the system will soon get a measure of your preferences." He flashed me an infectious smile. "I guess from your interest, you're comfortable with this level?"

I winced, a half-smile creeping onto my face as Helen came to mind. I hoped the wave of guilt that washed over me wouldn't spoil the evening.

But I needn't have worried. As I turned around, I was met with one of the most absurd sights I'd ever seen. Over a hundred people were dancing in perfect synchrony, their bodies moving as if they were part of a grand performance. As the deep bass of the music sped up, I watched in disbelief as the top halves of the dancers' bodies seemed to separate from their lower halves. They were still connected by what looked like thin cables, but they moved rapidly to the beat, hovering first over the bottom half of the person to their right and then over the one on their left. Their arms waved to the rhythm, and their hips shifted in time with the music. It was a chaotic ballet, arms entangled, disconnected bodies morphing and shifting positions at different speeds, creating a phantasmagorical scene that I could never have imagined in a million years.

It was so bizarre that it reminded me of a crowd of puppets on strings, but far more controlled. As I watched, my chest began to contract involuntarily, and I felt a bubbling laughter rising within me. I couldn't hold it in; it was the most ridiculous and hilarious thing I'd ever seen. I knew I wouldn't be able to control the spasms building inside me. Yep, I was going to laugh.

I bolted for the door, my friends trailing closely behind. I reached the bottom of the corridor before collapsing against the wall, laughter erupting from me in uncontrollable waves. Tears streamed down my face as I gasped, "Thank you. That was brilliant."

The laughter was infectious, and soon the others joined in. Between fits of giggles, Simon managed to say, "I knew you'd find it funny, Richard. You've been through so much lately; I'm glad it worked."

As I sat there on the floor, my laughter subsiding, my forearms resting on my knees and my head bent forward, a small group of women appeared through the main entrance and walked past us. One of the women caught my eye, and I felt a jolt of recognition. She was dark-skinned with strikingly sharp features, tall enough that she should have looked awkward, but she carried herself with an effortless grace. An unravelling ponytail half-held her mid-length brown hair away from her face, and her smouldering brown eyes locked onto mine. The moment our gazes met, a rush of pressure surged through my head, and the laughter evaporated, replaced by something far more intense. My whole body jolted back as if hit by a taser, and I slammed against the wall behind me. Waves of heat pulsed over my skin, and I felt my features melting under the weight of an overwhelming sensation. The woman looked back at me in confusion as she and her party passed through the entrance to the club, and just like that, the strange sensations ceased.

My friends rushed to my side as I hit the wall with a sickening thud. Simon knelt beside me, his voice low and reassuring. "Don't worry, Richard. I think I know what just happened."

Still shaking, I nodded as I took Simon's hand. "You're still learning to control your new senses. That reaction was normal, albeit magnified in your case because of your inexperience. That feeling you had was what people experience when they're looking to meet others who are compatible. She obviously has her senses tuned to seek out compatible partners, and you must have too."

"But I haven't turned anything on," I blurted out, confusion swirling in my mind.

"You just need some practice, that's all." Simon gripped my hand tighter, pulling me up. "Come on, we need to find her."

"What do you mean?" I protested, pulling back. "I'm not looking for a partner, Simon."

"No, you don't understand, Richard," Jennifer interjected, picking up on Simon's train of thought. "You might have subconsciously set your body to look out for anyone like Helen." She grabbed my other arm, helping Simon drag me back toward the club, her excitement palpable. "Richard, don't you see? There's a possibility she could be Helen. Who knows? She could be a re… born." She hesitated on that last word, because she was suddenly talking into space. I was already rushing back to the club.

"What am I supposed to say?" I asked, hurrying along the corridor, my heart racing.

"Just act like you would in the old days when you were picking women up," Simon advised.

"That's easier said than done, I was never any good at that."

"She knows you're compatible, Richard; she's not going to blow you out."

I paused outside the entrance, anxiety gnawing at me. "Okay, but what if she's not Helen? I couldn't ever consider getting involved with anyone else, and if I make an approach, she might think I'm looking for a partner. How would I let her down?"

"Deal with that if it happens," Earl chimed in. "You can't let this chance go by. You need at least to establish if she's been reborn."

As I stepped back into the club, I was confronted by a sonorous wall of sound, accompanied this time by a very familiar voice. It was Rod Bones singing "I Am a Natural Lover," and it wasn't just a recording they were playing. People were facing the stage, and there, as large as life, was a young Rod Bones, gyrating his hips and belting out the song in his iconic voice.

Jennifer shouted in my ear from behind me, answering the question racing through my mind. "Yes, it is him. He was revived about fifty years ago. What a hunk."

My eyes scanned the crowd for the mysterious woman, and I knew my friends were doing the same. Where would Helen be? My gaze immediately darted to the corners of the room, and there she was, next to the bar, talking to friends just as I remembered Helen at the school disco.

As I approached her, I hesitated, trying to control the strange feeling that was beginning to return. As it subsided, I took a deep breath and stammered, "H... Hello, I was wondering if... err... you'd like to dance?"

"I'd love to," she replied, smiling back at me as she held out her hand.

Then it hit me—I couldn't dance. "Err, but I can't dance. I mean, not in this body anyway." I stammered, trying to justify my statement. "I'm a Cryogen, and I'm not quite coordinated yet. Not that that would make any difference because I was never... God, I sound like an idiot."

"No," she said, her eyes sparkling with warmth. "You don't sound like an idiot. But I can guarantee you can dance. I assume no one has told you how all this works?"

"How all what works?" I Asked.

She pointed to the row of lights in the ceiling that surrounded the dance floor. "Do you see those lights?"

"Yes."

"As you pass through them, the system programs your body with the dance moves required for the music."

So that's what Jennifer must have been referring to when I mentioned I couldn't dance. "In that case," I said, holding out my elbow for her to join me, "may I have the pleasure?"

Out on the dance floor, a remix of "Someone to Live For" by Jamie Smallhouse thumped through the air, and I stood across from her, surrendering to the music. I instinctively began to rock on the balls of my feet, matching her every move. Unbelievably, my body even separated when hers did, and I managed not to laugh or feel sick.

As our bodies synchronised, and the pulsating energy of the club swirled around us, I realised that the night was far from over. The laughter, the music, the thrill of the unexpected—all of it was a reminder that life, even in this new form, was still full of surprises. And perhaps, just perhaps, I would find a way to navigate this strange new world, one dance at a time.

By the time we stepped off the dance floor, we were both laughing—not at the absurdity of the experience, but because of the sheer joy of it. It had been exhilarating, and I felt the now-familiar tingling sensation running up my arm as she held my hand and led me back to the seating in the corner.

I was acutely aware that my friends were keeping their distance, but they were never far away, and it warmed my heart to know the comfort of their presence. I was beginning to feel at home in this new world.

The woman introduced herself as Rachel Karr, but I barely registered her name, too captivated by her beauty. She was stunning, and I struggled to keep my eyes from wandering over her exquisitely slim figure. Yet, I thought of Helen and tried to steer the conversation toward topics that could reveal if she was Helen reborn. It seemed to be paying off.

She shared her love for science fiction and her interest in science and technology. "I'm so disappointed with the current consensus to retain everything from the cultures of the past above anything else," she said, her voice passionate. "Just because there's so much left over from previous times doesn't mean we can't create our own literature, art, and music." *So that's why they were playing music from my era.*

She had so much in common with Helen that I had to fight the urge to ask her outright. All the frustrations that had been building since my revival pressed down on me. *Tell her about yourself*, I thought.

"Since my revival, I've been trying to get involved with the Cryogen project so I can help as many people like me get a second chance. I'd like to meet as many of them as possible, seeing as there's only a finite number of us left."

I deftly omitted any reference to Helen, pausing, hoping that if Rachel was reborn, this would be her opportunity to reveal it. *Come on*, I thought, *take the hint.*

"Richard, there's something I should tell you," She began, her expression serious.

Here it is, I thought, my heart soaring. *Please, please.*

"Only," she stumbled, "my family is pure Manooran, and my parents are a bit anti-Cryogen. There are still some of us like that." She said it apologetically.

My heart, along with my mood, sank.

Chapter 21 – Maya and Mazood

If I'd ever had any patience at all, it had long since evaporated. My frustration at being unable to do something—anything—constructive to find Helen was beginning to ferment into a bubbling cauldron of anger. I could feel it simmering just beneath the surface, ready to erupt. It was as if the whole system itself conspired against me, erecting barriers at every turn. I hadn't yet learned to accept that everything in this new world moved at a different pace, a sluggish rhythm that felt foreign and maddening. Perhaps having eternity had dulled the urgency in these people? Whatever the reason for this glacial pace, one thing was clear: life was having a laugh at my expense.

I tried my hardest not to let this frustration spill over into my relationships with my friends, but the more reassurance they offered, the more my tension grew. I snapped at them, my words sharp and unyielding, rejecting everything they said. Each time I lashed out, I felt a pang of guilt gnawing at me, a reminder of the sadness and foolishness that accompanied my outbursts. But I knew it would only worsen until I could join the Cryogen project, gain access to their records, and begin to unravel the mystery of the revival process. I needed to feel as if I was doing something—anything at all—to find my wife.

The absence of Ankit and Ramoon only compounded my frustration. Despite the countless messages my friends and I had sent, there was still no response from either of them.

"This is ridiculous!" I snapped after yet another failed attempt to reach Ankit. I could feel the violence lurking just beneath my skin, a beast waiting to be unleashed. I'd never been a violent person, but this situation was straining me beyond belief.

"We all agree the situation is out of the ordinary, Richard," Earl said later that morning, his voice calm and measured. "But rather than winding yourself up like this, I suggest we wait a little longer and then try to approach someone else in authority."

Earl's sensible and logical approach was starting to grate on my nerves. *Did he never feel the weight of frustration or get wound up?* But deep down, I knew he was thinking clearer than I was, so I nodded and accepted his advice, even if it felt like swallowing a bitter pill.

"You'll see, Richard," Jennifer reassured me, her voice warm and soothing. "They'll be back soon, and before you know it, you'll be working on the project."

But it wasn't just the uncertainty surrounding Ankit and Ramoon that plagued my mind. Fate had thrown me yet another curveball in the form of Rachel, and I felt a gnawing guilt about the friendship that was beginning to blossom between us. After discovering her Manooran roots,

I'd not wanted to pursue our connection further. Yet, I couldn't shake the feeling that she saw me as a potential partner, and I was at a loss for how to navigate this new territory.

There was no denying it; I'd carried some cowardice from my previous life into this one. I'd been putting off confronting the issue, afraid to tell her the truth. I had to, of course, because the longer I delayed, the stronger my feelings would grow.

Never, since falling in love with Helen, had another woman affected me like this. I couldn't forget the way Rachel's fathomless eyes drew me in, promising undiscovered secrets. Every time her tongue wet her lips, I felt an overwhelming urge to press my own against them. She was breathtakingly beautiful, and that beauty didn't deserve the hurt I feared my continued contact could inflict.

But had I known her a little better and trusted in the strength that lay in her eyes—those eyes that seemed to hold the weight of ages—I wouldn't have worried so much. When I finally found the courage to tell her about Helen, she didn't cast blame; instead, she was considerate and caring.

A raised eyebrow was all that betrayed her surprise at my confession of fear. "It doesn't mean we can't still be friends," she said, her voice steady. "I mean, you're friends with Jennifer, aren't you?"

I wanted to explain that my feelings for Jennifer were nothing compared to what I felt for her, but I didn't want to raise any false hopes if she harboured feelings for me. So, unable to find any other argument against her suggestion, I simply smiled and said, "Of course we can be friends."

Rachel worked at the central energy grid that supplied India Prime, commuting daily from her parents' house. She was fascinated by all fields of science but specialised in quantum energy production. Her frustration with the general population's lack of interest in space exploration made her scathing at times, and I found myself drawn to her passion.

As I began to know her better, I wondered how much influence my new body was having on my feelings. I tried to suppress any emotions that might develop, but I couldn't control the physical reactions that accompanied my attraction to her. I'd never cheated on Helen, and I wasn't about to start now. These were conscious thoughts I repeated to myself, afraid that one day my subconscious might slip in one of those inappropriate thoughts—the kind you could never seem to erase once they appeared.

So, when I sensed the danger of thoughts that could harm my love for my wife, I retreated into a journal I was writing about our previous life, trying to reinforce my memories in case I had to share them with

Helen. Helen and I had both loved and worshiped life, but why did this new existence have to be so complicated?

Rachel had been hesitant to let me meet her parents, ashamed of their views and fearing their attitude toward Cryogens would drive me away. At times, she painted them as egregious xenophobes, and I found myself thankful for not receiving an invite.

"You'll learn, Richard, that there are many Manoorans who wish we'd never found you Cryogens because it reminds them that they're not human. The desire to assume humanity's mantle is so strong among some that the entire population of one of the new worlds has had their memories altered to make them believe they're the original humans. They think they're living on the first Earth alongside the rest of us, who they believe to be friendly visitors from space. The information system is advanced enough to maintain the pretence easily."

"Wow, it's not just the human race that was seriously messed up then?" I replied, incredulous.

"No," she said, "but as I've noticed you say sometimes, 'it takes all sorts.'"

In the end, it was Rachel's parents who invited me to meet them.

"I think they're worried you're some kind of nutter and want to vet you. Do you mind? I'm sure it'll only be the once."

"Of course not, I'd love to come." I thought I was being clever and joked, "It'll give me the opportunity to show them that we're not all bug-eyed monsters."

As soon as those words came out my mouth I winced.

She didn't laugh but looked at me with a wry smile. "I'll see you there then."

Realising I probably had nothing in common with her parents, I set out to learn a little about their area of expertise. I knew they were solar scientists researching the productive use of material within black holes. Oh dear, I thought, this is going to be far beyond me. But using the mind link with the system, I learned, on a very elementary level, that they had managed to access the minute dimensions wound up within the tiniest elemental particles found in the quantum foam that bound all the structure of space-time together. Then there was something about solving the riddle of the Heisenberg Uncertainty Principle, and that was when it became so complex my mind nearly shut down! I was right; this was going nowhere. But for Rachel's sake, I continued to attempt to absorb the information.

It was now possible to store data and draw energy from these dimensions, which they'd discovered were fundamentally linked to the dense cores of black holes. What I was learning was far beyond anything Helen and I had ever considered.

They'd even created something called a Solid String, an immeasurably thin but solid structure made from black hole material consisting of elemental strings condensed so much that they no longer vibrated, stretching through dimensions over many light-years. There was some connection with quantum entanglement and teleportation, and the energy required to manipulate these things was more than the entire visible energy within our galaxy. The numbers gave me a headache as they passed into and then straight out of my head (before it exploded!).

Regardless of the amount of energy required though, they now had access to an unlimited supply from the quantum dimensions. Manipulation at this end created an instant reaction at the other end, providing real-time communication across the galaxy.

I discovered they were communicating with beings who lived on the orbiting moon of their home planet, who had previously helped them escape to a better life. They were sending information as a reward for their help in the past, assisting them in re-engineering Manoora to cope with the absence of their species. Whatever I might think of Ramoon, the Manoorans, in general, were a caring and honourable race.

By the time I arrived at their home, I had to laugh at myself; I'd virtually forgotten everything anyway. It was just too much to take in, definitely more detail than I could absorb. I presented my hand to the green patch next to the entrance, and it flickered between blue and green to indicate that the people inside had been informed of my presence.

Rachel's head suddenly appeared through the door. "Hi Richard, come in."

Their apartment was much larger than mine, which was to be expected considering it was a family unit. Across the room, on a brown lounger, sat a man who looked about thirty, with a neatly trimmed goatee beard, looking as if he couldn't possibly be Rachel's father. But considering that outward appearance of age was now a choice, it was perfectly possible he could have looked younger than she did.

The man rose to greet me with a smile as I entered the room. "Hello, Richard—welcome to our home."

"Thank you, sir," I said, surprised at how polite I'd become. This society was definitely having a positive effect on me. "It's very nice to meet you."

"Likewise, do take a seat. My wife Maya will be out soon; she's just informing the system what food to deliver. She's proud of her choices."

"I'm sure it'll be lovely."

"Mother's choices always are," Rachel chimed in as she joined us.

Maya and Mazood Karr welcomed me into their home with smiles and pleasantries, which initially made me think Rachel's concerns were unfounded. They treated me with respect and were courteous to an extreme, unnerving me because I couldn't tell if it was genuine or patronising. But clarity emerged when they began discussing their work.

Rachel had told me that the general population, especially those with influence, were obsessed with not straying outside the solar system. Even though they had the technology to colonise other systems and traverse interstellar space, it was as if they were afraid to leave this place now that they'd found it. "All they talk about is how the population will never grow, so we don't need any more space." She'd told me. "Honestly, Richard, you'd think this solar system was their whole universe."

'Did you ever get the opportunity to travel to any of the other worlds in your first life?' Mazood asked, looking at me with intense interest and expectation.

"I'm afraid not; we'd only just begun taking the first tentative steps to terraform Mars when I passed away. There was a small colony on the moon, but apart from the orbiting hotels owned by private companies, there weren't many opportunities for the general public to move off Earth."

"Maya and I study the Sun," Mazood said as his wife walked into the room. "It's our long-term objective to control its burning and ultimately use a local black hole in a nearby star system to introduce matter in a controlled flow. Once we've mastered that, we can use the technology to keep the Sun stable and extend its useful life indefinitely."

"That sounds fascinating! I'd love to know more," I said, genuinely interested. "How would you get to and transport the matter, for example? But if you don't mind me asking, why are you bothering at all? Couldn't you just find another system to colonise?"

Oh dear, I'd done it again—put my foot in my mouth and pushed it right down my throat. In my mind's eye, I could see Helen laughing.

Rachel's parents both looked at me as if I were an absolute idiot who had just swung in from the trees. For a few uncomfortable seconds, they stared at me with open mouths, almost in disgust, as if they were utterly dumbstruck.

What had I said?

Then Maya spoke, her tone condescending. "We're not a primitive species," she blurted out. "We don't intend to become wanderers of the universe. We have everything we need here, and here is where we intend to stay."

I seemed to have hit a sore spot and quickly said, "I didn't mean to offend you. It's just that before I died, any talk of the future always included traveling outside the solar system."

Maya looked down at me as if being asked to communicate with a one-celled amoeba. With a noticeable sneer, she said, "That's because you probably thought the Sun would 'run out,' and you'd be forced to move on. No doubt a hypothesis arrived at by your scientists' incomplete equations, leading them to the wrong conclusions about the universe."

"You see, Richard," she continued, really getting into her stride now, hot and indignant, "what they left out was quite a significant part of the equation when attempting to explain the universe and predict its future." Tapping her temple with her forefinger, she said, "This… intelligence, Richard, that's the force that will ultimately master and control everything in existence—not your silly laws of nature and physics, and the extrapolations of what would happen if left on their own. Humanity isn't the only collection of chemicals that ever rose to consciousness, you know. And fortunately, we can think beyond you and not make the same mistakes."

The words "you" and "we" had a definite emphasis, and I felt I'd just been given a dressing down on behalf of my own race, even though overt references to the differences seemed to be taboo.

"Mother," Rachel said sharply, "I think something's ready in the dining room." She silently mouthed the words, "I am sorry," to me.

I'd learned many skills in my first life, and one of them was diplomacy. I knew I had to win these people back over, if only for Rachel's sake.

So, before Maya left the room, I managed to say, "I think what you're doing is amazing. You must remember I'm only using the limited knowledge from my past. I would never presume to think that what you're doing is anything other than improving the lives of all humans."

Maya paused and smiled to herself before walking through the wall, the inclusive use of the word "humans" doing the trick.

Mazood looked at me and raised his eyebrows. "Thank you, Richard. We Manoorans can be a little sensitive about certain things. I hope it doesn't come between us if you and Rachel stay friends."

He started to ask me about my revival when a buzzing sound at the entrance interrupted us, and the doorway became transparent from inside, revealing the caller standing as if staring at a blank wall.

And that caller was Ramoon!

"Richard, I think you know our friend Ramoon," Rachel's father said as Ramoon entered. "I thought it would be a good idea to invite him, so you didn't feel too uncomfortable."

In fact, my comfort level plummeted to new depths. I wanted to demand an answer from him about my rejection from the Cryogen project, but I bit my tongue and forced a smile.

"Hello, Ramoon. I've been trying to get hold of you, but all your systems said you were away on business."

"I'm sorry, Richard. I've only just returned."

Somehow, I didn't believe him. *How had Rachel's parents been able to invite him tonight, then?* I wanted to ask but didn't.

"Is Ankit back as well?" I was having difficulty concealing the underlying anger I felt, and I bit down on the other side of my tongue.

"Yes, and he said he'd be contacting you tomorrow."

"Only I wanted to speak to you about the Cryogen project, but I realise tonight isn't an appropriate time. Would it be alright to come see you as soon as possible? Would tomorrow be convenient?" The tension in my body was palpable.

"Of course it would. Why don't you invite Ankit along as well if he's free? He may have some ideas about where we can employ your talents."

He seemed to enjoy making that last remark just a little too much for my liking. I certainly had no intention of doing anything other than searching for my wife.

Maya invited us to the table, and I followed the others into the dining room. It didn't look vastly different from what I'd experienced in the past; a large oval wooden dining table (although I doubted it was wood) was surrounded by high-backed chairs. As we walked toward it, Maya took control, pointing to where she wanted each of us to sit. She placed me between her and Mazood, with Rachel on the opposite side of the table with Ramoon, as far away from me as possible. When we settled, Maya spoke toward the middle of the table and said clearly, "Please serve dinner."

Up to now, I'd been getting my food from the panel embedded in the wall and taking it to my small table to eat, but this was something entirely different. The food seemed to grow out of the table itself. One minute it was bare, and the next, cutlery and plates formed out of the table. In the dishes themselves, the food emerged, changing colour, shape, and texture, and then finally grew hot as steam rose into the air, carrying the wonderful aroma of Chinese cooking throughout the room.

"That smells delicious," said Ramoon, and Maya seemed to fawn under his praise.

"I know it's your favourite, Ramoon," she said, hardly able to conceal her obsequious tone.

I followed everyone else's lead, and as we finished each course, we placed our implements inside the dishes. Upon which the plates and remains of the meal melted back into the table before the next course appeared just as miraculously as the first.

When the last course was complete, not only did the plates disappear, but so did the table. As it absorbed what was on it, it too melted slowly down into the floor until it had gone completely. Even though we were still in them, the dining chairs began to reshape and move. We soon found ourselves sitting in a circle of comfortable armchairs, and where the table had once been, the flames of an open fire danced rapidly before us.

Only a small amount of heat reached us from the flickering image, but there was something wonderfully primitive about its amber glow that was so relaxing. The walls had disappeared, virtually transporting us to an opening at the side of a wide river, the moonlight and stars shining down from a clear night sky. I could hear the shrill of insects all around and smell the mix of fresh air and burning wood that surrounded us. It took me back to my scout days. But the scouts had nothing like the armchairs we were reclining on, and I'd certainly never been allowed to drink wine around a campfire.

Although Ramoon and Rachel's parents were outwardly pleasant, I couldn't shake the feeling of animosity emanating from them in waves. They wanted to know what I planned to do with myself, and when I said I wasn't sure at the moment, their disappointment was palpable. I didn't particularly want to raise the issue of Helen while I had outstanding issues with Ramoon about the Cryogen project.

But Maya took every opportunity to praise the superiority of their race, and it felt to me like she was doing it for Ramoon's benefit. "We mourned the passing of such a noble race as the original humans," Maya said. But there was an undercurrent of relief in her voice that her kind was able to end their long search and settle here. There was a distinct lack of genuine feeling behind their so-called sadness at the extinction of humanity, and even less delight when she recounted the story of discovering the Cryogens on the Moon. Throughout the evening, they lingered on the technological changes they'd added to human culture as if something had always been missing.

As a lull fell over the conversation, Ramoon leaned forward toward Maya, as if he had important news to impart. "Have you heard about Amira?"

I looked at Rachel and mouthed, "Who's Amira?" But Maya was quick to ask, "Ankit's wife? No, what?"

"It's reported that she's left him. The rumour is that they've fallen out, and she's opted to be reborn to get away from him."

"Oh, poor Ankit," said Rachel. "But isn't Amira's action a bit drastic for the breakup of a marriage? Shouldn't she be given counselling?'

I was surprised by the news. But it did explain why my friend had been so disturbed about the breakup of his relationship.

"She was a bit of a recluse," explained Mazood. "Not many people saw her at all; she didn't get involved in Ankit's work, and he was happy with that arrangement."

The conversation then seemed to turn naturally toward relationships and my intentions toward Rachel. Ramoon quickly picked up on the concern emanating from Maya, interrupting with a mischievous and malicious grin. "Have you told them about your wife, Richard?"

He didn't give me time to reply before eagerly going on to tell them about Helen.

I shifted uncomfortably in my chair as Maya's mouth lifted into a smile, and she seemed to come alive. "Oh Richard, that's so sad. You mustn't ever give up on her. She could be anywhere, just waiting for you to find her."

That did it; their intentions were blatantly obvious now. They didn't want my dirty Cryogen ways to sully their Manooran purity. After everything they'd been saying about how wonderful the new world was, where everyone believed they were human, and how one day they'd like to live there, I'd had enough. How could they bring Helen into this when I was sitting opposite Rachel, especially as I was beginning to have strong feelings for her? Their conversation was deliberately inappropriate, and their words angered me.

Holding my temper, I got up and made my excuses, thanking them for a lovely evening before leaving. Rachel walked down the corridor with me, apologizing for her parents.

"It's not your fault, Rachel; I shouldn't be as mixed up as I am. At least then no one could question my intentions."

She looked into my eyes and said, "Richard, I'll help you find out what's happened to Helen, whatever the outcome. As long as you don't mind me admitting I have strong feelings for you."

I gulped, "Err…" I started to say something that just wasn't there. Then I squeezed her hands and turned around, walking away.

I needed to resolve this as quickly as possible. There was something not quite right about it all. Somehow, I had to find out the truth. And as I thought once more about the sense of pleasure I'd detected in Ramoon's explanation of my desperate search for Helen, a sudden idea struck me about how and where I might be able to find it.

Turning around, I headed in the direction of the one person I knew who might be able to help.

Chapter 22 - Evidence

"Richard, it's private." Ankit's voice was firm, almost pleading, as we met the following morning to head to Ramoon's office. I could see the tension etched on his face, a mask of reluctance that hinted at the turmoil beneath. He was clearly unwilling to discuss his recent disappearance, only admitting it had been for personal reasons, not the business ones we'd all been led to believe. But I didn't want to pry. I already knew the general facts, courtesy of Ramoon, who might as well have broadcast the news across all the planets for all the discretion he'd shown.

As I mulled over the situation, I had to confront a troubling truth: my desire to highlight Ramoon's indiscretion was as strong as my need to express concern for my friend. I felt a knot tightening in my stomach, a mix of worry and frustration.

"I don't want to talk about Amira at the moment," Ankit asserted, his voice clipped.

"I understand, and I won't pry," I replied, my sincerity genuine. "It's just that I was worried about you when I couldn't get in touch. Both you and Ramoon went missing on the same day I received that message from the Cryogen project. It felt like... something was wrong."

I hesitated, gauging Ankit's reaction, hoping to glean his thoughts on the high official. Then I said, "I can't say I was particularly concerned about Ramoon, though; he doesn't come across as overly friendly to anyone who's a Cryogen."

The weight of my words hung in the air, and I glanced at Ankit, searching for a flicker of acknowledgment. He remained silent for a few seconds, as if processing my statement. It was clear he was uncomfortable with the conversation, eager to escape its grasp. Finally, with a note of finality, he said, "I can't speak for Ramoon. Perhaps he genuinely was on business, but as far as I'm concerned, I want to forget the last two weeks." He paused, his voice steadier now. "But I do appreciate your concern, Richard. Thank you."

Seeing him in such low spirits twisted my heart. I felt helpless, a bystander to his pain. So, I nodded in understanding and followed him in silence to the administration sector at the heart of the city.

When we entered Ramoon's office, the high official sat behind a long desk that shimmered like glass. I suspected it was made of synthetic diamond, a marvel of technology that Jennifer had told me they could now manufacture in large amounts. Behind him loomed a wall-sized vid-screen, displaying a vast expanse of space, with a familiar planet hovering in the distance.

"Manoora," Ankit said, as if reading my thoughts.

"Of course," I replied, my gaze fixed on the graceful home planet of my friend. "It's beautiful."

"It most certainly is," Ramoon interjected, pride swelling in his voice. For a fleeting moment, I thought I detected genuine warmth. "But looks can be deceptive, Richard. To many of us Manoorans, that image represents a reminder of the prison we've escaped from and the freedom we've finally gained."

That was about as much sincerity as we were going to get from Ramoon today. The familiar condescension returned, along with the disingenuous frown I'd come to expect. "Sit down, Richard. I've uncovered some information regarding Helen."

Stunned into silence, my jaw must have dropped. I'd come here to discuss my application to the Cryogen project, armed with a carefully crafted argument for why they should let me join. But now, my heart raced, and all I could manage to say was, "What is it? Have you found her?"

"Please, Richard. You need to sit down," Ramoon repeated, glancing at Ankit for support.

That said it all, didn't it? They couldn't have found her. If they had, he would have said so immediately. The words *"sit down"* felt like a prelude to bad news, a warning that something terrible awaited me.

I fell hard into the chair behind me, my eyes locked on Ramoon, demanding, "What?"

"I've uncovered records that show an attempt to revive Helen." He adopted that fake sincerity I'd begun to detest. "It failed, Richard. None of her organic material was viable. She couldn't even be reborn; they cremated her remains, I'm afraid."

The words hit me like a physical blow. "What?" I screamed—or shouted, I don't know. Before I could process my actions, I was on my feet, grabbing Ramoon by his jacket, shaking him. "That can't be true! You're lying! You're lying! She's not gone."

"Richard, Richard, please..." Ankit's voice cut through my rage, trying to restrain me. I let him pull my arms away and guide me back to the chair.

I pulled a deep breath into my fake lungs and lowered my eyelids, just as I remembered doing to calm myself in the past.

"I'm sorry, Ramoon," I said, struggling to regain control of my emotions, my gaze fixed on the floor. "I don't know what came over me. It's just... the system told me there was no record of any attempt to revive Helen. I don't understand."

"That's okay, Richard. I know you're upset. The system was referring to its current records when it told you that. It seems Helen was among the first batch of Cryogens we attempted to revive, before we kept detailed records. I managed to discover this by searching through earlier data held offline."

I blinked, my mind racing to process what I'd just heard. I couldn't believe it. I'd lost Helen. We had travelled through time together, only to be separated like this. How could I live the life we had both wanted, forever... alone?

I covered my face with my hands, but the tears wouldn't come. I was in shock, unwilling to accept the reality crashing down around me. Ankit's hand squeezed my shoulder, a silent gesture of comfort. The room felt eerily quiet, as if all sound had evaporated, leaving only the haunting echo of Ramoon's words: "They cremated her remains, I'm afraid..."

When I finally composed myself and looked up, Ramoon held the info-sheet he had referenced when delivering the news. It shimmered in the light from the planet behind his desk, taunting me with the power its contents held over my very existence. It represented the final, irrevocable separation from Helen. An overwhelming urge to see the words it contained surged within me.

"Can I have a look at that?" I asked, extending my hand toward it.'

But Ramoon snatched it protectively toward himself. "No, I'm afraid it's confidential."

"I'm sorry, Ramoon," I said, my voice laced with dejection. For a fleeting moment, I thought I saw a flicker of something sinister cross his face, a look I remembered from our first encounter. "I'm just in shock."

My mind retreated into denial, as if hoping that by pretending nothing had happened, it would all go away. I suddenly recalled my ulterior motive for being there and asked, "May I have some water, please?"

Of course, I'll get you some," Ramoon replied, eager for an excuse to leave the room, still clutching the info-sheet.

As soon as he stepped out, I turned to Ankit. "Would you go and speak to him for me? Try to convince him to let me see what's on that info-sheet. I need to see it before I can accept what I've just heard." I looked directly into his eyes, pleading. "Please."

Ankit sighed, then nodded, before following Ramoon out of the room.

Once they were gone, I stood up quickly. The news about Helen had shattered my world, and my mind was racing, completely off the plan I'd hatched the night before to access Ramoon's private files. All I wanted to do was go home, crawl into a corner, and die. But I forced myself to focus, knowing I had a short window of time.

When we'd discussed my plan, we'd considered our chances slim, but it was worth it if there was any chance of uncovering the truth. Now, however, it was far easier than I'd anticipated. In his haste to leave with the info-sheet, Ramoon had left his desk drawer open, and I could see into it through the transparent surface. Piles of similar sheets were stacked inside, as thin as the one he'd been holding. I didn't have time to ponder why he hadn't stored the information on the main system; I had to act.

I pressed the buzzer in my pocket, signalling Simon, who I'd recruited the night before, hoping his surveillance knowledge would give me an edge. Simon was waiting at his apartment, and within seconds, I heard an incoming vid-message followed by his voice in the other room. I estimated I had less than five minutes to find whatever I could—just a few minutes while Simon distracted Ramoon, plus the time Ankit would take trying to convince him to let me see that info-sheet.

I reached down and fully opened the drawer, revealing piles of info-sheets. Lifting a handful out, I spread them quickly over the desk and took out the recording device Simon had given me. It would store the information and transmit it back to his apartment.

I had no time to examine what I was scanning. My nerves were frayed, and I just wanted it to be over. However, I caught a glimpse of the word "suppressed" next to a list of names before the device captured the information, and I hastily returned the sheets to the drawer, replacing them with another pile.

When I finished, I sat back down, my heart racing as I waited for Ankit and Ramoon to return. A minute or so later, they walked back into the room.

"That was Simon," Ramoon said, his tone clipped. "He expressed concern that your obsession with finding Helen has been having a detrimental effect on you. I haven't said anything about what we've discovered. I thought you'd want to break the news to your friends personally."

'Thank you," I replied, struggling to inject sincerity into my voice.

As we left the office, Ankit explained that Ramoon had been adamant that I couldn't see the classified information on Helen. "I'm sorry, Richard. I did what I could. The best you can do is try to come to terms with your loss." He patted me on the arm. "Would you like me to come back to your apartment for a while?"

'Thanks, Ankit, but I think I'd like to be alone for now. I'll be in touch soon.'

I waited until he disappeared around the corner before turning and heading toward Simon's apartment.

All three of my fellow Cryogens were gathered around the main vid-screen, their expressions grave as they examined the information I'd transmitted from Ramoon's office.

"You've got to see this," Jennifer beckoned me over, urgency in her voice. "There's definitely something not right here."

They were looking at a list of names, each one marked with the word "Cryogen," and beside each name, the word *"suppressed"* loomed ominously.

I fought to keep my thoughts from drifting back to Helen, as if hiding from the facts would somehow make it untrue. But all the life seemed to have drained from me, leaving me hollow. "Yes, I noticed that when I was scanning them," I said, my voice barely above a whisper. "I wonder what it means." The protester's words echoed in my mind— *"Don't let them kill us all off—protect the humans."*

"But it gets worse, Richard," Simon said, stepping through the documents. He paused, his expression darkening as he came to one that bore the same list of names, including mine and Helen's. But this document held something far more sinister against each name.

A chilling proclamation that sent a shiver down my spine. My heart raced as the reality of our situation crashed over me like a tidal wave. We were not just fighting for survival; we'd been marked for extinction. I watched in horror as Earl read the ominous words aloud.

"TO BE DESTROYED!"

Chapter 23 – Second Goodbye

If anyone else had been able to see us in that moment, they might have thought it a touching scene, a tableau of friendship and grief intertwined. But for me, it felt like a raw wound laid bare, exposed to the world. I couldn't hide my distraction from my friends any longer. When I finally mustered the courage to share the news, the silence that followed was deafening, a heavy shroud that enveloped us all. Earl and Simon stood resolutely at my sides, their hands resting on my shoulders, grounding me as I sat there, finally allowing the dam of my emotions to break. Jennifer knelt on the floor, her arms wrapped tightly around my middle, as if she could physically hold my shattered heart together. The side of her head pressed against my chest, her eyes squeezed shut, desperately trying to wish away the terrible truth that had just been spoken.

Somehow, voicing the news about Helen in the presence of my friends had made it all too real. It was as if the act of speaking had released a torrent of grief that I'd kept bottled up for far too long. Tears streamed down my face, hot and unrelenting, as I recalled the words from the ceremony we had held when she first died:

Keep me in your heart and mind,
Keep safe my memories too,
And when you're lonely you will find,
I am there and part of you.

Tears are the blood of emotion. How true that is! It seems so easy to gauge the severity of a physical wound by the amount of blood it sheds, but emotional wounds are different. The volume of tears is hidden from all but those who contain them. Helen had once told me this after she lost her father, and now, in this moment of despair, I wondered how right she'd been. I could see no way to stem the flow of this emotional blood that threatened to bleed me dry. *Is this what happens when people die of heartache?* I thought, feeling the weight of sorrow pressing down on me.

My friends would have happily stayed there all night, their presence a comforting balm against my anguish, but eventually, I cried myself out. For now, at least. When I finally lifted my head, my voice trembled as I announced, "Look, I've got so much to think about. I don't want to seem ungrateful, but would you mind if I spent a few days on my own to come to terms with all of this?"

Their tear-filled eyes spoke volumes, but it was Simon who found the words. "Richard, take as long as you like. Nothing else is important now. You know where we are when you're ready, and we'll always be here for you, mate."

If I'd been a fly on the wall after I left the room, I would have seen Jennifer leaning against it, her expression pensive as she gazed at the doorway, as if she could still see me on the other side. "I hope he'll be alright," she murmured, her voice heavy with concern. "He's been so consumed by his search. I just don't know how this is going to affect him."

Simon's muscular arm wrapped around her shoulders, a protective gesture that spoke of his unwavering support. "He's a strong person, Jen. He'll get through this. We just need to make sure he doesn't withdraw from everything and give up on his new life. At least he's not alone. He's got us to help him through."

"We need to let him deal with it in his own way, though," Earl interjected, his brow furrowed in thought. "Apart from making sure he doesn't do anything rash, we should give him the space he's told us he needs. And in the meantime..." He held up one of the info sheets, his expression shifting to one of determination. "We need to consider what we're going to do with this evidence he retrieved from Ramoon's office."

"We're not doing anything with it," Jennifer said firmly, her voice cutting through the tension like a knife. Earl looked at her, bewildered.

"But this is evidence," he protested. "We have a duty to act on it."

"Yes, you're right. But we're a team, Earl. All of us, including Richard. I don't know how both of you feel about our group, but the four of us are about as close to a family as I'm going to get, and I don't think any of us should act independently." Her tone softened slightly as she added, "By waiting for a while, we can give Richard the time he needs to grieve, and in the meantime, we can think about what we're going to do with the information."

She paused, letting the weight of her words settle in the air, making Earl squirm slightly before she continued, "A little more time won't harm, will it?"

He sighed, bowing his head in defeat. "Very well. Let's leave it a week or so unless Richard comes back before then. But we can't wait too long to find out what Ramoon's intentions are. If we do, it might be far too late to do anything about them. In the meantime, get your thinking caps on. We need a plan of some kind for when we are ready to act."

After that night, I became a recluse, retreating into the shadows of my own mind. I made excuses whenever anyone tried to contact me, immersing myself in the depths of my grief. I hadn't even felt this way the first time Helen had died. Back then, I'd convinced myself that she still physically existed, that she was merely in that cryogenic chamber, asleep and waiting to be reunited with me. But this was different. There was nothing left of her—not just the body that housed who she was, but every single synapse in her brain that made her the unique woman I loved. It was all gone, swept away like sand through my fingers.

There was no more crawling into that corner of my mind where denial lived, welcoming me every time I called. The door was shut firmly for now, and I found myself locked out in a wilderness of grief, with nowhere to shelter. The cold, clinging embrace of sorrow wrapped around me, and I stayed there for as long as I could, hoping to drown in it, to end the misery I was convinced would never stop.

Then, as if life had a cruel sense of humour, another companion stepped forward to dull the pain. Time, the very thing that Helen and I had planned to cheat, now moved the unbearable pain of the present into the more tolerable sorrow of the past. Like a drug pusher no one can escape from, time offered the relief craved by all addicts, a relentless supply of change that dulled the sharp edges of grief.

No one can predict when it's right for someone to move on after losing someone they love. Everyone must find their own reasons to convince themselves that it's acceptable to continue living the life denied to the person they've lost. For me, it was my conviction of what Helen would have wanted. It would be a betrayal of everything she had hoped for if I gave up and threw this life away. This dream come true, even though it would never be a dream fulfilled for Helen now.

So, I concluded, I would live my new life for Helen, keeping her memory with me forever. At least the part of her that lived inside my heart would survive, just like in the poem from her funeral—*she'd be here and part of me.*

She'd always been stronger than I ever was; I'd always known that, and it was one of the many things that had drawn me to her. She would never give up, and I grinned as I thought of the strength within her that I'd perceived as *stubbornness*, and she had argued was focused determination. That was what she had taught me—the strength she had willingly shared and passed on, and what I now used to pull myself out of the dark place that threatened to swallow me for good.

As I smiled at these memories, I realised it was the first smile since learning of her death. Her radiant face, smiling back at me in my mind's eye, seemed to nod in approval, telling me not to feel guilty, encouraging me to go on.

Over the next few days, I began to emerge from the despair I'd sunk into, and the dark reverie that had settled over me began to lift. I started to wonder what sort of future lay ahead.

Inevitably, those thoughts of the future brought my mind to Rachel… oh, Rachel. While there had been a chance of Helen being alive, I'd been ashamed of my growing feelings for her, confused by the thoughts invading my head and the urges my body presented. Not that I blamed the new body; it was only mimicking the old one. From my experiences so far, there wasn't anything it couldn't do at least as well as my original.

But now, those feelings of shame and guilt were magnified a hundredfold. How could I let such thoughts cross my mind at a time like this? I was grieving for god's sake. Nevertheless, those thoughts and feelings for Rachel invaded my dreams, refusing to abide by any moral rules of decency.

I realised, of course, that I couldn't leave it too long if I wanted her to be in my life as anything more than a friend. If she began to believe I could never commit myself because of Helen, she might start looking for someone else. I knew she wouldn't have any difficulty in that respect. Besides, her parents would probably feel threatened by my confirmed loss and start seeking suitors for their daughter as soon as possible—anything to prevent what they'd see as a terrible blow to their family if I were to be part of it.

It took me just over a week to work through my grief and come out the other side. I'd shed most of my emotional blood, and the deep wound it left had finally begun to heal. Although I would happily live with the scar it would leave, I knew in my heart that Helen had released me to the future. I could take what I could of her with me, but I had to live the rest of my life. And if that life included Rachel, so be it. I knew Helen wouldn't want me to be alone.

So, I didn't know who had been more surprised—Rachel when I asked her to marry me, or my friends, who I suspected must have thought I'd had some kind of breakdown.

"Are you sure?" was the reply I got, and in the circumstances, had fully expected from Rachel. It was a little disappointing because what I really wanted to hear was a resounding "Yes!" without any hesitation and accompanied by enthusiasm.

"I've told you how I've dealt with my feelings and what I think Helen would have thought. It's what I want, Rachel. I know at first it will be difficult for us, and I'll probably make some stupid mistakes that will hurt you. But none of them will be intentional. You know how much I loved Helen, but I have to live with that love being in the past, and it will become a different type of love. I want to be with you now, and I know the love that I already feel for you will only grow stronger. I promise not to let you down, Rachel. Please say you'll be my wife."

The beaming smile on her face assured me of the response she was about to give. "Yes, I'd love to marry you, Richard." Smiling, I ran my fingers over her lips before drawing her to me, letting all my tensions drain away.

If only my friends had been as enthusiastic about it as Rachel. But considering how quickly all this had occurred, I could understand their reservations about my latest decision.

"You'll never get over Helen," Earl had said when I broke the news to them. "Are you certain you're doing this for the right reasons? After someone you love dies, it's only natural to feel lonely and seek comfort in another close relationship."

"But…" Jennifer interrupted, jumping in quickly, not wanting me to think that Earl was implying I might be using Rachel in some way, "if you've given yourself enough time to think about this and it's what you want to do, then we're pleased for you." I noticed her throw Earl an apologetic smile.

"I know you're all concerned for me," I said to them, "but Rachel and I have discussed this, and how I've dealt with my grief for Helen. She accepts it and knows that I'll never ask her to compete with a ghost. Helen's memories will stay with me for as long as I live, so in a way, she will live forever. But they'll never come between Rachel and me. I need to learn to live in this new world now, and the only person I know who can help me do that is Rachel."

Simon grasped my right hand with both of his and shook it vigorously. "Congratulations, mate."

Then Earl and Jennifer, in their own ways, did the same, showing me the support, they must have thought I needed for the decision I'd made. However, other than Earl showing his characteristic straightforwardness, none of them had expressed the real concerns that were beginning to grow in their minds.

As I stood there, surrounded by my friends, I felt a flicker of hope ignite within me. Perhaps this new chapter of my life wouldn't be so daunting after all. Perhaps, with Rachel by my side, I could forge a future that honoured Helen's memory while allowing me to embrace the possibilities that lay ahead.

Perhaps, perhaps….

Chapter 24 - Marriage

In the days that followed, I found myself engaged in a relentless battle against my own mind, desperately trying to barricade it from the haunting memories that threatened to surface. I busied myself with the tasks Rachel had set for our upcoming wedding, using them as a shield against the turmoil within. It was the only way I could navigate the labyrinth of each day. I clung to the belief that things would eventually improve; it was merely a matter of time. And I was determined to buy that time, no matter the cost.

For a fleeting moment, I managed to convince—no, trick—myself into believing that everything would turn out alright in the end. I didn't want to dwell on Ramoon or the Cryogen project any longer. I chose to ignore the sudden silence from my friends regarding the matter, blissfully unaware of their unspoken pact to withhold action until after my marriage. They were waiting for the right moment to pull me back into their fold.

"If he doesn't bring it up after the wedding, we'll act without him," Jennifer had conceded to Earl, her voice laced with concern.

Yet, even as my friends kept a watchful eye on Ramoon's movements, they were oblivious to the deeper currents swirling around us. Rachel's parents had begrudgingly accepted our marriage, but Ramoon seemed almost jubilant about it, as if he had achieved some clandestine victory. Maya and Mazood, without question, mirrored his enthusiasm, which struck me as odd. Their acceptance felt like a mask, hiding the disdain that still lingered whenever we were together. It hung in the air like a foul odour that everyone was too polite to acknowledge.

In a moment of desperation, I turned to Rachel, asking if there was anything we could do to make our marriage more palatable for her parents. She laughed lightly, "They'd be over the moon if they had a grandchild."

"Why not?" I replied, a spark igniting within me. "You've mentioned children before. I've always wanted them. If the process takes time, why don't we apply for one now and tell them."

"Are you serious?" Her eyes lit up, a mixture of surprise and hope dancing across her features.

"Never been more," I said, a smile breaking through the clouds of my thoughts. I couldn't help but think of the struggles Helen and I had faced in our attempts to have children. The pain of those memories threatened to resurface, but I pushed it away. *Stop it! Stop torturing yourself,* I admonished inwardly.

Rachel's excitement was infectious; she jumped up and down, her joy lifting my spirits higher than they had been since my revival. *This is my life now,* I reminded myself. *I need to live it fully.*

Choosing how to celebrate our commitment was no longer a straightforward task. The world had opened up to us, offering a kaleidoscope of wedding ceremonies from every corner of the globe. My lack of religious affiliation no longer barred us from embracing the rich traditions and symbols that had grown around them. Yet, the absence of strong beliefs made our decision even more challenging. I chuckled softly as I watched Rachel's bewilderment grow. "Why not have all of them?"

"What do you mean?" she asked, her brow furrowing in confusion.

'Why, does the ceremony have to be a one-off? We could have a Hindu marriage this year, a Christian one next year, a Muslim wedding the year after, and a Jewish one the following year. We could marry in every religion until we've covered them all!"

"Wouldn't that offend anyone?" she countered, her expression a mix of scepticism and concern. "Some people take their religion very seriously, and we'd have to consider how closely to follow the rituals. I'm not sure I want to wear sindoor on my forehead like many married Hindu women. And I'm not particularly fond of wedding rings either."

"I don't see why it should offend anyone," I replied, my conviction growing. "In my time, perhaps, but we'd be honouring their traditions, not disrespecting them. We can choose our own symbols to represent our marriage, even if they differ. After all, many people follow religious practices and traditions without being devout."

She hesitated, weighing my words. "Okay," she finally relented, "but only if we seek advice to ensure we won't cause any offense."

"You've got a deal," I laughed, my heart swelling with affection. "I'm serious about my commitment to you, Rachel. One wedding isn't enough to show you how much I want to be with you."

Her gaze softened, and I could see the realisation dawning on her. "You know, Richard, that's such a romantic suggestion. I can see why Helen wanted to spend eternity with you."

The grin on my face masked the tiny pang of sorrow that tugged at my heart. To stave off the swell of emotion, I leaned in and kissed her, and she responded with a longer, more meaningful kiss that sent warmth coursing through me.

Our application to adopt a reborn was accepted, and we were overjoyed at the prospect of having a child of our own—or at least what constituted our own child in this strange new world. We dove headfirst into the task of selecting attributes for our child, a way to compensate for the absence of natural development. We envisioned a girl, one who would inherit Rachel's delicate nose and my striking eyes, a blend of our racial backgrounds. We even had the option to choose her age, and we both agreed on a birth age of fifteen, the same as Rachel's.

We settled on the name Jane Maya, a tribute to my grandmother and Rachel's mother. I couldn't help but chuckle when she suggested a double-barrelled last name of Green-Karr. After I explained what a car was, we decided to stick with Karr, a choice that would surely endear me to Rachel's parents.

The average wait for a reborn was two and a half years, a blink of an eye for immortals like us. Besides, the application had served its immediate purpose of placating my future in-laws.

In the absence of my biological family, Earl, Jennifer, Simon, and Ankit took on the roles expected during the Hindu ceremony. We travelled to the surface to hold it outdoors, around a real fire, which was customary. I revelled in the opportunity to don traditional clothing that had long since faded from everyday wear. Rachel even accepted having the red dot of sindoor on her forehead for the day.

Out of respect for my long-gone family, my friends had gained permission to hold the ceremony in Sherwood Forest, near the place of my birth. Our marquee filled a clearing next to the ancient 'Major Oak,' said to have once concealed the legendary outlaw Robin Hood in its massive hollow trunk.

Inside the marquee, the sounds that would have once filtered through the brightly coloured fabric were muted by advanced technology. No open entrances adorned its futuristic structure; as people passed in and out through designated entrances, their advanced senses controlled the transmission of their voices, preserving the serene silence of the forest around us.

After family and friends made their toasts, including a heartfelt speech from Ankit, who still wore a shadow of sadness, I was taken aback when Ramoon stepped forward to address our guests.

"Everyone, could I have your attention, please? I have an announcement to make." Silence fell as confusion rippled through the crowd. The previous speaker had indicated she would be the last to speak.

"I know this is unexpected," Ramoon continued, his voice steady, "but I wanted to take this opportunity to share some good news with the happy couple on their special day." Rachel and I exchanged puzzled glances as he continued.

"As you all probably know, Richard and Rachel have applied to become parents. Normally, they would have to wait several years for the happy event, but…" He paused, letting the anticipation build. "I'm thrilled to announce that due to an exceptionally high number of people being reborn, your new child will be ready to join you by the end of the month."

If anyone had been watching us closely, it would have been impossible to tell whose jaw dropped the furthest. The room erupted in cheers, and the celebrations truly began, fuelled by the exhilarating news. I found myself so overwhelmed that I even hugged Ramoon, thanking him for his help.

Yet, amidst the revelry, whispers circulated among the guests, questioning how we could start a family so soon after our marriage. It was unprecedented, and no amount of joy could mask the suspicious glances exchanged between Jennifer, Simon, and Earl. They had already discussed their belief that Ramoon was doing everything in his power to keep me from getting involved in the Cryogen project. Only someone of his influence could have expedited our application so swiftly.

Later, my friends confided that they had kept their suspicions to themselves for the sake of our happiness. To everyone else, the speed of our application was attributed to the friendship between Ramoon and Rachel's parents.

As the evening drew to a close, Ankit approached us, clasping our hands in his. "You make such a wonderful couple, and you're going to be great parents. I'm sure you'll find true happiness together."

I sensed the weight of his words, knowing this must be difficult for him. Detecting an underlying sadness that seemed to drain the life from him, I asked, "Are you alright?"

"I will be after I get back," he replied, his voice steady but distant.

"Why? Where are you going?" I inquired, concern creeping into my tone.

"I've decided to take your advice, Richard, and take a break. I've managed to get permission to go to the surface and travel around India. I'm hoping it will help clear my head."

"How long will you be gone?" Rachel asked, her brow furrowing with worry.

"I'm not sure yet, but I promise I'll keep in touch."

As I watched him disappear through the side of the marquee, I made a silent wish to whatever gods existed in this time. I hoped his journey would revive the vibrant spirit I'd first encountered in him.

I wanted my friend back.

Chapter 25 - Family

Although this was my second family, it was my first time as a father. It hadn't been until Helen, and I reached the twilight of our lives that we finally realised the truth: the only family we truly needed was each other, along with those who loved us as fiercely as we loved them. By the time we retired, having children had become a relic of the past, a fading norm overshadowed by the enforced sterilisation policies designed to protect the wealth of the elite. Parenthood had been reserved for the privileged few, a cruel twist of fate that left many like us yearning for what could never be. Deep down, we both felt the ache of unfulfilled dreams, the bittersweet longing for the overwhelming joy of holding a child we'd created together.

And in a way, Rachel and I hadn't created this family—not in the traditional sense that would resonate with anyone from my time. Yet, it was the best we could hope for, and I was determined to embrace it fully. The more I pondered the concept of family, the clearer it became, family is defined by love, not by blood. Whatever the truth of our situation, that had to be enough for now. Biology was a long distant memory.

We settled into our home in India Prime, a vibrant tapestry of colours and sounds that felt both foreign and familiar. Quickly, we established a routine that brought a sense of normalcy to our lives. Jane, our fresh-faced, cheeky fifteen-year-old, was everything we had hoped for —thankfully devoid of the sulky attitude that plagued teenagers in my era. At home, she radiated confidence, a spark that made me wonder if she would eventually seek her own path in another society as she matured. Out in public, she adhered to the norms, but within the walls of our apartment, she shed her inhibitions like a second skin. I often found her wandering about the apartment naked, a habit that left me feeling decidedly uncomfortable. It seemed the system intruded less into the sanctity of home life, allowing for a freedom I'd long forgotten.

Beyond her carefree spirit, Jane was grounded and sensible, though a hint of shyness crept in when she was around others. I questioned whether this was a remnant of the rebirth process, but Rachel dismissed it as a simple lack of social skills. Her skin was a shade lighter than her mother's, yet she bore those distinctively sharp, classic Indian features that promised to blossom into film-star beauty as she matured. We had chosen her appearance, a decision made with the system's assistance, which would ensure she grew into the visage we envisioned. Not that it could stop her clicking her fingers and changing her features at will. Thank God that hadn't become a common practice; the idea of people changing their faces like outfits was unsettling.

Though Jane possessed the basic knowledge expected for her age, she lacked the rich mix of experiences that should have accompanied her previous years. Rachel and I were eager to fill that void, to weave her into the fabric of our lives. We initiated a regime of exploration and learning, determined to help her bond with us through shared experiences. We planned individual outings, each designed to introduce her to our passions and interests, to create memories that would last a lifetime.

As for her formal education, I was relieved that the dreaded 'school run' was a thing of the past. I remembered the tedious tales my friends had shared about their morning rituals, the chaos of getting children ready for school. In this new age, children were few and far between, rendering conventional schools impractical. I often wondered why anyone bothered at all when learning could happen even in sleep. Yet, the psychological undercurrents of society still pushed parents to simulate a classroom experience. Every household with a child boasted a small room equipped with a desk and chair, a mini holodeck that transported each child into a virtual classroom filled with their peers.

Like many parents, Rachel and I wanted Jane to share our interests. Rachel was passionate about science and seized every opportunity to engage Jane in her learning of maths and the wonders of the universe. I, on the other hand, was eagerly anticipating the day I could take her to a football match—a relic of my past that I'd only recently discovered still existed. I couldn't help but laugh inwardly at the absurdity of it all; Manchester United still reigned supreme at the top of the league, although it was now dubbed Earth League One. The most ridiculous part? Paul Auldham, arguably one of the greatest players to ever don the red jersey, was still playing! When I learned this, I closed my eyes and shook my head in disbelief. I didn't even want to know if it was the real Auldham, revived from the past, or merely someone using his body template. At this point, I was beyond being surprised.

Initially, I assumed every famous person I encountered was the genuine article. That was until I bumped into a young rock star who I knew for a fact hadn't been cryogenically suspended. It was then I learned that the estates of these icons had, at one time, owned their body templates and licensed them for use. Hundreds of thousands of copies of every recognisable figure from Earth's history now walked among us. Sure, there were more attractive versions than others, but the disorientation was palpable. If it hadn't been for the advanced senses built into these new bodies, distinguishing between them would have been impossible.

As I lounged in our new home, contemplating this strange new reality, I felt a sense of peace wash over me. It had only been a few months since my marriage, yet everything seemed almost perfect. I had what I'd always wanted to share with Helen. The sadness that tightened my insides each time I thought of her was gradually becoming less painful. I realised there would come a time when I could think of her, perhaps even speak her name, without the sharp pang of grief.

Yet, even as I entertained these thoughts, guilt washed over me like a cold wave. Deep down, I knew a fundamental conflict raged within me. I was torn between allowing the hurt of losing Helen to fade and clinging to it as if it were the last thread connecting me to her. Sometimes, I felt that the only way to cope with her absence was to slowly numb my feelings. But whatever path I chose, at least it was my only worry now. Everything else in the world seemed to be falling into place.

Or so I thought. Because just as this newfound sense of security began to envelop me, my old friend fate lurked in the shadows, waiting to strike. It seemed eager to reclaim its role in my life, to remind me that I was never truly beyond its reach. I'd let my guard down, lulled into a false sense of security, but fate had other plans. The card it was about to deal me was just one of many in its hand, all bearing my name.

Unbeknownst to me, in her room, Jane sat on the edge of her bed, gazing down at the drawer that housed her most cherished possessions. Among them were items her previous self had deemed important, remnants of a life she would not fully understand until she became an adult and reintegrated her past memories—if she ever chose to do so.

All she knew was that she had at least one previous life, and some of the objects before her were echoes from that time. The rest awaited retrieval from the growing warehouses scattered across the worlds, places where people stored their accumulated treasures from countless lifetimes.

With a sense of wonder, she pulled each item from the drawer, spreading them out on her bed for closer inspection. As she picked up one particular piece, her gaze lingered on it. The silver band of the ring formed a striking backdrop for the circle of gold that cradled two shiny blue stones.

They seemed to gaze back at her..................like a pair of familiar eyes.

Chapter 26 – How bad can it get?

Ever since the wedding, I'd noticed a peculiar shift in Ramoon's demeanour. He had become overly courteous, almost unnaturally good-natured towards me. While this change made me uneasy, it had a silver lining: Rachel's parents were beginning to warm up to me as well. I felt like I was walking a tightrope, desperate not to upset the apple cart for Rachel's sake. This newfound stability in my life was a fragile thing, and I was determined to nurture it. So, I'd skilfully dodged discussions about the evidence and the Cryogen situation with my friends. They had tried to engage me, but each time, I managed to steer the conversation away from those treacherous waters. What was the point of stirring up trouble?

Tonight, I was finally ready to relax in our apartment, savouring the first full day alone since the wedding. Rachel and Jane were off on one of their educational excursions to the surface, courtesy of Ramoon, who had suddenly become eager to wield his influence for our benefit.

Since discovering Helen's fate, everything had spiralled forward at an alarming pace. The transition from that harrowing moment to now felt like it had happened in the blink of an eye. Life was beginning to settle into a routine, but I knew that soon, I would have to confront the reality of my situation and consider what I truly wanted to do with my life.

Yet, a gnawing guilt tugged at my conscience. No matter how much I tried to avoid it, I would eventually have to discuss the Cryogen project with my friends. I needed to know what they intended to do with the information I'd unearthed in Ramoon's office. I couldn't put it off forever. But now that Helen was gone, everything felt less urgent. The fire that once burned within me had dimmed, leaving me feeling strangely apathetic.

I sat there, drink in hand, staring at the info-tablet I was using to jot down notes about the changes I envisioned for our new home. The apartment we had been allocated was a standard family unit, but Rachel and I were eager to customise it to reflect our tastes. We had decided to take our time, but Jane's impatience was wearing us thin. Her constant nagging about the changes she wanted had finally worn us down, and we agreed that each of us would make notes on our desired improvements before settling on a final plan. Our goal was to create a space where we could all feel comfortable and truly at home.

As I contemplated how a veranda could be attached to the apartment—somewhere I could sit in a rocking chair and lose myself in the virtual forest beyond the vid-wall—a sudden clunking sound broke my reverie. The doorway slid open, and an auto cleaner rolled in, its mechanical whirring filling the room.

Though the structure was self-cleaning, this little 'robot', as Ankit would call it, was designed to monitor the environment and eliminate what it deemed contaminants. I'd seen these machines in action countless times before, so I paid it little mind as it scuttled about, performing its duties.

Moments later, I heard a dull thud emanating from Jane's room, pulling my attention away from my designs. It was odd to hear anything from the other rooms, thanks to the noise reduction technology. I realised it was because the entrances in the walls had to actually open to allow access for the cleaning machines; they couldn't simply pass through the walls as we could.

Curiosity piqued, I walked over to where Jane's bedroom door had been, just as the auto cleaner was preparing to exit. "What was that noise I just heard?" I asked, my voice tinged with curiosity.

The quiet, almost disconcerting voice of the machine replied, "The bottom drawer of the cabinet next to the bed was half open. I attempted to shut it, but something was preventing it from closing, and further attempts caused it to fall to the floor. Nothing was broken, and I've placed the figure back in the drawer."

"What figure?" I inquired, my interest deepening.

"The colourful stone figure of the dancing female," it responded. "I've replaced it in the drawer."

"Err, thank you," I said, dismissing the conversation, unsure of how to respond. The machine rolled back through the door it had originally entered, embarking on its journey down the utility ramp to the storage room below our apartment. The door to Jane's room re-materialised, leaving me half in and half out of our daughter's bedroom.

Now, I was intrigued by the stone figure the machine had mentioned. I knew that those being reborn often took personal and sentimental items with them to their new lives, even if they wouldn't remember them until—or if—they re-integrated their previous memories. But it was in Jane's drawer, and I felt it would be a gross invasion of her privacy to look at it, especially since she hadn't mentioned it or any of her other possessions. Yet, the cleaner had described it, and I couldn't shake the urge to see it for myself. Surely, that couldn't do any harm, especially if she never knew.

With a distinct sense of wrongdoing, I crossed the room, feeling like I was about to read someone's personal diary. But the desire to see something that connected my daughter to her earlier life compelled me forward.

I knelt beside the bed and opened the bottom drawer.

There it was—the pink outstretched arm of a pirouetting ballet dancer seemed to reach out to me through a jumble of fashion glasses and a pile of small, brightly coloured purses. I lifted it by its delicate hand, marvelling at its beauty. It was crafted from different coloured stones, reminiscent of the statue of Robin Hood that my friends had taken me to see. Cold and smooth to the touch, it was heavier than it appeared. I wondered about its history and hoped that Jane would share its story if she ever re-integrated her memories. I turned it around, inspecting its delicate features, before deciding it was time to respect Jane's privacy.

I had no intention of rummaging through the rest of the drawer. I'd seen what I wanted and gently pushed the little ballerina back between the black and yellow bags from where I'd picked it up.

But as I moved the bags, a flash of blue caught my eye, glinting against the gold. Unable to resist, I nudged the yellow bag aside with my finger.

"That can't be!" I gasped, my heart racing. "No," I answered myself, "that's impossible."

I lifted the object, holding it in front of my face. Time seemed to freeze. I stared at it, much like a devout Christian gazing upon the Holy Grail. My mouth fell open, and tears began to form in the corners of my eyes before they started their journey down the sides of my frozen face. I couldn't believe what I was seeing. The two tiny sapphires of Helen's wedding ring sparkled from their circular gold setting, their steely blue reflections shimmering in the tears that now rolled freely down my cheeks.

Then, the full weight of the implication hit me like a freight train. I stood up sharply, my heart pounding in my chest. "NO," I shouted, the word echoing in the silence of the room. "No, No, NO!" I began to pace back and forth, repeating the word like a mantra, "no... no... no..."

I backed up through the bedroom door, my mind racing. I slammed my fist against the wall, as if I could physically knock the thoughts from my head. "No!" I banged, desperate to silence the chaos swirling within me. "No!"

Leaning against the wall, I felt my heart racing as I slowly sank to the floor. My head felt like it would explode. I couldn't handle the torrent of emotions crashing over me. We had never specified what type of reborn we wanted when we applied for Jane. It hadn't seemed important at the time. I'd accepted that Helen was gone and was just beginning to cope with that reality. But what Ramoon had told me must have been a lie. Why would he lie? I was married to Rachel now, and the thought made me feel sick. I couldn't bear to think about it, but the idea crept into my mind like a sly fox sneaking into a henhouse.

Our daughter could be my first wife! My stomach churned at the thought, mirroring the turmoil in my mind. I took deep, sharp breaths, fighting the urge to vomit.

I slumped on the floor for what felt like hours, clutching the ring that glistened in my hand. The more I looked at it, the more I felt Helen's presence, her hand pointing an accusing finger at me, demanding to know why I'd given up on her.

"What's happening to me?" I whispered aloud, closing my eyes to calm the storm within. Gradually, I began to regain my composure. I needed time to think. I kissed the tiny sapphires and placed the ring back into Jane's drawer, then walked back to the living room. Once there, I released a torrent of tears, unsure if they were tears of joy, sadness, or guilt.

After a while, when I could think a little clearer, I realised I had to decide what to do. My options were limited. I could carry on as if everything were normal and let Helen rest in peace. But even as that thought crossed my mind, I knew I could never find peace again until I uncovered the truth. And if Jane ever re-integrated her memories and they were Helen's... oh, I couldn't bear to think about it.

I certainly couldn't tell Rachel yet. It would shatter her heart, just as mine was shattering at that moment.

Though I'd tried to push it from my mind, I had to admit that this entire confusing mess was likely intertwined with the Cryogen issues. It was somehow connected to Ramoon and the protestors. I should have listened to my friends after all. I'd been in denial, selfishly focused on my own happiness. What a coward I'd been.

I needed to confide in someone about this, and right now, it was those very friends I'd been avoiding who I turned to for help. I arranged to meet them at Simon's apartment under the pretence that I was ready to discuss Ramoon and what we had discovered in his office. I wanted to wait until we were all together before revealing the horrifying truth I'd just unearthed about Jane.

Jennifer said she had been praying for my return, hoping I would help them uncover Ramoon's involvement in these suspicious events. But she never suspected it would be something as horrific as this that would draw me back to them.

"Oh, please, no..." was all she could manage after I shared my news. She was as shocked as I'd been, her forehead cradled in her hands as she stared at the floor in disbelief.

"Richard, this is terrible," Earl said, his voice heavy with concern. "We have to find out the truth before we talk to anyone else about this."

"I'd already decided that, Earl," I replied, nodding in agreement.

"We've been waiting for you to come to us about the protestors and the Cryogen situation, Richard," Simon added. "We didn't want to act without you. But I guess Ramoon's efforts to keep you occupied have been working."

"What do you mean?" I asked, confusion clouding my mind.

"I know you and Rachel have been over the moon about getting Jane so early, but we think Ramoon had more to do with it than you realise. What you've just told us makes it even more suspicious." He shook his head; disbelief etched on his face. "We thought he interfered somehow with your application process just to keep you from persisting in your attempts to be involved in the Cryogen project. He's certainly hiding something."

"I was just so happy with everything working out so well, and Rachel being so happy, that I never considered it. But it does seem likely now that he is involved in trying to keep me away from the Cryogen project. I just don't understand why he would arrange something as twisted as this. Is he really that sick?"

"We've got to do something to sort this mess out," Jennifer insisted. "We ought to go straight to Ramoon's office now and confront him."

"I'm not sure that's the right thing to do at the moment," Earl interjected.

"Alright, smart Alec," Jennifer shot back, her voice laced with irritation. "What's your brilliant idea?"

Earl looked around at us, catching our attention. "I suggest we attempt to contact the protestors and share the information we've gathered. I don't believe they're as paranoid as we've been led to believe, and they may have insight into what's really going on. We shouldn't tackle this alone."

"Do You realise how dangerous that could be?" she countered.

"I agree with Earl. But if that's the route we're taking, I want to keep Rachel and Ankit out of this for as long as possible," I said firmly. "They're not Cryogens, so they're not in any immediate danger. We need to keep this between ourselves until we uncover the truth."

"Alright," Earl said, "Let's all try to gather as much information as we can about the protestors. Then we'll reconvene tomorrow to devise a plan. Sound good?"

"Agreed," I replied, feeling the weight of exhaustion settle over me. "Right now, I'm emotionally drained and need to get some rest."

As I made my way back to my apartment, I couldn't shake the thought of how I would keep Rachel and Jane from sensing that something was terribly wrong. It would take Herculean effort to maintain the facade that everything was as it had been before I uncovered this dreadful truth. But for everyone's sake, I had to be strong.

That night, Helen visited me in my dreams. Her vivid image filled my vision, but it was a different Helen than I'd known—accusing and bitter. "I never demanded anything from you, Richard," she said, her voice dripping with disdain. "I asked for nothing more than you were willing to give, and I always gave you everything you wanted. Whenever you wanted, I gave, gave, and gave. But I was happy in the knowledge that I was your soulmate—the only person you'd ever love. But I must have been mistaken. After all, you weren't so loyal, were you? What sort of man could do what you've done to me? You gave up on me, Richard. Left me to the void, and I'll never forgive you. I hate you; I hate you..."

"Arrgh!" I shot upright in bed, drenched in sweat. But Rachel remained undisturbed, blissfully unaware of the turmoil raging within me. Had I shouted in my dream? I wasn't sure.

But one thing was clear: Ramoon had lied about Helen. And now, no matter how dangerous it might be or what consequences awaited me, I knew I had to contact the protestors. Tomorrow, I would try.

My search for the truth about Helen……..was back on.

Chapter 27 - Contact

Despite all our efforts, the situation looked no better when we reconvened the following day. I felt a gnawing frustration in my gut as I realised, we had uncovered absolutely zilch about the protesters. The silence surrounding them only reinforced my suspicions of a cover-up, a dark cloud looming over our investigation.

"I can't find any pattern in their appearances," Jennifer confessed, her brow furrowed with worry. "There's no way to predict when they'll show again. Their activities seem to be totally random." Her voice trembled slightly, betraying the anxiety that had settled in our small group.

"I've got nothing either," Simon admitted, his shoulders slumping in defeat. "I keep hitting a brick wall. The information system seems to be preventing anything about them from being revealed. It looks like they've employed an information blackout to stifle any support." His words hung in the air, heavy with the weight of our collective helplessness.

Jennifer nodded, her expression grave. "We should have expected it. They've learned from our past how powerful the control of information is in fighting your enemies. Remember how our governments won the war on terrorism by reigning in the excesses of the media, essentially cutting off the terrorists' access to the wider community? Terrorism only exists if people know about it. It was the most powerful weapon they had." Her voice was laced with a mix of admiration and bitterness, as if she were mourning a lost era.

Earl shrugged, bitterness dripping from his tone. "Yeah, I remember how controversial that was. What a price to pay." His eyes flickered with resentment, a reminder of the personal stakes involved.

Jennifer shot him a reproachful look, her frustration boiling over. "We were at war, Earl! How many 9/11s were prevented because of that sacrifice?" Her voice rose, echoing the tension that crackled between us.

"I was just saying…" he began, but she cut him off.

'We were at war," she repeated bluntly, her tone final, leaving no room for argument.

"You're being a little unfair, Jennifer," I interjected, trying to diffuse the tension. "It's not Earl's fault that society let the media get so out of control. It was the way of the world back then." I felt the weight of their gaze, the unspoken emotions swirling around us like a storm.

"Okay, okay," she sighed, her shoulders slumping in resignation. "We're all under stress; I apologise, Earl. I guess I am letting this all get to me." Her voice softened, revealing the vulnerability beneath her fierce exterior.

I glanced between Jennifer and Earl, feeling the palpable tension that had replaced the usual camaraderie among us. It was the first time I'd seen anything but affection between my friends, and it unsettled me. "Well, it was an emotive issue back then," I interrupted, trying to steer us back to the matter at hand. "And it obviously still is. But this isn't getting us anywhere. We need to think of a way to contact the protesters."

"I think we may have no choice but to bring Ankit and Rachel into this," Earl suggested, his voice steady but tinged with concern. "They may know something more or even have access to information that we don't."

"No!" I almost shouted, the urgency of my response making Earl recoil instinctively. Realising how harsh I sounded, I took a breath to steady myself. "Sorry, I didn't mean to be sharp, but I don't want to do that unless it's essential. I couldn't live with myself if I put either of them in danger." The thought of involving either of them sent a chill down my spine.

"Okay," Earl conceded, his expression softening. "I agree we should keep them out of this if possible. But we may have to consider it in the future. I think we should review our position at the end of the week. If we haven't made any progress, we bring them in?" The group turned to me; their eyes filled with expectation.

I felt a knot tighten in my stomach, unconvinced but unable to see any other way forward. "All right," I sighed, reluctantly agreeing. I'd just have to hope that something would come up before we had to risk putting Ankit and Rachel in harm's way.

As I walked home later that afternoon, the enormity of our task weighed heavily on my shoulders. The cities sprawled before me, vast and labyrinthine, allowing anyone who wished to become lost and wander for days without encountering another soul. The protesters could be anywhere —inside those concrete jungles, outside them, or even on one of the countless worlds orbiting the Sun. I shook my head, the thought striking me like a bolt of lightning. *Who's to say they weren't hiding on a moon or one of the asteroids?* The possibilities were dizzying.

Approaching my home, I couldn't shake the feeling that involving Ankit and Rachel might become necessary. If it came to that, I'd speak to Ankit first. Perhaps I could raise the subject in casual conversation, gleaning something from him without revealing everything. Yes, I'd do that. Why wait? If only I knew where my friend was.

He still hadn't returned from his travels around India, and the last update I'd received was a week ago when he was in Delhi. He could be anywhere now, lost in the vastness of such a large country.

Then it hit me—I wasn't using my new abilities. I could close my eyes and think of Ankit, just like I had in the library. Just like when I received that message from… I stopped short, as if I'd walked into a brick wall. "Idiot, idiot, idiot!" I shouted aloud, slapping my forehead with the palm of my hand. Of course! *Why hadn't I thought of it before?*

When I got home, I was relieved to find that Rachel and Jane were still out. I didn't know how I would have explained my frantic rush or my dash to the bedroom, followed by an enthusiastic dive onto the bed. I was convinced this would work, and I didn't want to waste any time.

I closed my eyes, focusing intently. Now, what did they say you have to do? Just think and imagine his face. I tried to conjure the image of the man I'd seen at the protest, the one who had lingered in my mind since that day. *What was his name? Yes, Jon. Jon Numan.*

"*Jon, where are you?*" I thought, trying to make the image clearer in my head, projecting my thoughts like a beacon. "*I need to speak to you.*"

Come on, senses, kick in for God's sake! I need to find this man. But nothing happened. I tried for almost an hour, concentrating until my head ached, before reluctantly deciding it wasn't going to work. I sat up, frustration bubbling within me. What was I doing wrong? The image had come to me while I was concentrating on Ankit, so it should have come even easier by focusing on Jon himself. Then it dawned on me—I was an even bigger idiot than I thought. It must have something to do with trying to contact Ankit.

I lay back down, determined to try again. This time, I did the same as I had in the library. In my mind, I called out to Ankit, asking where he was. I closed my eyes tighter, hoping that this would somehow amplify my new ability.

Suddenly, an alarming dizziness threatened to consume me, and I started to open my eyes in panic. Just a moment too late, because everything went black. One second, I was conscious, and the next, I was gone.

When I woke, it felt like the last stages of my revival in the white room. I felt surprisingly groggy, and when the mist cleared, the man standing before me was Jon Numan!

"Richard?" he asked, his voice a mix of surprise and relief.

I nodded, but my head fell forward, heavy and disoriented. I had to jerk it back, trying to shake off the fog that clouded my mind. Looking around, I realised I wasn't in my bedroom anymore. "Where am I?" I croaked, my tongue feeling swollen, the tightness in my throat altering my tone.

"Don't worry about the disorientation; it'll soon pass," Jon said, his voice steady. "We weren't sure if you were familiar with jumping. So, we fixed the template of this spare body to one belonging to a member of our group who's jumped to another planet."

I stared at him, my mind racing as if he were speaking a completely different language.

"What?"

"So, my guess was right then. You've never jumped before?" His eyes searched mine, looking for understanding.

The vacant look on my face must have been all the answer he needed. "Body jumping is a form of travel. It's mainly used to move between planets, as it doesn't require your physical body to move. It's possible to transmit the contents of your brain pod to a spare blank template, which reforms to your own image as soon as you've taken possession of it—essentially becoming you. And the body you've left behind gradually reverts to a blank template."

I looked down at my hands. They were darker and far larger than mine. "Why hasn't this body taken on my shape then?"

"As I just mentioned, we fixed it because we weren't sure if you'd ever jumped before. If you're not aware that you have to consciously will the new body to take on your own form, you could become trapped in a featureless shell."

"So will the body I've just left behind now be a faceless dummy?" I wondered, picturing Rachel and Jane's reactions upon finding a human-sized amorphous blob on our bed.

"Normally it would, but we've fixed that too." He frowned, his expression serious. "Yet another law we're breaking because it's not normally possible to fix a template on a body once the core conscience has left it. Our techs had to find a way to do it so we can carry out what we've got planned."

Once again, I was amazed—there was just no way to predict anything with any degree of certainty anymore. In fact, in this world, it seemed like surprise was the only certainty. I was learning something new every day, and it just kept getting more bizarre.

I swung my legs off the cot and took the hand that was stretched out to me. "We've been trying to contact you, Richard. But because we didn't have your body signature, we've not been able to get an accurate fix on you. So, we monitored Ankit for anyone attempting to contact him who wasn't on our records. And we knew when you started to practice using your senses that you'd try to locate him."

"How could you possibly know that?" I asked, my heart racing.

"Didn't someone suggest it at the library?" he replied, a knowing glint in his eyes.

Remembering what the librarian had suggested to Jennifer when I first got my senses turned on, I said, "You mean the librarian is a protestor?"

"No, but she is a sympathiser. We have quite a few of them in the Manooran ranks. Anyway, we know Ankit's body signature, so when you tried to link up with him, we were waiting to pick yours up. It wasn't ideal, so that's why the message was cut short, but at least we were able to communicate and get something across. Unfortunately, though, we couldn't completely establish your signature, and we've had to wait for you to try to contact him again. I knew it was just a matter of time before we could transport you here."

"And where exactly is here?" I looked around at the empty grey walls. It was hot, and a boiler room sprang to mind. A circular table and four chairs sat in one corner. Apart from those and the cot I was sitting on, the room was bare.

"This is part of our headquarters," Jon said, his tone matter of fact. "It's near the power core for the main water processing plant next to the cavern where the Manoorans first found us."

"You mean on the Moon!" I exclaimed, the realisation hitting me like a freight train.

"You know what they say about the best place to hide, Richard. It's in the place those looking for you are least likely to suspect."

Well, being close to the plant's power core explained the constant low thrumming sound in the background, I thought. *But what about the heat? It was sweltering*. Another reason a boiler room had come to mind.

"Can't you regulate this heat?" I asked, "Or is it this body I'm in?"

"I'm afraid not; we've had to learn to live with the temperature down here and our bodies self-regulate anyway. You've obviously not had to do this yet. If we did tamper with the heat, we risk being discovered by the authorities."

"So, if you can just transport people out of their bodies at will, why didn't you bring me here sooner?"

"No, we can't. That's not possible. The person we want to transport must want to make the jump or at least be receptive to it. That happened as soon as you actively started looking for us."

Then he looked at me, like a doctor about to deliver a bad diagnosis. Knowing what his next words would elicit, he said, "We knew you'd eventually try to make contact with us, Richard."

"How?" I asked, my chest pounding.

Then looking me directly in the eyes he said quite clearly.

"Because Helen told us you would."

Silence.

Chapter 28 – The Plan

Despite my efforts to maintain composure, I felt the rush of whatever passed for blood in this artificial body surge to my head, a hot tide of confusion and dread. If it weren't for the advanced support system keeping me upright, I was certain my heart would have faltered at the weight of Jon's words. But then again, I often questioned whether I even had a heart anymore.

I leaped off the table, my new limbs feeling foreign and unwieldy, and nearly stumbled, the unfamiliarity of this body disorienting. "What!!" I nearly screamed, my voice a gruff echo of its former self, a sound that felt alien in my throat. "What do you mean Helen, Helen who?" I demanded, fully aware of the answer that awaited me, yet desperate to deny it.

"Your Helen, Richard," Jon replied, emphasising the word "your" as if it were a lifeline thrown into turbulent waters, a tether to the past I so desperately clung to.

"Where is she?" I blurted out, my voice rising with a raw urgency that surprised even me. The artificial body I inhabited seemed to possess a remarkable control system, allowing me to channel my escalating agitation without collapsing under its weight. I gripped Jon's arm, desperation clawing at my throat like a wild animal. "I said, where is she?"

"Whoa, calm down, Richard, please. Let me explain what's happened. Are you okay, or do you need some time to settle?"

My hands tightened around Jon's arm, as if letting go would sever the fragile connection I felt to Helen, as if he were the last thread binding me to her. "Please, just tell me where she is."

"I wish I could, Richard, but the truth is we don't know. She was captured, and we have no idea if they're holding her somewhere," he paused, his voice dropping to a sombre whisper, "or if they've killed her."

Helen's wedding ring flashed in my mind, a haunting reminder of our bond, a symbol of love that transcended time. "Could she have been reborn?" I asked, the words tasting bitter on my tongue.

"Forcibly, yes. That's the fate of most criminals. But I'm hoping they think she's more valuable to them alive while we're still at large," Jon replied, his eyes reflecting a mixture of hope and despair.

Jon raised his hands, a gesture meant to calm me, but it felt like a futile attempt to soothe a raging storm. "Hold on, Richard. Before you say anything else, I need to show you something." Reluctantly, I unclenched my bulky hands and let him go. He moved to the far wall, speaking softly to it, words too quiet for me to overhear, as if he were invoking some ancient magic.

I watched him return, my chest pounding as the wall began to glow with an ethereal light. The image that materialised was a portal to the past, pulling me back over a thousand years. I was staring into the eyes of the woman I'd last touched a millennium ago, her gaze piercing through the veil of time.

The 3D image of a youthful Helen hovered against the wall, her features just as I remembered them from our twenties. Those classic traits that transformed her plain face into something stunningly beautiful, her poise radiating the confidence of the woman I'd married so long ago. The sound of her voice, even in this digital form, reached out to me like a siren's call from the depths of time, echoing in the chambers of my very soul.

"Richard," she began, her voice soft yet filled with an urgency that transcended the years. She paused to draw a breath, as if gathering strength for the words that would follow. "If you're looking at this message, then I am either dead or missing. But I don't care about that because it means you're alive, and that's all that matters to me. If I am missing and there's a chance of finding me, then Jon will help you; just as I hope you'll help him. Listen to him, Richard. We're all at risk, and we need to find the truth and expose it. It's the only way we'll ever be safe and hopefully be together again."

She swallowed hard, reaching out with her hand as if to touch me through the veil of time, her fingers stretching toward me in a gesture of longing. "If you find that I am dead, Richard, then I want you to know that I still love you more than anything. And I was thinking of you when I closed my eyes for the last time."

As the image faded and the illumination from the wall dimmed to match the rest of the room, I realised I was gripping Jon's arm again, but this time for support, my knuckles white with tension. The simulated muscles in my forearms began to knot, and I let go, sinking back into my chair, the weight of my emotions pressing down on me like a heavy shroud. My feelings were a tempest, and this new body was merely a vessel for the storm. I blinked back tears, unsure if they were born of joy or sorrow. Helen's message filled me with elation, yet the spectre of her possible death loomed large, casting a shadow over my heart. Finding her wedding ring in Jane's possession wasn't definitive proof that she was Helen. But if she was, what about Rachel? Who did I truly love? Should I even be thinking these thoughts? Oh God, how cruel was fate going to be?

I needed to focus on something other than the chaotic party of confusion and turmoil raging in my mind. Nodding at Jon, I croaked out what Ramoon had told me about Helen's revival, omitting my suspicions about Jane and guiltily explaining my marriage to Rachel, the guilt gnawing at me like a persistent itch.

Jon regarded me with sympathy, his expression a mirror of understanding, a silent acknowledgment of the turmoil swirling within me. I couldn't imagine any other reaction he could muster in the face of my predicament. He didn't mention Rachel, but simply said, "Ramoon has obviously been trying to throw you off the scent. Given your current situation, I'd say he thinks he's done a pretty good job."

"You'd better tell me everything, Jon. I've got a million and two questions," I insisted, my voice steadying as determination began to replace my fear.

He walked to the wall behind us and requested drinks from the panel before sitting back down beside me, the tension in the air palpable. "The story of the protesters is complicated," he began, his voice steady, yet laced with urgency. "When the Manoorans first discovered the store of preserved humans on the far side of the Moon, most of them were thrilled and wanted to integrate us fully into their diverse societies. Their long-term goal is to reach a point where everyone identifies as human. For some reason, they seem to despise their origins and what they once were, as if the very thought of their past is a stain on their identity.

"But there's a minority among them, some of whom have gained significant influence, who don't want us Cryogens walking around, reminding them that they're not true humans. They fear 'contamination' and worry that we might resurrect the old, hateful ideologies that led to our downfall. I suppose they're terrified we'll bring about the same fate for them that we inflicted upon ourselves, a cycle of destruction that seems destined to repeat."

I nodded, fully aware of humanity's failings. If the human race hadn't changed dramatically since my time, then the Manoorans had every reason to be concerned, their fears rooted in a history that echoed through the ages.

"When they first began reviving us," Jon continued, "most attempts were successful. Almost all survivors retained their memories. But that's changed, and it's difficult for us to prove why. The people working on the project are only trained to perform individual tasks, so none of them have access to all the records and research. Only a select few high-ranking officials have that level of information, and they guard it jealously, as if it were a treasure worth killing for.

"It all started when Ramoon and his faction began a concerted effort to take over the project, which they've now accomplished. As soon as they gained full control, suddenly most Cryogens were deemed unviable and consigned to rebirth. They claim it's because they're trying to revive individuals preserved using outdated techniques, but we suspect otherwise.

When Ramoon joined, he assigned new personnel—his own people—to the final stages of the process. The existing staff were shuffled away from that area, their expertise rendered useless. It was all done with alarming haste, and while he isn't openly anti-Cryogen, the whispers we've heard suggest he's orchestrating a systematic attempt to eliminate us, a silent genocide cloaked in the guise of progress."

None of this surprised me. "My friends and I have gathered evidence that supports that, Jon," I said, recounting the information I'd unearthed in Ramoon's office.

He listened intently, excitement flickering in his eyes, a spark of hope igniting in the darkness. "That will certainly bolster the evidence we've already compiled against him and his group. I can't wait to see it."

"I'll send it to you as soon as I can," I promised, determination hardening my resolve.

Jon took a sip of his drink, his gaze steady, as if he were weighing the gravity of our situation. "But it doesn't end with what he's doing at the Cryogen centre. Even those who have been reborn and settled are starting to go missing. We've been tracking them for the last decade, and slowly but surely, they've been meeting with mysterious accidents. Remember, it's nearly impossible to destroy one of these bodies completely, a fact that only adds to the horror of what's unfolding.

Most citizens aren't aware of the connections between these deaths because they're not conscious or concerned about any individual's racial background. But one by one, they're exterminating us—first the un-revived, then the reborn, and eventually, it'll be us. We're the only hope for saving what's left of humanity. We must expose Ramoon's plan and remove him and his people from the Cryogen project, or we risk losing everything."

"So where does Helen fit into all this?" I asked, my heart racing, the stakes rising with each revelation.

"She was successfully revived about twenty-five years ago and immediately began searching for you. She joined the Cryogen project for the same reasons you have, driven by love and desperation. But when Ramoon arrived, she grew suspicious and started asking questions about the new team members he'd brought in. Naturally, Ramoon didn't appreciate that and began making her life difficult.

"That's when she reached out to us. We'd just begun forming our group, and she feared becoming one of Ramoon's victims. She believed joining us was the best way to give you a chance at revival. Then, fifteen years ago, she was captured and taken away. We have no idea if she's being held captive, treated like a criminal and forcibly reborn," he paused, his voice heavy with dread, "or even destroyed."

I no longer believed the last option was possible, not after finding her wedding ring. I didn't show the emotion I thought Jon expected. Instead, I simply asked, "So how come my revival was successful if Ramoon has been interfering with the process?"

"We have a sympathiser working on the project, Richard, but she must be extremely careful. It's only at the moment they open the pods that there's any indication of the identity of the person inside. We instructed our contact to look out for the items Helen said you would be taking with you, particularly your distinctive wedding ring."

I glanced down at the new wedding ring that had replaced my original, guilt washing over me like a cold wave.

"Did your contact slip a warning message in with my belongings?"

"That's right. We thought it wise to make you wary of those around you. When she eventually came across your pod, she was able to interfere with the process and ensure you were revived. It was when you began sharing information about yourself and asking questions about Helen that Ramoon grew suspicious. Now we suspect he'll do everything in his power to get to you because of your connection to Helen and hers to us."

"That explains my feelings about him," I said, realising I would have to show more emotion if I wanted to keep my knowledge about Jane hidden. "But you're convinced Helen could still be alive?"

"I hope so, Richard. Even if they've put her through the rebirth process, there's a chance enough of her essence remains for her to be reintegrated. It's only if that hasn't happened, or if they've completely destroyed her, that she'll be lost to us forever."

"Will you help me find out what's happened to her, Jon?"

"Of course, Richard. It's one of my highest priorities. She's a good friend and one of the most valuable assets of this group. Our leadership isn't half as strong without her."

I smiled, recognising the description of the woman I loved. Or was that one of the women I loved? The complexity of my feelings twisted in my chest, a knot of longing and confusion.

"The problem we face is that the information we need to uncover what happened to her, and the information we need to expose this entire operation, is stored in the same place: the main information hub. Only the highest-ranking officials have access to it through their terminals. So, what do you say, Richard? Will you help us save humanity and find Helen along the way?"

"If Helen told you anything about me, Jon, you already know the answer to that."

"Yes, I do," he said, extending his hand to me, a gesture of solidarity and trust. As I shook it, he added, "Welcome aboard."

The protesters' plan was audacious: to fix the template of one of the Manooran high officials after they'd jumped out of their primary body, using it to gain entry to their terminal and access the main information hub. This would allow them to retrieve the data that would expose

Ramoon's involvement in the attempted extermination of the Cryogens and, hopefully, provide answers about Helen's fate.

"However," Jon said, his expression turning serious, "to accomplish this, we need access to the schedules that will tell us when these high officials are planning to jump to different locations."

"And how will you obtain those?" I asked, curiosity piqued.

Jon gave me a knowing look, a glimmer of hope shining in his eyes. "That's where you can help us, Richard."

"Oh?"

"The schedules are stored in the system and are only accessible to Manooran officials of a certain rank. We don't have any contacts among Manoorans of that rank. But you do."

"Ankit?" I offered, a smile creeping onto my face at the thought of my old friend. I'd never been invited to Ankit's apartment before, and considering how private and secretive my friend was, I knew it wouldn't be as simple as Jon had suggested.

Just before jumping back to my own body, I envisioned Helen's face, a beacon of hope amidst the chaos. I smiled at the thought and recalled a misquote from our favourite comedy duo from the early twentieth century. We had exchanged those words countless times, and they echoed in my mind once more, a reminder of the bond we shared.

"*Well, here's another fine mess you've gotten me into.*"

Chapter 29 - Deception

I wondered if anyone in the entire history of humanity had ever faced the gut-wrenching task of telling their current partner that their first love—the one they believed was lost to the void of time—might still be alive. And if they had, I was certain they had never compounded that devastation by revealing that the child they had created together could be that very first partner. It was absurd, a cruel twist of fate that left me paralyzed with dread. How could I possibly break this news to Rachel? So, I took the coward's way out and didn't.

Instead, during the agonising weeks I waited for Ankit to return from the surface, I gradually introduced my other friends to Jon. I had no choice; once I shared my encounter with him, their eagerness to join the cause was palpable. They were all buzzing with excitement, relieved that at last, something was happening after the frustrating delay in acting on the evidence we'd uncovered.

But their disappointment was a heavy weight in the air when Jon only asked them to support me in my attempt to extract information from Ankit's terminal. I could see Earl's face fall; he'd been expecting something more significant, something that would put him at the forefront of our mission.

"But it's good to have you with us," Jon assured them, his voice steady and reassuring. "I know you'll be valuable assets to the group. I just don't want to expose you to any risks unless it's absolutely necessary."

Earl turned to me; his brow furrowed with determination. "In that case, we'd better start formulating a plan for when Ankit finally shows up."

Yet even that conversation couldn't distract me from the storm of unfathomable questions swirling in my mind. Was Helen truly buried deep within Jane's psyche? If so, what was Ramoon's role in all of this? Why would he want me to adopt her? Was it all just a sick joke fuelled by his hatred for the successfully revived Cryogens? And why did he seem intent on our destruction? I had no idea where this tangled web was leading, but I felt certain it would culminate in a heart-wrenching choice between the two women I loved. The thought of that decision haunted me, a shadow lurking in the corners of my mind, whispering that I already knew what my choice would be.

Regardless of how my personal life would eventually unfold, my resolve to stand with the protesters was unwavering. I would do whatever Jon asked of me while maintaining a respectable front to everyone else in Open Society. I would act undercover, just like the librarian, blending in while plotting our next move.

Ankit's return was characteristically understated. One morning, he simply appeared at our apartment, as if the weeks of absence had been nothing more than a fleeting dream. Rachel was at work, and Jane was engrossed in the education booth, learning about the chemical reactions that birthed life from the primordial soup of Earth's pre-genesis. Ankit stood there, a familiar smile gracing his face, as if nothing had changed.

"I've come to see how married life is treating you, Richard." His tone was upbeat, a stark contrast to the turmoil swirling within me. "It's not too early to call on you, is it?"

"No, no, Ankit, come in and make yourself comfortable. It's great to see you back. I've missed you. In fact, we all have."

"Thank you, I've missed you all too." His smile was genuine, and for a moment, I felt a flicker of normalcy return.

We settled in the dining room over coffee, and I ordered breakfast. The aroma of freshly brewed coffee mingled with the scent of warm pastries, that appeared from the table filling the air as we basked in the virtual sun rising beyond the walls.

So, I thought to myself, all I had to do now was get myself invited to his apartment—a place I'd never been, and where, given my friend's recent domestic upheaval, I doubted he would want anyone to visit.

The holiday seemed to have worked wonders for him; he appeared more relaxed and confident. Although I didn't broach the subject of visiting his home immediately, by the time he left that first visit, I was convinced I would eventually succeed. I managed to persuade him to join us several more times over the following days, under the pretence of wanting to hear all about his travels through India. Each story he shared was more fascinating than the last, drawing me in deeper.

During these visits, I seized every opportunity to drop blatant hints, hoping to secure a return invitation. I caught strange looks from Rachel and Jane, but I pressed on. Eventually, the casual invitation came, almost as if it were an afterthought. "You'll have to come over to mine some time."

I could barely contain my excitement. "Yeah, that'd be great! We'll do it this weekend then. We can watch some of the inter-planet Olympics. You'd like that, wouldn't you, Jane?"

"Definitely!" she chimed in, turning to Ankit with wide eyes. "That'll be okay, won't it, Uncle Ankit?"

Unable to retract his invitation, especially with Jane's eager eyes upon him, he had no choice but to agree. "Yes, I'd love you all to come over."

Getting invited had proven to be the easy part. Now, I had to concoct a convincing excuse to gain access to Ankit's information terminal. Even my other friends were struggling with that one.

But the first part of my plan had succeeded, and I would have felt triumphant had it not been for the gnawing discomfort of deception. I didn't like keeping Ankit in the dark, but I had to weigh the potential gains against the risk of his reaction if he discovered what we were up to. It was either this or tell him the truth. And while I believed he would support us, I didn't want to drag him into this mess if I could avoid it. Jon was adamant that he didn't want Ankit to know what was happening. No, I had to bite my tongue and stick to the plan.

Ankit's apartment was reminiscent of Earl's—flowery and feminine, a testament to Amira's influence. I wondered if he'd truly come to terms with her departure or if this was merely a reflection of his denial.

As we sat down to our meal, I cursed myself for not having thought up a convincing excuse to access Ankit's terminal. I'd have to spend the rest of the evening racking my brain for a plausible ploy.

After we finished eating, we settled in the main room, watching the 'Stone Tossing' competitors. They hurled their round stones toward a circular hole in the green, an ancient Muslim sport that had gained immense popularity throughout the solar system. Though none of us understood the complex nuances of this modern version of the game, it was easy to tell when someone succeeded. Get the ball in the net, get the stone in the hole - simple.

Jane sat on the floor in front of Ankit, Rachel, and me, munching on a bowl of crisps, utterly engrossed in the action unfolding before us. As clips of various sports flashed across the screen, she turned to Ankit and asked, "Are there any sports where it's admissible to body jump, Uncle Ankit? There are a few I wouldn't mind experiencing without practicing myself."

"Not allowed, Jane," he replied, his tone serious. "There was some abuse of it in the past, apparently. People were giving the owner of the body advice and all that."

I looked from Jane to Ankit, confusion clouding my mind. "What are you talking about?" I'd only heard the term "jumping" used to describe travel. "I don't understand what you mean. The only thing I know about jumping is that it's a form of traveling. And that you can't forcibly take someone out of their body."

"You've obviously been doing some homework," Ankit said, just as I realised it was Jon who had given me that nugget of information.

"Oh... yes," I said defensively, trying to explain away my knowledge. "Someone mentioned it in conversation. I haven't asked the system about the subject yet." I offered that just in case they had ways of checking. After all, Jon had told me to be ultra-careful about what I said.

"Well, like all developments," Ankit continued, "some people will find ways to abuse it."

"Do you mean that you can be forcibly taken out of your body then?" I pressed.

"Not that I am aware of, but as Jane has just alluded to, travel isn't the only use for that technology. After being developed, we found that it was possible to 'jump' into another occupied body, if it was receptive to it. It effectively created two consciences in the same body, both able to communicate with each other and share the experiences and feelings of the host body."

Exhibitionists and voyeurs had found it entertaining over the years, as many people left themselves open to being *jumped* by anyone at any time.

"Oh wow, that must be really weird. But doesn't the body become confused having more than one person telling it what to do?" I asked, my curiosity piqued.

"No, only the core conscience has control of the body. The 'passenger' can only communicate with the host and experience all the feelings from the body."

"But surely that's not considered abuse of the technology, Ankit. It's just harmless recreational fun, especially if the two people involved are consenting adults."

"It was the abuse of that particular way of using the technology I was referring to, Richard. The worst case was that of Harold Schmitt, a tour guide in South America."

"Why, what did he do?" Rachel asked, becoming more interested.

Ankit glanced at Jane, who seemed as curious as we were. "Jane, I'm sorry about this, but I'm going to go into intimate mode while I talk to your mum and dad about something a bit sensitive."

"Oh, okay," she said slowly, disappointment flickering across her face. But she pointed to the vid-screen, murmuring, "I'll carry on watching till you're finished."

"He was a serial rapist," Ankit said, his voice low and grave. "And he was able to carry on with his despicable activities because of the help from some extremely important people in the community where he lived."

Intrigued, I leaned forward. "Was he blackmailing them then?"

"Not exactly, but he did have information they all wanted to keep secret about the way he satisfied their vile fantasies."

"Oh," I said, the realisation dawning on me. "You mean he—"

"Yes, he was letting them jump into him when he was stalking and violating his victims. The technology doesn't just allow one person to jump into a body. When they finally caught Schmitt, the system trapped fifty-eight other consciences inside him."

"Oh my God, that's awful," Rachel gasped. "Those poor women. Being raped by one man must be life-destroying. What must they have gone through when they found out every single disgusting second of it was being enjoyed by a whole group of sick, depraved men?"

"It wasn't just women who got raped, Rachel," Ankit corrected her. "And the jumpers weren't just men either. Sick minds like that don't conform to any norms we might recognise."

I wanted to wipe the horrific images Ankit had just painted from my mind forever. The idea of sharing experiences with those close to you was fascinating, but it never ceased to amaze me how some people could twist new developments into something grotesque.

The conversation had completely distracted me from the game playing out on the vid screen. Just as Ankit ordered another drink, I asked if I could access my journal through his information terminal. "I want to record my thoughts about what you've just told us before I forget. Is it all right if I use your study? I can leave you in peace to watch the games?"

"Of course," he replied.

It had worked, and I hadn't even had to think of the excuse myself.

But any feeling of achievement was quickly overshadowed by a wave of guilt that washed over me as I entered his study. I managed to access the terminal by following the instructions Jon had given me. I tried to retrieve the schedules of the high officials, but just as I began to think this uncomfortable experience would soon be over, a message flashed on the screen: *"You are not authorised to access this information."*

Drat! I thought to myself, what do I do now? Jon had assured me the information would be available. I tried several more times, but the same results greeted me each time. Reluctantly, I decided to abandon the attempt.

I left Ankit's that night feeling like I'd failed and somehow, indirectly, let Helen down.

"Don't be downhearted," Jon told me when we spoke the following day. "If you'd been with us for the last few years, Richard, you'd be used to disappointment by now. It makes you realise that you just have to get up and carry on." Then, as an afterthought, he added, "Helen taught me that, actually."

"I'll tell you one thing, though. It means that Ramoon must be even more suspicious than I originally thought. He must have removed rights to that information from all Cryogens, regardless of where they tried to access it. In which case, we need to get a Manooran to access the information instead. The problem is that none of our sympathisers have the right access level through their home terminals or know anyone who has."

"Then I'll have to risk telling Rachel," I offered, my chest rising at the thought.

"Are you sure, Richard? I wouldn't ask you to place her in any danger if you felt uncomfortable with the idea."

"I know her well enough to be sure she'll help us, Jon. If it's the only way to get the information, then I'll speak to her about it."

And then I thought to myself; *it's going to be easy, compared to telling her that Helen may still be alive.*

When I returned home, it took me a while to gather the courage to speak to Rachel. It wasn't until Jane had gone to bed that I finally approached her in the main room.

Standing directly in front of her, my face inches from hers, I said, "I have something to tell you and something to ask you, and I hope I am right in guessing your reaction."

She looked at me quizzically. "This sounds serious. Go on."

"You know I love you, don't you?"

"Yes, but what's this about, Richard? You're scaring me."

I held her then, squeezing her tightly to me. Laying my forehead on her neck, I whispered, "I am in such a mess, Rachel. I don't know what to do. Helen—"

"I know," she interrupted, her voice soothing. "There are bound to be days like this. I understand, and I'm sure Helen would. It's going to take some time."

As I felt the warmth of her body against mine, I knew I just couldn't tell her. How could I? If Helen wasn't alive and none of this was true, then Rachel would have gone through all of this for nothing. Why should I hurt her for no reason? I needed to know for sure before I ruined her life. No, I just couldn't bring myself to say anything about Helen.

So, wiping my eyes, I explained about Ramoon, about the protesters, and the information we'd discovered at Ramoon's office. I told her it was all getting to me, making me feel confused and upset. After I finished, I sat there looking at her expectantly, considering how close I'd come to possibly destroying our love.

It took a moment for her to process everything, but then she said, "To be honest, Richard, I've never liked Ramoon. He's always treated me in an offhand sort of way. If your intuition was that I'd help, then you were right. I just wish you'd come to me earlier." Her words made me feel even worse about what I was concealing from her.

We knew it wouldn't be easy this time. We had to find a legitimate reason to get Rachel access to Ankit's terminal, as it was unlikely a situation would arise that would provide me with another chance.

When we ran the idea that we'd come up with past Simon, Jennifer, and Earl, they all thought it was a great plan.

Simon's reaction was reflected in the huge grin that spread across his face. "I thought those things had gone out of fashion, Richard, but I'd put money on Ankit being up for it. It'll be a novelty and a new experience for him, who knows, you might be starting a fad. As long as you're sure he'll be up for us all coming along too?"

"Leave it to me," I assured him.

Maybe it was because we had already taken that first step into his inner sanctum; I wasn't sure. But it was far easier to get an invite back when I suggested it again. Perhaps Ankit was finally starting to relax.

When I proposed having a small party for him to bond with my other friends, Ankit was almost enthusiastic. It was something people didn't seem to do anymore, but he agreed to get together as soon as they were all available. So, the party was on. Ankit seemed to be finally coming out of his shell and moving on.

Simon was the last to arrive, and after Ankit provided him with the beer he loved, the subject of parties came up. Rachel asked me, "What sort of things did you do at parties in your day?"

"Well, we used to listen to music and dance, of course, but we also played party games."

"Games!" Rachel feigned surprise.

"That's right. Not all games are for children you know."

Jane jumped in eagerly. "Yes, please! Can we play some?"

"What sort of games, Richard?" Jennifer prompted me.

"Well, we used to play one called *Spot the Leader*," I explained. "One person leaves the room and is the guesser. You put on some music and choose one person to lead the others in clapping or dancing. The leader has to change the rhythm and which body part to clap against regularly, and the others have to follow until a pattern is established. Then the guesser comes back into the room and guesses who the leader is. It's not as easy as it sounds."

"It sounds like fun to me! I'll go first then," Rachel said hastily, almost appearing nervous. "I'll pop into your study if that's all right, Ankit?"

"Certainly," he replied, smiling at her enthusiasm.

"Do you mind if I access my records through your terminal while I'm waiting for you to shout me back?"

"Of course not. Help yourself."

Rachel later told me that as soon as she entered Ankit's study, she crossed the room and nervously entered the details Jon had given her into the terminal, hoping it would be over quickly. She was awash with nervous energy. But as she selected the final option that should have brought up the information, she was met with the same message I'd encountered.

It seemed there was no access to the information for anyone below a certain rank, not just Cryogens. Just as I had, Rachel tried a few more times before eventually giving up.

When she returned to the living room, she went along with the game for appearance's sake and waited until Ankit took his turn to go into the study.

As soon as he was out of sight, Jane was once again tuned out of our conversation. Rachel explained that she hadn't been able to access the information.

"Oh well," Earl said, trying to sound optimistic. "At least we tried. Jon will just have to come up with another plan."

"Is this what you've all been trying to get at?" Ankit's demanding voice came from behind us, and he stood there waving an info-sheet.

We all exchanged furtive glances, guilt washing over us, and I suddenly felt overwhelmed with shame.

"Ankit, I am so sorry about this. Will you let me explain, or are you going to call the authorities?"

"I think you'd better explain. Jane, would you go into my study for a few minutes while we talk?"

When Jane left, looking utterly confused, I timidly revealed our suspicions about Ramoon and the evidence we had found in his office.

"You know as well as I do," Rachel said almost pleadingly, "that there is an anti-Cryogen element in our society, Ankit. Even my parents are a little like that."

"Very well, I admit that I've had my doubts about Ramoon for a while. There are many adjectives I could use to describe that man, but harmless isn't one of them. If he's up to anything, then it should be brought to light. And because I consider all of you to be my friends, I am willing to help you." He held out the info-sheet to us. "You can give this information to your contacts and tell them I am available if there's anything they want me to do."

Jennifer was ecstatic. "Really, Ankit? Oh, thank you!" She clapped her hands excitedly.

"Thank you, Ankit," Rachel said, kissing him on the cheek.

After we left his apartment, I reflected on how fortunate I was to have the support of these wonderful people, who I was beginning to love.

But unbeknownst to me, standing in the centre of the main room of his apartment, Ankit was staring at the floor as if he bore the weight of the world on his shoulders. He had just finished talking to the vid screen on the wall, which displayed the image of Ramoon.

As Ramoon glared out of it, he said, "Well done, Ankit."

"Your wife will be pleased…"

Chapter 30 - Capture

I was a little disappointed, to say the least, at Jon's reaction when I told him the news about recruiting Ankit to the cause. I'd expected a spark of enthusiasm, a glimmer of hope, perhaps even a fist bump in celebration. Instead, Jon's face twisted into a mask of scepticism, his brow furrowing as if I'd just suggested we jump off a cliff.

"Are you sure about him, Richard? We can't afford to leave ourselves exposed now that we've come this far," he said, his voice laced with an edge of distrust that cut deeper than I anticipated.

"Yes, I promise you, Jon. I've never known anyone as honourable as Ankit. He'd lay down his life rather than betray the people he cares about," I insisted, my heart racing as I tried to convince him.

"And you haven't given him any information about us, or this facility?" Jon pressed, his eyes narrowing as if he were searching for cracks in my resolve.

"No, don't worry. You can relax. I knew you'd want me to play it close to my chest, so I told Ankit that any detailed information would have to come from you. And anyway, he only pledged his support; he never asked questions. Honestly, you don't have anything to worry about when it comes to Ankit."

"Alright," he said, his tone still half-hearted. "In that case, I suggest I meet with this friend of yours. After all, he'll be the highest-ranking Manooran we'll have working with us. And anyway, a meeting will give me the chance to assess his sincerity."

You're going to take some convincing, I thought, but I smiled in appreciation at Jon's cautious display of confidence in my decision to ask Ankit to help, even though I hadn't really had a choice. We could have just asked him to keep quiet, of course, but surely it was better to have him on our side.

"I'll let him know you want a meeting," I said, my voice steady despite the unease bubbling in my stomach.

As I made my way out of the facility, a wave of anxiety washed over me about reaching the jump point that the protesters used to move in and out of their headquarters. Jon had gone out of his way to assure me that jumping was safe and straightforward... yeah! It hadn't gotten any better for me since the first time I'd done it. I always felt sick, both at the anticipation of it and during the process. I wondered if I had the future equivalent of a fear of flying. At least that's what the experience felt like to me.

The Moon had developed considerably over the years. Where there was once a forgotten storage site, there was now a thriving city, pulsating with life and energy. The jump point was some way from the headquarters, nestled in a busy shopping area. It was hidden in a large storeroom in the basement of a shop run by a sympathiser. This place contained all the spare bodies they needed, a veritable treasure trove of potential. To avoid being followed, it was considered safer to jump in and out of this location and then take a different route to the headquarters on each visit. Of course, it was possible to jump directly into the headquarters, as I'd experienced myself. But the jump point provided additional security. And now that I'd become adept at jumping, I had no option but to adopt their security protocols.

When I finally met Ankit to share the news about Jon wanting to meet, I was taken aback by his underwhelmed reaction. I'd completely misjudged the responses I'd expected from both these men.

"I thought you were looking forward to helping us find the truth, Ankit?" I said, trying to draw him out of his distracted state. "Look, I don't want to put you at any risk. Should I tell Jon that you've changed your mind?"

That seemed to bring him back from wherever his mind had wandered. He blinked and said, "No, I am sorry, Richard. Thank you for setting this up. If Jon lets you have the details, you can pass them on to me, and I'll make myself available." He smiled, but it was a smile that didn't quite reach his eyes, a façade that hinted at something deeper lurking beneath the surface.

I sighed inwardly. *Ankit still hadn't gotten over Amira*, I thought. He was just not admitting it to himself.

Two days later, Ankit and I were walking down the familiar main corridor of the library, on our way to meet Jon. The faint humming of the air conditioning system, or whatever the equivalent was, gently chased the silence into the background. It also masked the thumping that sounded like it was coming from my heart, a relentless drumbeat of anxiety.

I'd never displayed any criminal tendencies in my previous life. Even the high jinks I was involved with as part of the gang at school were far from criminal. No, this was the first time I'd ever felt like this.

But laws are just rules created by people. There's nothing natural about them. So, is it wrong to break them if you think they're unjust?

It was yet another one of those dilemmas that were difficult to get your head around. That old saying that one man's terrorist is another's freedom fighter echoed in my mind. It must be down to the degree of action that people were prepared to take. Surely there must be a point beyond which most people would agree it was wrong to go. And that has to be part of human nature. I hoped so, anyway, for humanity's sake. Or what's left of it.

As we approached the end of the corridor, where Jon had arranged for a room to be available, I felt a knot tighten in my stomach. The librarian looked at us knowingly over the spectacles that were perched precariously on the end of her nose. Nodding towards the very end of the corridor, she almost whispered, "The last room on your right. You've got an hour."

As we approached the room, I once again thanked Ankit for his support. "I know what you're risking for us, Ankit, and we'll never be able to thank you enough."

He just nodded, but I made a mental note to try to get him to open up more about Amira. His depression seemed to have returned, and if anything, gotten worse. He now looked as tormented as I felt every time I thought of my situation. It couldn't be good for him bottling it all up like this.

When we entered the room, it was empty. Jon and the two men who were going to accompany him would arrive slightly later and use separate doors from adjoining rooms, avoiding the risk of using the public entrance.

As we waited for Jon to arrive, I contemplated telling Ankit about the ring I'd found among Jane's possessions. After all, he was becoming almost like a brother to me now, and it might give him something additional to think about and take his mind off Amira. However, as I was trying to formulate the right words, two doors opened on opposite sides of the room. A man appeared through each. Both were unfamiliar to me, and as I was about to ask them if they were Jon's colleagues, a third door began to materialise. It must be Jon.

Instead, the man who stepped through was yet another stranger. And as I was about to say, "Where's Jon?" a booming voice filled the room and vibrated the very walls.

It was only one word, but to me, it sounded like it came from the throat of hell itself.

"NOW!!" it echoed around us, a command that sent shivers down my spine.

The room trembled as if the very foundation of reality had shifted. The ground beneath me shook, and my legs buckled before giving way. Even the strength contained in these new bodies couldn't keep me upright under the force of this... whatever it was. *Was it an earthquake*?

Everything became chaotic around me. Five other entrances appeared in the walls, and upholders came storming through them, shouting loudly and pushing everyone to the floor. I'd only seen this sort of thing happen on TV before and never imagined it could be this frightening. I followed all the orders screamed at me, and I soon found myself lying face down on the floor, where I'd been thrown, with my hands bound behind my back. A vice-like grip on my neck pushed the right side of my face into the cushioned flooring.

Then the room stopped shaking, but something inside of me was simulating the effect of a sudden increase in adrenaline. The pounding in my chest was having an equal effect on my body – did I have a heart. I could also feel it in my head. I saw the three protesters held in the same position as me, but where was Ankit?

I managed to move my eyes to look up at the men who were still standing. And there, in front of me, unharmed by the upholders, was Ankit! My friend couldn't keep eye contact with me and looked away in shame as I realised what had happened.

I closed my eyes, hoping it would all go away. I would have bet my life on Ankit's loyalty just moments ago. The disappointment I now felt was almost enough to distract me from the enormity of what was happening. And I may very well have just bet my life!

As I struggled with my bindings and the hand that was clutching my neck, Ankit knelt beside me. The strained quality of his voice was almost pleading for forgiveness. "I am so sorry, Richard," he managed to choke out as if he were about to cry. "I had no choice. Ramoon's got Amira. She hasn't left me at all. He's holding her captive and blackmailing me into helping him with his plan. He won't let her go until he's caught all the protesters. Please forgive me."

In the short time I'd known this man, I'd come to appreciate all his qualities and virtues. I understood that only something like this could have led him to betrayal. I hadn't been wrong about him after all, I told myself. Ankit would probably lay down his life for those he cared about, but he would betray everyone to save the one he loved. I knew I'd have done the same for Helen, Rachel, or Jane. How could I have been so stupid?

"Take care, Ankit," I said, my voice filled with genuine warmth and sincerity. And looking over at the three men who'd entered the room, I wondered what Ramoon would say or do when he found out that he'd not captured Jon after all. "And be careful," I added, my heart heavy with the weight of our shared fate.

I wondered what the penalty was for colluding with the enemy. Was I facing being reborn? Or worse still, would Ramoon really try to destroy me completely? Whatever the official charges they would use, I knew I was in serious and deadly danger.

With our arms restrained, the four of us protesters—because that's what I'd now officially become—were marched through the door to captivity. We were unceremoniously bundled through the public entrance of the library and joined by a fifth. The bound figure of the librarian, being pushed forward, struggled against her restraints and demanded to know why they were taking her.

Ramoon had used Ankit well.

Chapter 31 - Imprisoned

I'd been drugged or perhaps turned off—whatever it was that could be done to these bodies to render them unconscious. When I finally woke up, I knew I hadn't just drifted into a normal sleep. The last thing I remembered was being herded, along with my fellow protesters, into a large container that had mysteriously appeared outside the library. Then, everything had gone black, as if someone had flipped a switch in my head, plunging me into darkness.

As I lifted myself onto my elbow from the cot, I found myself on, I scanned the surroundings, my heart racing. For a fleeting moment, I thought I was back in the sterile white room, that clinical prison of my past. But then it struck me—most institutional rooms probably looked like this, devoid of warmth and personality.

When my eyes finally adjusted to the harsh brightness, I realised this space was smaller than the white room, and there were no signs of a doorway or a vid-screen on the walls. Just to confirm that my eyes weren't playing tricks on me, I stood up and approached the opposite wall. "I'd like some coffee, please," I said, my voice echoing in the silence. No response came, nor did any panel appear to present me with a drink.

Defeated, I lay back down on the cot, closing my eyes in a desperate attempt to reach out to Jon. My advanced senses, once such a boon, were now muted. They had turned those off as well. *I should have expected that*, I thought bitterly.

So, this must be what prison is like in the thirty-third century—my senses, along with my freedom, stripped away. Blast! I felt utterly useless. I couldn't even communicate with the others who had been captured alongside me, to ask why Jon hadn't shown up.

How long would they keep me here? What legal rights, if any, did I possess? Was I entitled to the equivalent of a phone call? Whatever I expected—or didn't expect—I was overwhelmed by a gnawing sense of danger. If Ramoon was orchestrating the deaths of all Cryogens, what fate awaited me? A nasty accident, I was sure.

At least the room they had confined me in mimicked the daylight cycle of the surface, just like the white room had. Constant light would have been torture, and I was relieved when the lights finally dimmed, allowing me to sink into a more natural sleep.

When I woke, a pungent smell assaulted my nostrils. It was the unmistakable aroma of cooked food. The scent of scrambled eggs not only tickled my nose but also ignited a fire in my stomach, reminding me just how hungry I truly was. I rolled over and spotted a steaming bowl of food on the floor by the opposite wall. Next to it, propped up and facing me, was an info-tablet. To my right, I noticed a small room had appeared in the corner, which I assumed was a bathroom.

I walked over, my heart pounding with a mix of anticipation and dread, and retrieved the objects, bringing them back to my cot. I placed the tablet down, but my stomach growled louder than my thoughts, demanding my attention. I had to satisfy this primal need before confronting the more pressing matter of the info-tablet.

As I devoured the food, I couldn't help but reflect on the psyche's strange nature. I knew I didn't need to eat to survive; they couldn't starve me to death. Yet, the hunger was insistent, a reminder of my humanity, and I had to quell it before I could focus on the tablet.

Once I finished, I placed the spoon into the empty bowl and returned it against the wall. Sitting back on the cot, I touched the power button on the tablet. It expanded in my hands, and the familiar, now repellent face of Ramoon appeared on the screen.

"Hello, Richard. I hope you're enjoying your little rest. We won't be inconveniencing you for long, I can assure you. I just wanted to bring you up to speed with a few things."

I braced myself, my heart racing as he continued. "I expect you must be feeling rather smug knowing Jon is still safe and sound. But although I must admit to being disappointed that he's a lot less trusting than you, it's not been a complete disaster. I've been legitimately able to take you into custody, and we also have the other protesters to interrogate. Including that traitorous librarian."

His words dripped with malice, and I felt a surge of anger. "Your numbers are dwindling, and that's enough to satisfy me for now. And don't worry about Rachel and Jane. I've confined them to Maya's house, where I am confident, she will keep them under control. I am not sure if they're involved with your illegal activities yet, but I am sure I'll find out. Maya and Mazood have done nothing to hide their distaste for their daughter's choice of partner. So, I am certain they'll find out the truth and show her the error of her ways."

I sat upright when Ramoon mentioned Rachel and Jane. It sounded like he didn't know that anyone other than me was involved. Had Ankit managed to keep everyone else out of this? The less Ramoon knew, the better. I had to tread carefully, ensuring I didn't reveal what I knew about Jane.

"As for Ankit," Ramoon continued, "well, what can I say? He's far too soft; he really does care for you, Richard. I had no choice but to take the action I did to assure his loyalty."

He held one of his hands in front of him and clicked his fingers, as if reminding himself of something. "Oh yes," he said, "and by the way, I just thought I'd show you what we'll be doing to you in about a week's time."

The screen went blank for a second before a torturous image appeared. The librarian lay on her back, clad in a pitch-black bodysuit, tied spread-eagled to a low plinth in the centre of an empty room. My heart raced as I focused on the image of the woman, clearly in great distress. An ominous outlet on one wall roared to life, resembling the engine jet of a plane.

As the engine ignited, a massive plume of fire engulfed the screaming figure. It was over in mere seconds, but the horror of it seared into my mind. When the jet cut off, the image focused on the only thing left in the room—a gleaming object rolling around on the floor, slowly coming to a halt. Ramoon's voice returned, dripping with satisfaction.

"That's all that remains of the people we want to remove, Richard. By the time we've finished, this person will be reborn, running around in a new body. Unaware of any of her previous experiences or that she ever knew a Cryogen. And like the Manooran she is, she'll believe and act like a new model human; just like every Cryogen we do this to."

My stomach churned at the thought as he continued. "You should have been satisfied with your new life and forgotten the Cryogen project. Believe me; it would have been a lot safer for you. I'll see you soon, Richard…" And with that, the screen flicked off.

For a few seconds, the shape of Ramoon's face lingered in my mind, a haunting reminder of the man responsible for the chaos in my life. For reasons I couldn't fathom, he had made me give up on Helen, and he thought nothing of destroying anyone who crossed him. The rage boiling within me was palpable; I'd have gladly put him in the same place as the librarian given the chance.

The next day, I awoke to the enticing aroma of another delicious breakfast wafting through the air, but this time, no info-tablet accompanied it. Ramoon must have gained as much satisfaction as he wanted from that first message.

But when I picked up the bowl and turned around, I was surprised to see an info-tablet after all, propped up against the wall at the foot of my cot. My heart raced with hope as I retrieved it, ignoring the persistent messages of hunger that bombarded my senses. I turned it on, expecting another message from Ramoon, but instead, my spirits lifted when Jon's face suddenly appeared on the screen.

"Richard, I'm sorry I didn't trust you when your friend Ankit set up the meeting. But as it turned out, that was a good call on my part. One of our sympathisers has managed to get this message to you. We're working on a plan to get you out, but it's going to be difficult. I'll get word to you as soon as I can."

My heart raced at the prospect of hope. "We can't afford to communicate openly because of the security in the systems. But you can record a message on this tablet and leave it where you found it. Our contact will retrieve it during the night."

"Say nothing to Ramoon about Helen. The less he thinks you know, the better."

After I recorded my message, I lay down on my cot, praying that Jon could act quickly enough. I stared up at the stark white ceiling, its overpowering whiteness conjuring an image of Helen in my mind. I smiled up at her, feeling a mix of love and longing. I didn't know how this would all pan out, but I knew she had a lot of explaining to do.

"Goodnight, Helen," I whispered, closing my eyes. Her image lingered in my mind, and like a beacon it began guiding me back to our earlier life, to the choices that had led us both to this strange and perilous place.

Chapter 32 – A Love Affair Extraordinaire

Throughout the time leading up to our marriage, Helen continued to fascinate me with her quirky views on the world. Each day spent with her felt like unearthing a hidden treasure, revealing layers of her personality that both intrigued and delighted me. It wasn't long before I realised, I'd found the person I wanted to be with for the rest of my life. I convinced myself she felt the same way too. At least, I prayed she did, because my proposal was anything but conventional. I risked looking like an absolute fool if my assessment of her feelings was wrong.

I'd arranged, and paid for, a ride on the Big Wheel at Nottingham's annual 'Goose Fair.' As we ascended, the world below transformed into a kaleidoscope of vibrant neon lights, illuminating the vast expanse of the recreation ground just outside the city centre. This fair, a beloved tradition that had, at the time, been considered the biggest traveling fair in Europe, was a spectacle of joy and chaos, with laughter and screams mingling in the crisp October air.

High above the noisy crowds, the tantalising aroma of hot dogs, caramelised onions, and mushy peas wafted up to us, mingling with the cool breeze. The rides below continued to thrill their passengers, their joyous screams echoing against the night sky. As the wheel came to an abrupt stop, Helen jumped slightly, her eyes wide with surprise. I turned to her, my heart racing, and said reassuringly, "It's alright, Helen—don't be frightened. I arranged this because there's something I want to say."

Taking a deep breath of the cold air, I summoned the words I'd been rehearsing for weeks, each syllable heavy with meaning. "Helen, I love you more than I ever thought I could love anybody. In fact, I worship you. You surprise me almost every day when we're together. I love your strength, your unwavering commitment to what you believe, and especially that infectious laugh of yours. I could never tire of being with you. In fact, I feel alone when you're not with me." I paused, searching her eyes for a flicker of understanding, and then said, "Look behind you."

As she looked over her shoulder, a smile blossomed on her face, illuminating her features as she recognised the group of familiar faces standing on the hillside, looking up at us with wide grins. I'd gathered our friends, each one holding up a self-illuminated letter, the novelty of that year's fair. One by one, they turned the letters toward us, revealing the words, "Helen—will you marry me?"

Her eyes watered as she turned back to me and nodded vigorously through her tears.

We were married the following year. After all, what was the point in waiting? We both knew this was it, the culmination of our shared dreams. The only disagreement we'd ever had—if it could even be called that—was about the wedding ring. I'd envisioned a classic gold and diamond ring, a symbol of purity that I thought reflected her essence perfectly. But Helen had fallen in love with an unconventional silver band, adorned with two bright octagonal sapphires nestled within a circle of gold. It just didn't seem right to me; she could have had any ring in the store, yet she chose that one.

"When we're not together, this will remind me of looking into your eyes," she'd told me, her voice steady and resolute. "It's the one I want." And that was good enough for me. I wanted to return her romantic gesture, so I chose the same design for myself, but with emeralds that matched the colour of her eyes—deep, vibrant, and full of life.

The only other unconventional aspect of our wedding was Helen's choice of flowers for the reception. Each table was adorned with arrangements dominated by dandelions—her favourite flowers. While everyone else considered them weeds, she adored them, and somehow, that didn't surprise me at all. It was just one of the many quirky things that had made me fall in love with her.

Throughout the late nineteen eighties, I continued to work at the bank, and together, Helen and I made sound financial decisions, prospering during the boom years. We saved and invested wisely, and even through the slump of the nineteen nineties, we managed to acquire a couple of investment properties in the city and some shares in the newly emerging dot-com businesses.

Although I was the one working in a bank, it was Helen who possessed a remarkable talent for following the markets. She had the foresight to move all our investments to the housing market before the dot-com bubble burst, placing us in a strong position to weather the economic disaster that began its disastrous collapse in 2008. Our investment portfolio, though diminished in value, still generated a decent income, allowing me to take advantage of a generous redundancy package from the bank.

Helen had started out with very different aspirations. Her social conscience led her into a caring profession, and she began working in a rest home. Even when it became clear we didn't need the money, she continued her work. It eased her conscience to know she was helping others. "These people could be my grandparents," she often said, her voice tinged with compassion. "And someday, this will be me. Someone must protect their dignity and give them the care they deserve."

"I'll give up work when the first baby arrives," she'd promised, her eyes sparkling with hope.

But our attempts to start a family had all come to naught. Like so many things in life, it just wasn't fair.

"It's not your fault," she said tenderly, kneeling in front of my sobbing form. "It's just one of those things." Holding my hands, she continued, "One in seven couples, they said. One in seven—that's a lot of couples who can't have kids."

"I know, but it's me, Helen," I managed to say through my tears. "I can't give you what you've always wanted."

She cupped my face in her hands, wiping my cheeks dry with her thumbs, her gaze unwavering. "We talked about this possibility when I didn't get pregnant. We agreed it wouldn't matter if it were either one or both of us who couldn't have children. Don't feel guilty about this, Richard. We've got each other, and I love you more than anything in the world, and I'll never stop."

"It's different when you know it's you, though, Helen. I can't help thinking I am not a complete man."

"I know, that's a natural thing for anyone to think. I suppose I'd have similar feelings if it had been me." She brushed my hair aside and gave me a gentle peck on the lips. "But you know that's not true. We'll get through this together, okay?"

We fell into each other's arms, where, if either of us had possessed the power, we would have stayed forever, cocooned in our shared warmth.

We discounted adoption after IVF treatment failed, and Helen avoided the subject of a surrogate father. Perhaps she thought this would be like rubbing salt into my wounds. I decided if she didn't mention it, I'd never raise it, and she never did.

Our shared interest in science and science fiction had led us to discuss the possibilities of future treatments from stem cell research and cloning. But after a while, we seemed to stop talking about it, resigning ourselves to the inevitability of it all.

Although I never told her, I thought of it often. It was during those moments that I became overwhelmed by the blow to our hopes and dreams. It had crushed my wife's spirit, and although I would do anything to give her the baby she so desperately wanted, there was nothing I could do. So, on those occasions, I locked the door of my office, put my head in my hands, and cried.

After we retired, I mentioned cloning again. "But I don't think it'll ever happen in our lifetimes," I said, "and besides, we're far too old now."

"But what if our lifetimes were longer and we stayed younger than we are now?" she countered, her eyes sparkling with excitement.

"What do you mean?" I looked at her as if she'd gone crazy.

"Have you ever thought about being frozen when you're dead?"

I laughed, "You mean like Walt Disney?"

"Yeah, that's right—cryogenics. It's becoming popular now, and I reckon if our investments keep growing, we could afford it."

"I know you have some wacky ideas, Helen, but this one is way out of the ballpark. And there's no guarantee with it, is there?"

"No, but look at it this way. We've got no kids to leave our money to, and if we die and get buried, that will definitely be the end. We'll be gone for good—stone dead. It's not as if either of us believes in an afterlife. But if we get frozen, then at least there's a chance. Even one in a billion, billion, trillion is a better chance than none at all."

I thought she'd overdone it on that last bit. "And" she said, "if it worked, we could be together in a better world—a world where we'd be able to have the family we've always wanted." She looked at me expectantly as I gazed thoughtfully over her shoulder. "...And we'd be together for a whole new life."

Everything went silent as I contemplated her words, and I could hear her breathing in anticipation.

"Alright," I finally sighed, "there's no harm in looking into it, is there?"

Her face lit up with a grin that could rival the sun. "I've already got lots of literature for you to read, and I've downloaded material from the internet."

'I'd expect nothing less from you, Helen Green," I said, grinning back at her.

We joined the Balcor Life Extension Foundation on the recommendation of friends. After conducting extensive research about the company online, we handed over our money. Shortly afterward, we received our lockets, which we proudly wore around our necks. These lockets contained the information to inform the medical profession what to do when we were declared legally dead. We also made friends with other like-minded individuals through a networking site on the internet.

Most of our existing friends accepted our decision, as they had similar interests or simply accepted, along with our families, that we were both barking mad. Helen's mother quoted the often-used colloquialism and started to refer to us as a couple of *"daft bats."*

It became a private joke for us to whisper to each other before drifting off to sleep, "Darling, wake me in the future."

As the years progressed, so did technology, and stem cell research began to offer new opportunities to many young couples who found themselves in our position. It at least gave us increased hope that if a future society could bring us back, it would probably be able to offer us the thing we most wanted.

However, by the time we'd lived well into our retirement, we truly began to fear for the state of any future human society. Most of Helen's crazy predictions had come to pass and were no longer considered extreme. Most of the population had succumbed to the 'King's New Clothes' psychological tactics of the interested parties of capitalism. Those who could afford to bombard the public with messages designed to enforce their desired views and had the money to buy the support of greedy and corrupt politicians.

The world's wealth was concentrating into fewer and fewer hands, while more and more of the planet's population laboured to support this shift. Cultures clashed, and fanatics turned to terrorism, tipping societies into ever more extreme policies. The twin towers fell, Iraq and Afghanistan erupted in conflict, and the Korean War brought China and the US face to face. Then Iran carried out what they'd threatened for years and obliterated Tel Aviv, the nuclear fallout poisoning many of their Arab neighbours and throwing the world into chaos.

The internet, like so many other inventions, had been used for both good and evil. From global democratisation and the downfall of oppressive regimes everywhere to the proliferation of child abuse and the desensitisation of the public to pornography, extreme violence, and cruelty.

Yet, some things gave hope. The Global Information Tax allowed universally free access to all content while rewarding the makers and owners based on its use. It satisfied both the big corporates, who had been obsessing over what they considered the theft of their property, and the new generations who saw information as their right.

For people like Helen, the blocking technologies that emerged provided a glimmer of hope for the future. They had the potential to force content creators to develop new business models. As the public gained the ability to stop any exposure to advertising or content they didn't want to see, companies were compelled to produce advertising suitable to be 'called up' only at the request of the customer.

Media creators began to discuss ways to modify their content to 'penetrate' the blocking systems, seeking greater exposure and a larger share of the information tax.

Mainstream media would surely become less extreme and shift back to what it was in its earlier years, especially now that people had started to reclaim control over what their passive senses were exposed to.

Exercising real choice.

That was the world we'd left behind. And we prayed to a God we didn't believe in that the society we hoped to awaken in would be one that had learned from its past and its many mistakes.

Chapter 33 – The Procedure

After Helen died, I continued to live in the house we'd lovingly made into our home. Each creak of the floorboards echoed with memories, and every corner held a whisper of her laughter. Almost a decade slipped by in a haze of solitude, a relentless passage of time marked only by the absence of her warmth. It wasn't until I became terminally ill that I found myself moving closer to the facility that would undertake the procedure I'd come to believe in so fervently.

Fortune smiled upon me, for the practice of cryonics had gained traction, and a centre had opened in the UK. This meant my family and friends could gather around me, their presence a comforting balm as I approached the end of my earthly journey. I'd been deemed an ideal candidate for preservation by Balcor, a beacon of hope in a world that often felt dark and unforgiving. Being on the premises would give me the best chance possible, allowing the technicians to exploit the narrow window between being declared legally dead—when my heart finally ceased its relentless beating—and the moment my brain would succumb to the irreversible grip of death. Those precious minutes would be my lifeline, a chance to restore circulation to my brain, giving it the best possible opportunity to endure the procedure.

Many cryonics patients, those who opted for preservation—or "Frozen," as the public often referred to it—found themselves at the mercy of time, undergoing the procedure hours after their hearts had stopped. They pinned their hopes on the promise of future technologies, dreaming of a day when the damage inflicted upon their brains could be reversed. We had become known as "Cryogens," a title that felt almost sacred, as if we had elevated our beliefs to a new form of religion. We wore the locket provided to us with as much pride as Christians wore their crucifixes, and I often found myself surrounded by fellow Cryogens who preached the gospel of science with fervour.

The gradual advances in reviving lower life forms after suspension lent our cause a semblance of respectability. Space agencies around the globe began to discuss the potential of using this technology to send humans to distant planets, igniting a flicker of hope in our hearts. Even the spectre of significant brain damage failed to shake our unwavering belief in the capabilities of future generations to revive us in pristine condition. It was as if science had become our deity, and the promise of an artificially achieved heaven our ultimate salvation.

No, there was nothing you could say or show to devout followers of science like us that would ever cause us to waver in our faith. Not even the chilling footage of the procedure that awaited our bodies after death.

When I finally succumbed, I was blissfully unaware of the cold reality that awaited me. They placed my body in a grey metal bath filled with ice water, the temperature plummeting rapidly, a stark contrast to the warmth of life I'd known. I felt nothing as they artificially restored blood circulation, allowing protective medications to course through my veins, a desperate attempt to safeguard my most vital organ—my brain—giving it the maximum chance to survive the impending procedure.

I remained oblivious as they drained the blood from my body, washing it away with a cocktail of chemicals before gradually replacing it with a cryoprotectant solution. This was the alchemy that would allow my tissues to vitrify instead of freeze, preserving me at the temperatures required for the procedure. It was common knowledge that any ice formation within the cells during this phase could wreak havoc, causing cellular damage that future technologies might find insurmountable.

When Helen had undergone the process, they had used liquid nitrogen at a bone-chilling -196 degrees Celsius to preserve her body. But for me, they would employ a new vapor-phase procedure, allowing preservation at a higher temperature, further minimising the risk of deadly ice formation. The process was in a constant state of evolution, gradually gaining acceptance among an ever-growing minority who dared to dream of cheating death.

But death had claimed my body, and when the technicians finished their work, they placed me inside a cryogenic suspension container, side by side with the one holding my beloved wife. There, I was expected to remain until the time came for my resurrection.

What we had failed to consider was the growing indifference of a future population, one that could extend their own lives through other means and might find little interest in the long-forgotten few. It had never crossed our minds that no one would ever attempt to revive us.

That was the measure of our belief, and that was how Helen and I had arrived at this juncture. She had been preserved for nine long years before I joined her on this surreal journey. The empty darkness enveloped me, but not before I could whisper to the vision of her smiling face that danced before me.

"Darling, wake me in the future."

Chapter 34 - Rescue

As the days dragged on in this suffocating solitude, the weight of my incarceration pressed heavily upon me, inviting a flood of memories from my past life to seep into my consciousness. With little else to occupy my mind, I found myself sprawled on my cot, reliving vivid episodes that had once defined me. It was astonishing how much I recalled—like stumbling upon old friends after years apart, the warmth of familiarity washed over me, making it feel as though we had only just parted ways. Perhaps memories linger in the recesses of our minds, waiting patiently for the right moment to resurface. Whatever the truth, they were here now, lurking in the shadows, eager to be summoned. It felt like the most constructive way to pass the time, especially since my only distractions were the meagre bowl of food that appeared each morning and the rare updates from Jon.

But as each day crept closer to my so-called 'execution,' a gnawing anxiety began to build within me, escalating to a point that felt like it could launch me into orbit. I could almost feel my new body responding to the stress, and I wondered if I might freeze up entirely, like the old PC I once owned. I hoped someone would be there to reboot me if that happened.

On the sixth morning, I was jolted awake by a strange noise, reminiscent of an old-fashioned coffee percolator sputtering to life. As I blinked away the remnants of sleep, I glanced across the room and was taken aback—the floor, about four feet away from the opposite wall, was shifting and morphing, as if the very fabric of this bizarre world was alive. Bars began to rise swiftly from the ground, stretching upward until they merged seamlessly with the ceiling. I stared, bewildered, at this sudden transformation, wondering why a wall of bars had materialised to separate me from the rest of the room. But I didn't have to ponder for long.

Ramoon strode through a door that had inexplicably appeared on the opposite side of the room, standing just beyond the bars. He cast a glance in my direction, his expression a mix of amusement and disdain. "I wanted to deliver the news to you in person, Richard. The day for your 'rebirth' has been set for tomorrow. You'll pose no further danger to my plans. Once we've captured what remains of the resistance, there will be no one left to take their place." His eyes narrowed, and he leaned closer, emphasising his next words with a chilling intensity. "I am going to make sure of that."

He took a breath, stepping forward, and the wall of bars shifted ominously with him, inching closer to me.

"What's even more amusing," he continued, a smirk playing on his lips, "is that none of you truly understand the real reason behind your fight. You believe our motivation for wanting you Cryogens out of the way stems from a disdain for what's left of the original human race. That we don't want to share our future with a pitiful handful of survivors, constantly reminding us of what we once were."

"That's exactly why you're trying to kill us all off," I spat, unable to contain my contempt for this man any longer.

"Hardly," he replied, his tone dripping with condescension. "When we abandoned our world in search of another home, our numbers were nearly half a trillion. The useless bodies we despised were suspended in time, waiting for an unknown length of time. Does that sound familiar, Richard? It should, because it's what you Cryogens and we Manoorans have in common."

I pondered the striking correlation between the fate of the Cryogens and what some would call these celestial cuckoos.

"Only a few Manoorans were revived during our journey to Earth," he continued, his voice taking on a more sinister edge. "They were the ones who monitored our progress and set us on the path to visit you. They planned to interact and communicate with your species. But instead, they had to watch in horror as your petty wars and selfishness led to your extinction."

"I've heard all this before, Ramoon. Save your breath. I know how you came to take over our planet, like the thieves you are. And how you hate all Cryogens for reminding you that you're not real humans."

"True, it was too good an opportunity to let go. The template for your artificial bodies had advanced enough for us to adopt easily. Your system and everything in it was designed to serve this form. As you were all dead, there was no ethical reason not to adopt and adapt what you'd left behind."

"And you think we're going to play on those ethics and try to make you give up your new lives?" It was a statement, not a question. "You're wrong, Ramoon. That is such a sad and cynical view of what we humans are, and it's a million miles off the mark. This system is big enough for us all. Neither of our populations can grow, and there's so much space. I'm sure we can evolve into the single race that many of your kind want, including you."

"If only that were the case, Richard, I wouldn't have bothered with any of this. I know that no Cryogen has ever expressed a view that what we did was wrong. However, it's not your current manifestation that worries me."

Confusion washed over me. "I don't understand, Ramoon. What are you talking about?"

"There is an element of truth in the belief that we Manoorans can't accept what we used to be. And it's true that we envy what you were. But it's a different reason my group is trying to eliminate the last remnants of the original human race. When we started to revive the people we discovered on the Moon, our instinct was to transfer their mindsets into the artificial bodies we were using; bodies that your entire race had previously inhabited. But astonishingly, no one has ever questioned whether we could revive any of them in their biological form. And the answer to that question, Richard, is yes. We could successfully revive most Cryogens in biological form."

"I still don't understand. Why would any Cryogen want to be revived in biological form?"

"For the same reason humans, in the past, lived the first few decades of their lives in biological form." He paused for effect, letting the weight of his words sink in. "So, they could reproduce, Richard. You Cryogens could procreate and grow in numbers. Small at first, but eventually, over time, you'd outnumber us. And in biological form, unlike in these artificial bodies, there'd be nothing for our system to control."

The realisation hit me like a sledgehammer, a cold wave of dread washing over me. "Oh my God!"

"So, it's sinking in then," he said, his voice dripping with satisfaction. "We're not just trying to get rid of a few reminders of a previous time."

"NO!" I shouted, my voice echoing in the small room. "You're trying to commit genocide! That's just as bad as if you'd invaded our Solar System and exterminated us in the first place."

As Ramoon slowly advanced toward me, the wall of bars moved forward as well, as if they were just as frightened of this monster as I was. "I'd gladly do that, Richard, to save my kind. Do you think I want a race such as yours—who wiped themselves into oblivion—being resurrected and contaminating us? You original humans were capable of such extreme behaviour. Occasionally, seeming little less than your ancient gods in the way you conducted yourselves. Those were the attributes we admired so much, that drew us to you. Yet, more often than not, you allowed all those admirable virtues to be overwhelmed by your greed and individual selfishness." He shook his head; a look of disdain etched on his face. "No; everything that was bad about you, we've controlled. That would all be released again. Your petty cultural squabbling and insistence that you know how everyone else should live—just because it happens to be the way you live your own life—cannot be allowed to return."

I backed away, leaning against the wall at the foot of my cot as Ramoon pointed at me, his finger like a dagger aimed at my heart. "You'll be one of the last of your kind," he said, his voice dripping with malice. "Tomorrow, when I watch what's left of your body burn, I'll be a step closer to saving my race."

Feeling a surge of defiance I said, "That may be a bit difficult, Ramoon," hatred lacing my voice.

"And why is that, Richard?" he asked, a smirk creeping onto his face.

"Because I won't be here," I said, leaning back and sliding through the wall behind me.

Chapter 35 - Fugitive

Jon's face was ashen by the time I finished explaining the real reason we were under threat of extinction. The pallor of his skin was stark against the cluttered backdrop of his office, a chaotic mix of illuminated screens that mirrored the turmoil in my mind. He wore that look—wide-eyed and bewildered—that people get when they stumble upon the answer to a question that has haunted them for years. His fingers rubbed his temples, as if trying to bring something to mind.

"Why on Earth didn't anyone think of that?" he exclaimed, his voice a mixture of disbelief and frustration. "I can't believe we missed such an obvious motive." He still looked dazed, as if the weight of our revelation was pressing down on him. "If we hadn't been able to create that doorway behind you, or if we'd delayed it for just another day… well, you'd be gone, and this would have remained buried forever. It doesn't bear thinking about."

I sat in a chair in front of Jon's desk, the leather creaking beneath me, trying hard not to dwell on how close I'd just come to death. "I know," I replied, my voice steady despite the storm of emotions swirling within me. "I'm still thanking my lucky stars that your message got through yesterday. I can't believe how timely it was. It's a good thing the door you opened wasn't visible. I knew it had appeared just when Ramoon started to spill the beans, but I couldn't bring myself to use it right away. I had to stay and hear everything he had to say. And it's a good thing I did. I only wish I could have seen the look on his face after I disappeared."

"This makes the situation a lot more dangerous for all of us now, Richard," Jon said, his brow furrowing deeper. "The secret's out of the box, so to speak. And now Ramoon knows we're aware of what we're fighting for; he'll be desperate to get to us."

He looked at me, bemused, as if grappling with the enormity of our predicament. "I can't believe it," he exclaimed again, his voice rising with urgency. "We've been fighting to preserve what's left of humanity, not knowing that we could actually revive it completely. It raises the stakes to a different level altogether. We can't afford to fail now."

"I know," I sighed, the weight of our reality pressing down on my chest. "But what worries me more right now is what Ramoon will be willing to do to capture us. Do you think Rachel and Jane are safe where they are?"

"I believe so, for now," Jon replied, his tone measured but laced with concern. "Don't forget, Rachel's parents are among Ramoon's closest friends. So, I don't think he'll try anything at the moment. They're not his concern if he can get you out of the way. But I wouldn't count on that staying the case for long."

There was a steely resolve in his gaze as he continued, "One thing is certain, though. We need to bring our plans forward. It's too dangerous to continue with our original timetable. Ramoon will be furious that this got out, and he's almost certain to double his efforts to find us."

"Luckily, our tech people have discovered how to interact with the general information system without being detected," he added, a flicker of hope igniting in his eyes. "That's how we were able to create the doorway for your escape. They're currently working hard to make things safe enough for us to make our final move. But this has changed everything. We can't afford the luxury of making things safe anymore. We're going to have to take more risks. Even so, the earliest we can attempt a move is a week away. In the meantime, I'm going to call a halt to any public activities. We can't afford to slip up at this late stage. We've got to keep a low profile and focus on the plans."

The next few days were a nightmare for me. I was no longer in Ramoon's prison, but the memories of my first life were replaced by the relentless challenges this new existence was throwing at me. I'd done everything I could to avoid confronting the mess I found myself in, but fate seemed determined to present me with impossible choices.

I felt like a ship caught in a storm, tossed between contradicting emotions and conflicting desires. I wanted everything: Helen back at my side, sharing the life we had dreamed about together, but also Rachel, my new wife, and Jane, my wonderful daughter. The very thought of Jane not being my biological daughter only deepened the turmoil within me. I loved her as fiercely as any father could, and that love only intensified the revulsion I felt when I tried to reconcile it with my feelings for Helen.

If Rachel found out, she'd be devastated—who wouldn't be? She wouldn't want to stay with a husband who had re-found his first true love, especially when she discovered I'd kept the possibility of Helen being alive from her. She'd probably lose Jane as well, even if, as likely, Jane opted to retain her current life. After all, no one could demand that she revert to Helen. I was on the brink of losing them all unless I kept quiet about my suspicions and let Helen go. But how could I continue to raise Jane as my daughter when I knew that Helen could be trapped inside? And anyway, when Jane matured, she could decide to reintegrate her previous self.

I couldn't stand what this was doing to me. It was a 'lose-lose' situation, and for the first time, I seriously considered whether Helen and I had done the right thing. Guilt seeped into every corner of my personal life, and it was only exacerbated by the realisation that my subconscious had chosen Helen over Rachel. Oh God, this was horrible. I was keeping the truth from Rachel just in case Helen was really gone, allowing me to carry on without hurting her. What kind of man did that make me? It felt like I was treating her like second best. Another wave of guilt crashed over me.

I was overwhelmed by unanswered questions, and until I had the answers, my life felt like a chaotic mess. My heart was heavy, and dark shadows loomed around it. I felt that now-familiar, suffocating fear that I was going to lose everything. And always, hovering in my mind, was the vision of Helen, her eyes filled with disappointment, admonishing me for giving up on her.

I loved three women, and whatever the outcome, the only guarantee I could foresee was that one way or another, all of us were going to be hurt. I clenched my fists and pressed them against my forehead. "This stinks," I said out loud, my voice cracking with frustration. "I can't win."

"That bad, huh?" a voice broke through my spiralling thoughts.

I jumped, startled. I hadn't been aware of Jon entering the room and watching me. But this was a good opportunity to ask if they could open a channel of communication with my family, just as they had done with me in prison. For all his assurances about their safety, I was desperate to hear from them.

"I was just coming to see you, Jon." I stood up to face him; fingers crossed behind my back as I made my request to contact Rachel. As Jon responded, I closed my eyes and once again thanked the God I didn't believe in. I thought, *I'll have to actually start believing in you if you keep delivering like this.*

"Richard," Jon said, his voice steady, "I've already been thinking about Rachel and Jane's safety. I've authorised a plan to get them out of Ramoon's reach, one not dissimilar to the one we used to rescue you. We've already smuggled an info-tablet in with a message letting them know you're safe."

A rush of relief washed over me. "Thank you, Jon."

"You're welcome," he replied, pausing before continuing, "I don't want to pry, Richard, and tell me if you don't want to talk about it. But you've never said anything to me about your new family and what you intend to do if we're successful in eventually finding Helen. Have you considered it?"

I looked at the ground, despondent. "I don't know what to do, Jon. I've thought of nothing else since finding out that Helen is still out there somewhere. I love them both, but I might have to make a choice. Usually, life presents a natural change in the feeling of one love before you can give yourself over to another. Death is often one of those occasions. But what do you do when you fall in love again and then find out that the person you loved and thought you'd lost is still alive? I never believed someone could love more than one person like this at the same time..." I looked into Jon's eyes, desperation creeping into my voice. "But I do."

Even voicing my feelings made me feel guilty as hell. How could I put one above the other? I truly loved them both, differently but just as strongly. I knew I was going to be forced to make a choice, and that meant hurting someone I loved deeply. My voice cracked as the familiar sting of tears threatened to spill over.

I sank into the chair opposite Jon, trying to hold back the tears that seemed to be the only physical way to express the confusion swirling within me. Jon moved to sit next to me, placing a reassuring hand on my shoulder. I leaned forward, elbows on my knees, palms cupping my face, feeling the weight of the world pressing down on me.

"Can I tell you something personal about myself, Richard?" Jon said, his tone shifting to one of empathy. "I don't know if it will make you feel any better, but at least you'll see that other people have sometimes gone through similar torment to what you're experiencing now."

I nodded, too emotional to speak, my heart racing as I braced myself for his story.

Jon took a deep breath, as if preparing to share a great confession. "Before I was frozen, I was in love with two people. But it wasn't by accident, like in your situation; it was out of necessity. You see, I'm attracted to both men and women, and my particular orientation means my emotional and physical attraction is equally strong for both. I know there are plenty of people like me who find themselves drawn more one way than the other, but the way I am dictates my needs. And it's a fact, despite the bigots who tried to deny people like me existed. I know my own feelings."

He paused, his gaze distant as he recalled the past. "I thought I could suppress half of what I am and just conform, but I wasn't happy. That attempt to conform forced me to satisfy that other half of me by having affairs. Then I met Adam, and that's when I found myself in love with two people."

Jon's voice softened, filled with nostalgia. "He knew about my wife and was happy sharing me. After all, I'd been open with him from the start, and he understood the extent of what I could offer. But Julie knew nothing, and I knew I had to tell her, even though in my mind, I wasn't giving her any less than I would if I hadn't been seeing Adam. I knew it was wrong. But I was frightened of losing her, so I delayed. I made the stupid mistake of listening to people who thought they knew how I should live, and what I needed better than I did."

I leaned in, captivated by his story, wanting to understand the depths of his experience. "What happened, Jon?"

They made me feel like what I was doing was dirty and wrong somehow, that I had to make a decision because I couldn't possibly need a man and a women. I was confused in their eyes. I had to like either one or the other; nothing else existed. And if I thought differently, then I was just selfish and greedy. I was going to hurt everyone I ever loved. I had to conform to some kind of vision of normality that they had in their heads."

Jon's expression darkened as he continued, "Then one of my so-called friends decided they had some sort of moral duty to interfere. Driven by their own morals, of course. They weren't concerned about Julie not knowing about Adam. They wanted me to make a choice as if being with more than one person was somehow criminal. They told me I had to make a choice. Otherwise, they were going to tell Julie about Adam. They were happy to destroy our lives because it didn't fit into their acceptable templates."

I sat up, fully engaged, wanting Jon to know that I didn't share the views his previous friends had held. "What happened next?"

"I decided to tell her myself. I loved her enough to guess how she'd react, but I wasn't sure. I wasn't concealing the truth for selfish reasons; I just couldn't face the possibility of hurting her. But in the end, she understood. Her only concern was whether it meant she'd see me less or that I'd love her less."

"So, they both accepted the existence of each other then?" I asked, intrigued.

"Not only that, but they eventually became firm friends, and we all moved in together."

"And what happened to the friends who'd interfered?" I pressed, eager to know the outcome.

"They didn't stay friends for long. Julie and Adam saw to that; they didn't appreciate anyone interfering in what they considered their business."

"But it could have worked out differently. Julie could have left you."

"Exactly, but I couldn't have done anything about it. Society had put me in that situation by not accepting my differences, and then it tried to make me feel guilty. All I was doing was waiting for the right time to put things right while those around me were constantly trying to tell me how I should live my life."

Jon's words resonated deeply within me. "All I can say, Richard, is that circumstances have put you in this situation, not any deliberate deception on your part. It's up to you to decide when it's the right time to explain it to the other people involved."

"So, you told Julie about Adam because it was the right time to do it, and it was going to come out one way or another. I guess that's the situation I'm in with Helen and Rachel. So, I need to talk to Rachel about Helen's possible survival and my feelings."

"You'll know when you're ready, Richard. Hopefully, we will find Helen, and if we do, you can tell them both how you found yourself in this place. Let them judge the love you've got for them and the circumstances that have put you where you are. Perhaps the situation will sort itself out without you having to make a choice. And if either, or both, of them decide they can't live with the situation, then you'll know. I can't guarantee your story will end up as happily as mine did, but it will be resolved one way or the other. And that's what you need right now more than anything, Richard. Resolution."

"So, what happened to Julie and Adam then?" I asked, curiosity piquing again. As soon as I'd asked, I regretted it, seeing Jon's eyes glaze over.

"9/11 happened. They both worked in the South Tower."

"I'm sorry, Jon," I said, my heart heavy with empathy. I hugged him tightly, grateful for his support. "Thank you anyway. You've given me some hope and made me feel so much better."

Later that night, I received the info-tablet they'd smuggled to Rachel. It looked different from the ones I'd seen before—like a palm-sized black tile. I thought this must be their version of a smartphone. They'd been very popular in my time, so I hoped it wouldn't be too difficult to use.

Just by looking at it, I could tell it was far more advanced. It resembled a thin piece of smooth black slate, its highly polished surface reflecting my inquisitive stare back at me. On its front, embedded in the screen was a circle the size of a one-euro coin, which gave a good impression of a power button. A very good impression, as it turned out. Because when I reached out to press it, the circle raised itself slightly to meet my finger, as if sensing my impending contact.

As soon as I felt the button engage with my finger, the device began to grow. It doubled in size and doubled again, and the screen—if you could call it that—was like looking into a box. It gave the impression of great depth, covering an area of about twelve inches, even though what I'd initially picked up was no larger than the palm-sized mobile phone I used to own. For a fraction of a second, as it sprang to life, I thought I was going to see the same old operating system that dominated my time. The thought of what state this civilisation would be in if it had to rely on that crossed my mind, and I couldn't help but smile, thinking, *we'll see how many times I have to reboot.*

No operating system appeared. Just a blank grey space that looked like I could reach into it. But before I could act on that urge, Rachel's smiling face emerged in the space.

"Richard, Jon said he'd give you this message. We were so relieved to hear you were alright and managed to escape from that vile man. Jane and I were going through hell while you were in there. Now you're free, we've been confined to my parents' house. Luckily, they've just gone away on a research trip around Mercury because ever since this blew up, they've been horrid to both of us. Almost as if we weren't family. It's as if we were strangers. It really upset Jane. Let me know what's going on if you can. Otherwise, take care, darling, and send us a message as soon as you can."

She blew me a kiss, and before the image faded, I could swear I felt the draft from her breath. I began to think of what response I could send. I was certainly glad that her parents were away; I hadn't liked them from the start. But I was surprised at how Rachel had said they'd treated them. I wondered how easy it was to divorce your feelings from someone you knew ultimately wasn't your own flesh and blood. I had no experience, but from my previous life, there was a perception that many stepparents were cruel to their stepchildren compared to biological ones. But then again, the saying about blood just wasn't relevant anymore.

There were only a few more days to go before the culmination of the plan. If it was successful, it could reveal the whole truth about Ramoon's activities and end his despicable campaign for good. Everyone at headquarters was acting positive and upbeat, and in the meantime, I had my lifeline to Rachel.

The confidences I'd shared with Jon had really helped me too, but I was conscious that I hadn't revealed my suspicions about Jane. Somehow, I just couldn't bring myself to put it into words again. But it made my situation a great deal more complex than Jon's life had ever been.

Yes, just a few more days to go, and if the plan brought success for the protesters, it would probably bring answers for me. The question was, would they be the ones I wanted to hear?

Just a few more days....

Chapter 36 – Death in the Family

I hadn't spoken to my Cryogen friends since before my capture at the library, but Jon had assured me they were not under any suspicion. They were safe, if they kept a low profile. "That's what I've instructed them to do," he said, his voice steady but laced with an undercurrent of urgency. "They know you're safe, and although they're eager to help in any way they can, I've asked them not to attempt any further contact until we get in touch. We've lost too many good people, including the librarian, who was one of the essential links in our support group. So right now, we have to direct all our focus on getting our hands on the information to bring Ramoon and his people down. Before they can do any more damage to what's left of us original humans."

As I sat in the main conference room, the atmosphere was thick with tension. The oval table gleamed under the harsh fluorescent lights, and I faced Jon, flanked by nine or ten other core organisers. Behind me, a small crowd of supporters stood, their faces a mix of hope and anxiety, waiting to listen to the discussion that was about to unfold. The air was electric, charged with the weight of our shared purpose.

Jon stood up, his presence commanding attention. He scanned the room, and as if on cue, silence enveloped us. He began what must have been a well-rehearsed explanation of the plan, his voice rising and falling with the cadence of a seasoned orator. He meticulously outlined the responsibilities of each person involved, making them repeat their roles to ensure everyone was acutely aware of what, when, and how they were to act. "None of us can afford to fail," he declared, his eyes blazing with conviction. "Not now that we know what's at stake."

It was Jon's involvement in the plan that made me sit up and stare in disbelief. I'd known they were going to take over the body of one of the high officials, but had I just heard right? The official's body that he was planning to transmit himself into was Ramoon's! My heart raced as the implications crashed over me like a tidal wave.

Apparently, the high official was due to travel to India Central in a few days, and as usual, he'd jump there, leaving his original body unattended and ripe for the taking. The protesters would set a fix on it before inserting Jon's consciousness. He would then have a matter of hours to retrieve the data using Ramoon's access, sending it back for further transmission to the distributed information services on all the planets. Once that happened, it would be available to everyone, and no one—least of all Ramoon—would be able to stop his foul plan from being revealed.

It all sounded like a well-thought-out plan, certainly more elaborate than the one I'd used at Ankit's to gain access to his system. But my brow knitted together as I absorbed the gravity of it all. I raised my hand, just as I'd been taught to do in school over a thousand years before. Somehow, this didn't seem out of place, considering that most of the people in the room were from that time.

"Err...," I muttered, waving my arm, "there's just one problem with your plan, Jon."

Everyone's heads turned in my direction; surprise etched on their faces. Jon looked worried, his brow furrowing. "What have you spotted, Richard?"

"Well, from what I gather, you're the most valuable member of this group, and as there's a risk of this going wrong, I don't think it should be you we transmit." My voice trembled slightly, but I pressed on, feeling the weight of their gazes.

Jon's shoulders dropped, a flicker of relief crossing his features. "I would never ask anyone to risk something I wouldn't risk myself, Richard," he replied, his tone earnest.

"I don't think there's a person in this room who would ever doubt that Jon. None of us would question your commitment to this cause. So, there's no need for you to prove anything. But if there's any risk that we could lose you, then it's not a risk worth taking, especially if there's an alternative."

People began to nod, murmurs of agreement rippling through the crowd behind me. I stood up, emboldened by their support. "I suspect anyone could be briefed to do what you're intending. And as I am the newest member here, I think I am the person you could all afford to lose."

"I am not sure—" Jon started, but he was interrupted by what looked like a teenager sitting on his left, his voice cutting through the tension like a knife.

"Let him finish, Jon; he's speaking a lot of sense." Then, turning to me, he said, "Go on, we're listening."

"I'd like to volunteer to undertake this part of the plan," I continued, my heart pounding in my chest. I looked around at the rest of the people in the room, their faces a mix of scepticism and hope. "If that's acceptable."

By now, everyone was wholeheartedly behind me, and Jon could see he didn't have a snowball's chance in hell of arguing against my proposal.

"I am reluctant to let you do this, Richard," he said, taking a deep breath as if he were about to commit to a life-threatening decision. "But I can see the logic behind what you're saying, so if it's okay with everyone else, I'll accept your offer."

The agreement was unanimous, and as the meeting dispersed, a few people came up to me, slapping me on the back and shoulders to show their support and appreciation. I was truly a protester now. *And I am coming after you, Ramoon,* I thought, a fire igniting within me.

After everyone had left the room, I remained seated, contemplating the enormity of what I'd just committed myself to. I was going to be in the body of the person who had tried to have me destroyed. All I had to do now was memorise my part of the plan...

Returning to my room, I felt a wave of nervousness wash over me, a sense of loneliness creeping in. But my mood lifted when I discovered I'd received another message from Rachel.

Boy, did I need it; I'd been looking forward to seeing her smiling face and hearing news about her and Jane. It couldn't have come at a better time.

I turned on the device, and the smile that was beginning to form on my face gave way to shock. Rachel was staring back at me; her face streaked with tears. A forced smile told me something was seriously wrong. My heart raced, and my first thoughts were of Jane. But before I could react, Rachel's image began to speak through her sobs.

"Oh Richard, I've just been informed that my parents have died in an accident." Her voice cracked, and I felt a surge of helplessness wash over me, unable to reach out and comfort her as she struggled to find her words. "Their ship went too near the Sun and got caught in its gravitational pull. Nothing survived; everything's gone. I can't believe it. I'll never have the chance to make them love Jane or me again." Sobbing overwhelmed her, and all I could do was stare at my heartbroken wife as she mourned the loss of the people she loved.

As she wiped the latest wave of tears from her eyes, she looked out of the vid-screen and paused. "They weren't alone, Richard. Ankit was on the ship too." My heart sank as she said this. "I didn't know; I... I can't even think why he'd be with them. They're all gone, Richard," she began to cry again, forcing herself to look at the screen. "I miss you so much. I wish we could be with you. Send me a message as soon as you can."

When the screen went blank, I frantically searched the information system for news on the accident. Deaths were so infrequent in this society; only something that could breach the integrity of the evantium brain pod could end a life. The accident was reported widely on all planets, and a morbid interest had developed in the story.

Maya and Mazood had been undertaking research on the Sun's corona, and the Mag-Grav shield protecting them and their ship had failed, tipping them helplessly into the fiery grasp of the star. Their aborted attempt to jump to the base on Mercury only succeeded in bringing their molten end to the attention of the station in orbit around Venus. Along with Maya and Mazood were Ankit and two other research assistants from the base on Mercury.

My heart pounded as I continued to read the report. I couldn't believe it; I didn't have much love for Rachel's parents, but I cared deeply about how she felt. And in my mind, a suspicion began to grow about the real cause of the accident. If it was true, then my involvement with the protesters could be indirectly responsible for these deaths. How would I ever be able to face Rachel again if that proved to be true? The feeling of hatred for Ramoon began to swell within me, stronger with every passing second.

My main sense of loss, though, was for Ankit, my friend. The gentleman who, even though he had been forced to betray me, I knew cared. Gone forever, forcibly separated from his wife, dying knowing he'd never see her again. I could only imagine how terrible that would feel if it had been Helen or Rachel.

Ankit was the first person I'd seen in this world of immortals, and yet in such a short time since then, he had been taken by death—the very thing I thought I'd left behind. It seemed death would claim its prize after all. For if life could last forever, that's how long it was prepared to wait.

Then a thought struck me. With Rachel's parents out of the way, Ramoon had no reason not to harm Rachel and Jane! *My god*, I thought, as I began to run in the direction of Jon's room, *they're in deadly danger*.

We had to get Rachel and Jane to safety before Ramoon could do them harm.

Jon didn't say anything when I barged in and hurriedly explained what had happened and the increased danger, I feared my family was now facing.

"Okay, Richard, try to stay calm," Jon said, gripping my shoulders, his gaze steady. "This changes things again. I'll get onto the techs straight away and tell them to focus entirely on the plan to get Rachel and Jane to safety."

"Thank you."

"You don't have to thank me, Richard. We're all family, and we'd expect this for any of us."

"If there's anything I can do…"

"What you can do," he said, pushing me toward the exit, "is get back to your room and try to get some sleep. You can't afford to risk making the jump if you exhaust yourself."

"I doubt if Little God will let me rest tonight," I muttered under my breath.

"Little God?"

"Oh, nothing," I said, walking away, "perhaps another time."

When I got back to my quarters, I sat looking into the distant horizon through the vid-wall in my room. The weight of my decisions pressed down on me, and I knew that whatever happened next would change everything.

And Little God offered up dark thoughts of what I should do to Ramoon's body once I got possession of it.

Chapter 37 - Safety

Every second stretched out like an eternity, each tick of the clock mocking my impatience. It felt as if the very fabric of time had warped under the weight of my concentration, slowing to a crawl. Was it truly possible that time could bend in response to the intensity of my thoughts? Or was it merely an illusion, a trick of the mind? As I stood there, waiting for the techs to breach the threshold of Rachel's parents' house, the minutes dragged on, each one heavier than the last. Why was it taking so long? There was no room for delay. We needed to act swiftly, especially if they intended to replicate the same technique, they'd used to rescue me. The urgency of the situation pressed down on me like the talons of a great bird, sinking into my shoulders, holding me in a vice-like grip of anxiety.

When the techs finally signalled that they were ready, it felt as if a tightly wound coil inside me had suddenly unravelled. A headache began to throb at my temples, a cruel reminder of the tension that had built up during the agonising wait. I cursed the very notion of simulating such a stressful experience.

Now, all I could do was hope that Rachel would follow the instructions we'd sent her without hesitation. There was no time to wait for a reply; every second counted. If anything went awry now, it could be our last chance before Ramoon made his move to India Central. I could only imagine how furious my escape must have made him. In fact, I suspected it had driven him to orchestrate the deaths of Rachel's parents and Ankit. But I was still a million miles away from grasping the full extent of his rage.

Unbeknownst to me, Ramoon was seated in his office, fixated on a recording of Rachel in her parents' living room. He knew it was illegal, but he had long since abandoned any regard for the law. Armed with override codes that only a select few Manoorans possessed, he had taken full advantage of his power. Proof it seemed that emotional beings could not be trusted with such authority over others.

Ramoon was convinced he was fighting for the survival of his race. Ever since he had captured me, he had kept a watchful eye on Rachel's parents' home, monitoring it more closely than the law allowed. He anticipated that we would attempt to rescue them, and he had even predicted that we would use the same method that had worked for me. He acknowledged that we had grown cleverer, but he was not just clever; he was cunning. His initial instinct had been to place as many of his men as possible in and around the adjoining buildings. But then he realised that we would likely expect that, which might deter us from making any attempt at all. He needed to let us get close. After all, Rachel would have to meet someone, and Ramoon suspected—and hoped—that someone would be me.

So, he left the adjoining buildings unguarded. Instead, he decided to use the very structures themselves against us. He had the walls of Rachel's parents' home and the surrounding buildings programmed so that if any interruption occurred, a check would be made to determine if Rachel and Jane were alone. If they were, the exits would function normally. If not, the walls would be disabled, and the trap would be sprung. This devious plan was designed to allow Rachel to reach her rescuers, and Ramoon hoped it would be me. Anyone else would simply be a bonus.

The instructions in the last video message had reached Rachel, and as she listened, I could imagine her eyebrows raising in response to some of the more outlandish directives. Thankfully, she was intelligent enough to understand that every instruction had a logical purpose, no matter how ludicrous it seemed at first. That evening, she explained the plan to Jane using their 'intimate' mode, a communication method they had adopted since the tragic loss of her parents. They both felt a sense of discomfort, as if unseen eyes were watching them. It was ridiculous, she knew, but they felt safer acting as if someone were present. "Hopefully, if this works, we should be with your father tomorrow," Rachel had said, her mind laced with a mixture of hope and trepidation.

'I hope so. This place is seriously starting to give me the creeps," Jane had replied.

Early the following morning, just before the time they were supposed to make their move, Rachel had one last task to complete. She stood at the information terminal in her parents' private rooms, pressing her left hand against the screen. The matter in her fingers, palms, and wrist seemed to meld with the surface, until it was impossible to distinguish her hand from the screen. This was how her parents had set up access to their private files, and since their death, the system had transferred access rights to their legal heir—Rachel.

Her instructions from Jon had been explicit. She was to wait until mere minutes before their departure and transfer all her parents' private files to an info-tablet, which she would take with her. They were certain that this activity would be registered, so speed was of the essence, and timing was crucial.

As the download completed, Jane stood anxiously, clutching a small bag of personal possessions that she was allowed to take, slung over her shoulder. She held a similar bag belonging to her mother, ready to grab as soon as Rachel finished. "Hurry, Mum," she communicated, her foot tapping nervously as if counting down the seconds until they could escape. "I want this to be over."

"Finished... quick, run!" Rachel urged, her words a mix of excitement and urgency.

They quickly reached their destination, and Rachel looked at Jane, nodding toward the wall as if to say, "You first." In an instant, Jane disappeared, and two seconds later, so did Rachel.

Minutes later, Ramoon stood up from his desk, having just been informed of the download at the Karr household. He slammed his fist on the desk, nearly shouting, "Gotcha!" But as he looked up at the guard who had delivered the news, his triumphant smile began to fade. The guard didn't seem as pleased as he should have been.

"How many of them did we get?" Ramoon demanded, not giving the guard time to answer. "Have them brought straight here!"

The guard remained motionless, a look of fear creeping across his face.

"Well, man," Ramoon barked, "what are you waiting for?"

The guard's brow furrowed, as if he were terrified to deliver bad news.

"Well?" Ramoon shouted, his patience wearing thin. "How many did we catch?"

With a timid voice that trembled with subservience, the guard finally managed to say, "None, sir."

As the guard stood there, quaking in his boots, he had no idea that just moments earlier, Rachel and Jane had found their balance among the cleaning machines, waiting silently for their next job. They had effectively escaped through the rubbish chute, which was just an access route for the cleaning machines. After manually prying open the conventional door and squeezing through, they had slid down a steep ramp into the storage room for the machines that cleaned the house.

I'd always loved the Star Wars movies and had suggested the plan, thinking it was reminiscent of Luke's daring rescue of Princess Leia.

Rachel and Jane had spotted me waiting a few feet away. "Quick!" I pointed to another service entrance. "We need to go through here." Then I whispered under my breath, almost to myself, "Before the walls start moving in."

They hurried over to me, and together we navigated the maze of entrances in the underground basements, slipping through the conventional doorways that separated the rooms occupied solely by cleaning machinery. No one paid attention to these machines, nor did they care where they came from or where they went. Not even those who had set a trap for Rachel and Jane.

"Was it really essential to come down through the utility ramp, Richard?" Rachel asked, her voice tinged with indignation. "It was so undignified."

"I'm afraid so," I replied, trying to keep my tone light. "We had to avoid using the adjoining buildings, if possible, in case Ramoon had set a trap. This was the quickest way to get you far enough away for us to feel comfortable opening a virtual doorway." I smiled, "And it worked."

When we finally reached the safety of our headquarters, we rushed to meet Jon in his office. He watched as the three of us seized the first opportunity we had to embrace, hugging and kissing each other with a mix of relief and joy.

Jon stepped back, allowing us to finish, then extended his hand toward Rachel. "May I?" he asked, nodding toward the info-tablet.

"Of course," Rachel replied, handing him the tablet that now contained the information from her parents' files back on Earth.

"I think you all ought to get some rest and freshen up. Why don't you meet me back here in two hours?" he suggested, holding up the info-tablet. "Then we can find out if there's any relevant information in this thing."

"Not before I give you a big hug," Rachel said, wrapping her arms around a startled Jon. "Thank you, thank you!"

"You're welcome," he laughed as we left the room.

As we walked away from Jon's office, Rachel gestured to her body and said, "Isn't it strange how much you carry over when you jump from one body to another? You'd think I'd feel bright and fresh in this new body. But in reality, I'm still exhausted and feel like I could sleep for a week. And even though this body I've jumped into is clean, I still feel as dirty as the one I left behind."

I put my arm around her as we approached my rooms, squeezing her tightly. "Don't worry; you'll feel as right as rain after a long hot shower," I assured her, winking.

Two hours later, when we entered Jon's office, he was at his desk, chin resting in his hand, engrossed in studying the information Rachel had brought from her parents' home.

"Jon?" I called softly.

"Hmmm?" he responded, looking up as if emerging from a deep reverie. He pointed at the info-tablet. "There's some interesting stuff here, but nothing more than we already knew." He turned to Rachel. "It covers your parents' interest in joining the Community of Humanity and their desire to erase their memories of being Manooran. They clearly didn't have a fondness for us Cryogens, and they were extremely close to Ramoon."

"But there's nothing to connect them to his plans, right?" Rachel asked hopefully. "I'm relieved to hear that. What do the records say about me?"

"There are a lot of gaps here, Rachel," Jon replied, his tone serious. "They've transferred selected files to a secure area on the main information hub, which I suspect even you won't be able to access. I believe those files will implicate them in his plans for the Cryogens. I'm sorry," he added apologetically, "but I can't see any other reason why they'd move information from their personal files onto the main system."

Rachel's head drooped, a look of embarrassment washing over her. "That's okay, Jon; I suspected as much anyway. I can't say it's not a disappointment, though." I noticed Jane squeezing her hand in support.

"As far as you're concerned," Jon paused, "there's nothing other than the usual references to them having a daughter named Rachel. There's not much detail."

"That's great," she said, her voice tinged with bitterness. "Not only were they in cahoots with Ramoon, but they were also so ashamed of my existence that they couldn't even be bothered to give me any space in their reference files."

"I don't think that's the case," Jon said, trying to offer her some hope. "If our plan is successful, I'm sure you'll find other files relating to you when we gain full access to the system. There must have been other information attached to the files they transferred."

She offered him a sceptical smile, unconvinced. "I think you're wrong, Jon. I believe they were trying to erase anything that would link them to being Manooran. Remember how deluded and obsessed they were with wanting to see themselves as human? These types of Manoorans want to forget where they came from, so they gradually wipe out all records relating to the past before they submit themselves to have their memories altered. If my parents wanted that, then what must they have thought of me marrying Richard?"

I looked at Rachel, my heart heavy with sympathy. "Don't beat yourself up about it, Rachel. If anything, what's happened to you is my fault for coming into your life."

She hugged me tightly, and for a moment, words failed us both.

But then I turned to Jon, curiosity gnawing at me. "You've both mentioned this Community of Humanity. What exactly is it?"

"It's the fiftieth planet, Richard," Rachel explained. "An alternative society where all Manoorans have had their memories altered, and they genuinely believe they're humans living alongside us. I mentioned it before at my parents' house."

I nodded, recalling her earlier words. "Their history has been rewritten to show it happened the way they'd hoped when they first travelled to Earth—only with them as the humans."

Jon looked up at us, his expression serious. "It's no use pondering this any longer today. We'll find out more when we gain full access to the system, and unless Ramoon alters his travel plans, that'll be tomorrow." He turned to me, perhaps realising he could be parting me from Rachel for good so soon after our reunion. "Are you ready, Richard?"

"It can't come soon enough for me," I replied, bitterness creeping into my tone as I thought of Ramoon.

But it was more than just Ramoon that weighed on my mind. As I shuddered, the thought of the next day loomed ominously ahead of me. Even if my entire world didn't come crashing down, I was certain my whole life was about to change again—forever.

Chapter 38 - Jump

I was acutely aware of the precariousness of my situation, more so than anyone around me could possibly fathom. Jon, with his perceptive nature, seemed to grasp the turmoil that churned within me, torn between my affections for both Helen and Rachel. Yet only my friends—those who had been cast aside in this chaotic narrative—understood the full weight of my knowledge about Jane. They were absent from the scene, leaving me to wrestle with my demons alone. No one truly comprehended the labyrinth of thoughts that twisted and turned in my mind.

It felt like a catch-22, a cruel paradox with no escape. Each time I contemplated the impending decisions I would have to make, a fresh wave of shame washed over me, deepening the chasm of my despair. The circumstances were conspiring to force me into the role of a villain, a designation I knew I didn't deserve. The thought of being perceived as that person—someone who would hurt the very women I cherished—gnawed at my conscience, igniting a firestorm of outrage within me. How could I possibly make things right? I'd never wished to inflict pain on anyone.

I racked my brain, searching for a reasonable course of action that might spare the feelings of the women I loved, but each option felt like a betrayal.

It was only the incredible construct of my new body that kept me tethered to reality. Without it, the mounting mental exhaustion would have already driven me to the brink of collapse. I clung to the hope that if everything went awry tomorrow, at least I would have had one final night with my new family, knowing they were safe and out of harm's way.

As I drifted into a restless sleep, my arms wrapped around Rachel, Jon's words echoed in my mind: *"Let them be the judge of your love for them and of the situation you find yourself in."*

Sleep came fitfully, plagued by nightmares that clawed at the edges of my consciousness. I dreamt of frozen bodies, a faceless Data with cogs and wheels whirring behind lidless eyes, my parents and best friend Pete emerging from cold, sterile pods, and the agonising screams of the burning librarian. Each image was a haunting reminder of the stakes at play.

When morning light crept through the cracks of my reality, I awoke with a sense of urgency. My mind raced as I replayed the plan over, and over, a mantra of necessity. There was no room for error; everything had to unfold flawlessly.

Finally, I lay down on the couch, the interface attaching itself to my forehead, and I steeled myself for the truth. Would I uncover the reality about Helen, even as I held another woman's heart in my hands? The outcome of this journey was beyond my control, but as I waited for the transfer, a singular thought consumed me: *would I ever return?*

Meanwhile, Ramoon was a tempest of fury. The destruction of the guard who had delivered the bad news hadn't quelled his rage. "I WANT THEM DEAD!" he bellowed at the two men standing before his desk, his voice a thunderclap in the sterile room. "I don't care how you find them or what you have to do, but everything must be obliterated, including them. We need to eliminate these threats once and for all. There's far too much at stake." He inhaled deeply, attempting to regain his composure. "I'll return tomorrow, and I expect results."

The guards stiffened, the taller of the two responding, "Leave it to us, sir. The prisoners have begun to talk, and we have fresh leads we're confident we can follow. We've initiated a search around the power core that feeds the main water processing plant on the Moon."

"Good," he snapped, his gaze piercing. "Because I assure you, you have no idea how displeased I'll be if you fail." He dismissed them with a curt nod, and once they were gone, he turned his attention to the hovering planet on his vid-screen. More calmly he said, "The outcome of this will dictate the future of our race. I refuse to let ours be overrun. We are the best of humanity. I want all the originals destroyed."

With a touch, he made the image fade, his thoughts drifting to Richard. A small, sinister smile crept across his face as he recalled how he had orchestrated the complete destruction of that meddlesome first wife of Richard's. She had been inching too close to the truth, and he couldn't afford to let her live. Satisfied, he walked into the adjoining room to prepare for his Jump to India Central.

Unbeknownst to him, the protesters were monitoring his every move. As soon as he made the jump, they rechecked the systems linked to me and initiated the process.

Everyone had assured me that Jumping wouldn't be unpleasant, but they had lied. Each time I underwent the process, I felt a wave of nausea wash over me. This time, it felt as if my entire being was being drawn into a singular point near my heart, like a tiny black hole had opened and consumed me. My head exploded with pain, my stomach churned violently, and then... nothing.

When I finally opened my eyes, I looked down at my hands, disbelief washing over me. "It worked. I can't believe it."

I rose, scanning the room for the vid-screen. Ramoon was supposed to be away for the day, but I couldn't take any chances; I had to move quickly. I longed for this to be over, to return to my own body—this strange existence was becoming unbearable.

I stepped into the main room, where the terminal awaited. My hand reached into the wall, and the vid-screen flickered to life, recognising my presence. "Welcome, Councillor Ramoon," it greeted me. "What can I do for you today?"

A lot, I thought, urgency propelling me forward.

It took nearly an hour to track down the files I needed and transfer them to a backup location. I was so engrossed in my task that time slipped away unnoticed. I prayed that these files contained the damning information we sought.

Finally, as I finished, a wave of relief washed over me. I made my way back to the room where I'd entered this body, a smile creeping onto my face at the thought of what 'Little God' had suggested I do now that I was in control. I looked down at myself, tempted by the possibilities. But deep down, I couldn't bring myself to act on it. After all, it was merely a shell, a vessel for Ramoon to inhabit. No, I just wanted out. I was relieved this part was over, and with a smile, I closed my eyes, bracing myself for the familiar, terrible sensations of jumping back.

But nothing happened.

I waited, eyes still closed, but the expected shift never came. I shouted the thoughts in my head, just as instructed: "READY TO TRANSFER," I added a desperate "please…"

Still, nothing.

After several more attempts, I opened my eyes, dread pooling in my stomach. I was still in Ramoon's room, and the sight of my hands confirmed my worst fears. "Oh no," I breathed, panic creeping in. "What's gone wrong?"

I rose and walked back to the terminal in the main room, hoping to send a message to Jon. As I approached, a curious sensation washed over me—a feeling of foreboding, a psychological discomfort that prickled at the back of my mind. Just as I lifted my hand to present it to the screen, a terrible sound erupted from behind me. It wasn't terrible in the conventional sense, but it was terrifying to me because I never expected to hear a voice that should only have come from the mouth I now possessed.

"I've got you this time, Richard," Ramoon's chilling voice echoed from behind me.

My breath caught in my throat, and for a moment, I was frozen in place. I stood utterly still, terrified to break the spell and provoke a hasty reaction. I didn't want to die—not like this, not because of a mistake on my part. I remained rigid, desperately searching for a way out.

Summoning my courage, I slowly turned around, repeating a silent prayer: "Don't let this be happening, don't let this be happening."

But when I faced him, my nightmares materialised into reality. I was staring directly at another Ramoon!

"Et Voila," he said, a satisfied smile stretching across his face, arms thrown wide to acknowledge the duplicate body. "I always keep a spare template here at the office. The system, although rather slow today, has done its job of alerting me to the access of my files and your possession of my primary body. But best of all, it has successfully trapped you inside." He brandished a gun, pointing it directly at me, and my gaze locked onto it.

Following my stare, he continued, "Normally, weapons aren't allowed, but if you wield enough power, it's astonishing what you can do. This one creates a sticky plasma called Plasmex that will entirely envelop a body and consume it, including the brain pod and whoever's mind it contains. And I am going to relish using it to eliminate you."

"It's too late, Ramoon," I somehow found the courage to say, my voice steady despite the fear coursing through me. "I've transmitted the information, so your little plan to destroy all the Cryogens will be exposed within hours." I forced confidence into my tone, adding, "I suspect you'll be reborn, but if it were up to me, I'd take that gun you're holding and obliterate everything you are."

To my surprise, the reaction I anticipated didn't materialise. Ramoon remained unfazed, his smile unwavering. *He should have been trembling in fear!*

"I afraid you never got the information out, Richard. My system is designed to intercept anything transmitted from here, holding it in a buffer until I issue a secondary command for it to be released. And before you can stick your hand in there again and utter the words 'secondary transmit,' I'm going to reduce you to nothing more than a puddle of slag."

A punch of despair hit me in the gut. The realisation that everything I thought I'd achieved was slipping away sent me spiralling toward panic.

But somehow, I managed to maintain a façade of confidence. "I don't care about that, Ramoon. You can't keep this silent forever. The rest of the protesters know what they're fighting for now, and it won't be long before they expose you and your vile group of supporters for what you truly are."

To my astonishment, the smile on his face widened. "You mean the ones based near the power core for the Moon's water processing plant?" he asked, his tone dripping with malice. "Right at this very moment, it's under attack from my guards. Within hours, your comrades and their pathetic notion of reviving your obnoxious race will be nothing more than a distant memory—and a pile of ash, just like Maya and her insufferable husband."

Defeat washed over me, draining the fight from my spirit. After coming so far, was this truly the end?

But hearing Ramoon mention Rachel's parents ignited a fire within me. "So, it was you then," I spat, fury surging through my veins. "I suspected you were involved in their deaths."

"Oh yes, it was me," he replied, a twisted satisfaction in his voice. "Their loyalty to the cause was becoming a liability. A shame, as they were once very loyal. In fact, Maya was responsible for destroying your first wife for me."

"What!"

"Yes, she was obedient back in those days, but allowing you to marry Rachel..." He spat the words as if they were poison. "That was unforgivable. It revealed her true nature—weak and guilty. I suppose she thought she was making amends in her own mind, replacing the wife she had snatched from you and vaporised."

That was it; I'd made my decision. If I got the chance, if he let his guard down, I would rush him. I had nothing left to lose. Strangely, I felt a calmness wash over me, surprising me because I'd never considered myself particularly brave. But I would die if I did nothing. I had to keep him talking until I found my opening.

"And what exactly did Ankit do to deserve your murderous wrath?"

"Ah, yes, poor Ankit. That was never intended. He wasn't supposed to accompany the Karrs on their doomed mission. I didn't even know he'd joined them until after the event. Apparently, the fool decided to tag along at the last minute, so even if I'd wanted to, I couldn't have stopped him without risking exposure. Besides, he was always a shaky ally, only willing to act under duress while I held Amira. He's not such a loss to the cause." He chuckled darkly. "I suppose his death was a bonus."

Ramoon's gaze remained fixed on me, the gun unwavering. I realised I wouldn't get my chance to rush him after all. This truly was the end.

"This is all academic anyway, Richard, because in a few seconds, you won't exist." He straightened his arm, aiming the gun directly at me, and pulled the trigger.

Instinctively, I slammed my eyes shut, bracing for the end. I would never see the people I loved again, but in that fleeting moment, their faces flashed through my mind. I wanted them with me at the end. I heard a strange whooshing sound, and—oh God, I could smell burning. I was going to die by being slowly melted!

I clung to the images of Helen and Rachel as I gasped what I thought was my final breath. Then, admonishing myself, I thought, "Don't be a coward. Open your eyes—don't let him see you afraid. YOU'RE HUMAN!" Defying my fear, I opened my eyes to confront my murderer.

But where Ramoon had stood, there was now a grotesque parody of a human figure, covered in what looked like glowing volcanic lava. Suddenly, it solidified, cracked, and crumbled to the floor, revealing a hand holding a similar gun protruding from the opposite wall.

As I looked over at the hand, it grew an arm, and my eyes widened in amazement as the rest of the body emerged into the room.

"Ankit!"

Chapter 39 – The Truth Be Out

The friend I'd thought was dead, vaporized on Rachel's parents' spaceship, stood before me, facing me with a gun in his hand and a smile that danced across his lips like a flickering flame.

"Did I get the right one? That is you isn't it, Richard?"

Shock coursed through me, a jolt of disbelief that quickly morphed into a realisation: this was Ankit's uncharacteristic attempt at humour, a desperate attempt to lighten the gravity of our situation.

With near-overwhelming delight, I surged forward, arms wide open, ready to embrace him. But his smile vanished like smoke in the wind, and he recoiled sharply, hands raised defensively as if I were a wild animal ready to pounce. He didn't want any hugs from a body of Ramoon's, even though he knew I was trapped inside.

I halted abruptly, confusion swirling in my mind. "I thought you were dead."

"I'll explain later Richard, did you send the information?"

"Oh." The weight of his words hit me like a tidal wave, and I remembered what Ramoon had said. I turned to the terminal on the wall, my heart racing as I placed my hand against its cool surface. I made the connection and uttered the words, "secondary transmit." Relief washed over me like a warm tide when I heard the response: "transmit successful."

"That's it," I said, a sense of accomplishment swelling within me.

"Good. We must go. Follow me," he commanded, turning on his heel and striding away.

All the reservations I'd felt when Ankit first uttered those words seemed like echoes from a distant past. I just wanted out, so I nearly leaped after him. But the shadows of uncertainty loomed large in my mind, and as we hurried down the corridor, I couldn't help but ask, "Where are we going?"

"We need to get back to headquarters, if it's still there."

"What do you mean?"

"They discovered it, Richard. Ramoon's thugs have laid siege to it for the last few hours. I barely managed to escape. I just hope the information you sent gets out in time to save them."

My heart sank at the thought of Rachel and Jane, two of the people I cared about most in this chaotic universe. A thousand questions clamoured for attention in my mind, but as soon as I opened my mouth to speak again, Ankit cut me off. "Save all the questions for later, Richard. We need to concentrate on getting back. If anyone speaks to us, you need to pretend to be Ramoon. Say you've come back from India Central early because you heard I'd turned up. I'll explain the rest."

"Okay, but how are we going to get back to the Moon? I couldn't jump back from Ramoon's office."

"I've brought a tech with me who can get us back to the Moon, but it will only be in your current manifestation. So, you'll have to wait to get back to headquarters before you can shed that body."

As we hurried to meet up with our contact, I caught glimpses of recognition in the faces of some people we passed, and I silently thanked the stars that no one stopped us or spoke.

When we finally emerged from the jump point on the Moon, the familiar shapes of the headquarters loomed ahead, casting long shadows in the dim light. A row of containers, reminiscent of those used after my arrest, lined the entrance. Anxiety twisted in my gut as we approached, and I couldn't shake the fear that Ramoon's thugs had already imprisoned many of my friends within those cold metal walls. I hoped Rachel and Jane were alright.

We paused in the shade, watching as upholders emerged from the headquarters, leading bound prisoners in front of them. My heart raced, and I stood frozen, afraid that even a whisper from my lips might shatter the fragile silence and alert the law to our presence.

Then Ankit spoke, his voice low and urgent, as if he were deciphering a hidden truth in the scene unfolding before us. "They're not protesters," he said, his eyes narrowing. "They're arresting Ramoon's henchmen!"

I was relieved and started to move out of the shadows.

But Ankit's arm shot out to bar my way, 'Richard,' he said, 'you're still in Ramoon's body. You don't want to be arrested again, do you?'

"Oh yes, of course." The realisation that I'd grown so accustomed to Ramoon's body that I could forget I was in it made me feel nauseous.

"We need to wait till they've gone."

Then, like a beacon in the darkness, Jon appeared, talking openly to one of the upholders. As we watched, they shook hands, and the convoy of containers began to move off. Jon turned to walk back into the headquarters.

"Come on, I think we're safe," Ankit urged, stepping out of the shadows and sprinting toward Jon.

"Jon!" Ankit shouted, eager to attract his attention. He didn't want me to walk into the headquarters in Ramoon's body without everyone knowing the truth.

"The first thing we need to do is transfer you back into your own body," Jon said, his tone serious. "You won't last long around here looking like that."

I could hardly contain my relief when, half an hour later, I opened my own eyes. Looking down at Ramoon's now lifeless form, I watched as it slowly began to lose its features, fading away like a forgotten dream. And although it didn't matter anymore, I turned to the technicians and said, "Make sure it's totally destroyed, won't you?" I wanted every vestige of that man erased from existence.

Jon assured me that Rachel and Jane were alright, but even so, I could hardly wait to see them.

"Everyone's gathering in the conference room in an hour," Jon said. "I'd appreciate it if you didn't mention what happened at Ramoon's until then. But bring everyone with you."

As I made my way to my quarters, I marvelled at the progress the domestic robots and self-cleaning mechanisms had made in restoring the headquarters to its original state. By the end of the day, no one would be able to tell that a full-scale battle had raged here only hours before.

I spent most of the next hour pouring my heart out to Rachel and Jane, expressing how much I loved them and the worry I'd felt, thinking I might never return. I carefully avoided the details, respecting Jon's request, but I could see in their eyes that they understood the trauma I'd endured.

"We've been trapped here for ages," Jane exclaimed, her excitement bubbling over. "I wanted to join in and fight with the rest, but no one would let me."

"Not everything is a game, Jane," Rachel replied, her gaze filled with the same concern I felt about the society our daughter might one day inhabit, especially given her streak of exhibitionism.

Later, when we entered the conference room, I was struck by the transformation. The oval table had been removed, and a dividing wall had slid open, doubling the room's size. Chairs filled the space, and a long table stretched across the front, where the main leaders sat. As I walked in, Jon gestured for me to join them.

Ankit, Rachel, and Jane sat facing me in the front row. When the room filled, over one hundred people were present, a mix of Cryogens and Manooran sympathisers, all waiting in anticipation for an explanation.

As the room fell silent, Jon stood up, commanding attention. "For those of you who don't know what's happened today, two significant events have occurred. This sanctuary," he said, gesturing to the walls and ceiling, "was discovered by Ramoon's thugs. And as many of you know, because you were involved, we literally had to fight for our lives."

"Secondly," he continued, "our plan to retrieve the evidence needed to bring down Ramoon succeeded, and because of that, the attack on us by his men failed. They've now all been arrested." After a dramatic pause, he added, "...and Ramoon has been destroyed."

Ripples of excited relief swept through the room, but Jon raised his hands for calm and continued. "In a moment, I'll be asking the man involved in that," he said, looking directly at me, "to tell us what happened. But first, I need to inform you that I've had contact with the rest of the Manooran High Officials, and they've assured me that we're no longer in any danger. They've requested some time to consider all the information and its consequences. I've agreed to a reconciliation meeting with them next week in this very conference room, and I want all of you to attend."

"Now, Richard, would you be able to tell us what happened with Ramoon today?"

I stood up, my heart pounding as I recounted the story I'd already shared with Rachel and Jane, but this time, I added the details I'd left out. As I recalled Ramoon's words about Maya's involvement in Helen's death, I noticed a shadow of sadness fall over Rachel's face, and a gasp rippled through the room. Jon's head lowered in solemn acknowledgment. I chose not to mention Ramoon's twisted idea that Maya had willingly allowed Rachel to marry me as compensation for her murderous deed. That felt wrong somehow. Instead, I smiled at Rachel, silently conveying my understanding of her pain.

"And he thought you dying was a bonus," I said, glancing at Ankit.

Ankit stood up, his voice ringing clear. "Well, I'm glad it was a bigger bonus than he expected then." Approval murmured through the crowd, and he turned to Rachel, his expression sincere. "I'm sorry I used your parents' accident to hide from Ramoon. But it was the only way I could guarantee he'd leave me alone and release Amira."

Then, addressing everyone again, he continued, "After I managed to get a friend on Mercury to falsify my being on the Karr's ship, I contacted Jon and explained everything. He kindly offered to help me hide," he said, turning back to the top table, "even from you, Richard."

"I knew we had to keep your existence secret, Ankit," Jon added. "When we came under siege and found that we couldn't retrieve Richard, it seemed the right thing to send you to Ramoon's office and bring him back. You had the right access, and if anyone saw you and Richard, he could pretend to be Ramoon, and you could construct some story about your death."

Jon turned to the room once more. "If anyone has lost someone they love during this struggle, I want to assure you that we're all here for you. The sacrifices we've made today have helped save humanity. All we can do now is wait to see what the response will be from the authorities and consider what we want to happen next. Because when we meet with them again, we'll be helping to make fundamental decisions that will affect everyone living in this solar system. I want all of us to have a say in those decisions."

"To that end, we intend to arrange meetings for all Cryogens between now and next week to coordinate our demands. So, until then, I suggest you all take advantage of the time to relax and enjoy the freedom we've won."

As the applause faded, the room began to empty, and I turned to Jon. "Have the authorities given you any indication of what they propose to do?"

"I don't think they've had time to process it all, Richard, especially the prospect of a revived biological human race."

"But you do think we're safe now, don't you?"

"I'm not sure what to think. You know for yourself that there's more than one Ramoon out there. Let's just hope there are none with his influence."

"Amen to that," I replied.

Chapter 40 - Aftermath

I think it's safe to say that once a thought crosses a mind, it cannot easily be forgotten. And once that thought is voiced, it can never be unsaid. In this age of technology, information spreads like wildfire, propagating across multiple systems, leaving no trace of its origin. Once intelligent eyes have gazed upon it and understood its content, it becomes a permanent fixture in the collective consciousness.

So it was that the uproar and rage swept across the planets, as swiftly as the news of Ramoon's insidious plans had leaked out. The information coursed through the solar system like a shockwave, igniting questions that poured into the central committee like a torrential downpour. How had the all-powerful system been breached? What had prevented the committee from becoming aware of Ramoon's clandestine activities? What were these codes that allowed anyone to override the system, and who had access to them? These questions gnawed at the integrity of a system that was supposed to be free from human intervention. But they were not the only questions. The guilt-ridden, age-old arguments about the Cryogens and the original humans began to resurface, like ghosts from a past thought buried.

In the days that followed, authorities on each planet scrambled to set up meetings with representatives from their societies. They needed to discuss and agree proposals to present at the reconciliation meeting with the Cryogens and their supporters. The urgency was palpable, a frantic energy that buzzed in the air like static before a storm.

Even before any formal response came from the authorities, all Manoorans involved with the protesters, at whatever level, were granted full amnesty. Apologies flooded in from various corners of the system, a deluge of remorse. The Manoorans couldn't do enough, it seemed, but the true extent of their guilt would have to wait until the reconciliation meeting to be revealed.

I had hoped that all my personal conflicts would resolve themselves alongside the unveiling of Ramoon's plans, but those hopes had not materialised. I was left utterly confused by Ramoon's chilling reference to having Helen destroyed, and there had been no time to uncover the layers of that story. Compounding my frustration was the fact that I still hadn't received the unrestricted access to the main system that I desperately needed. In fact, access had been restricted even further, a direct consequence of the Manooran's shock at what they considered the system's failings.

Freedom of information and access to the system, especially concerning the Cryogen project, was one of the proposals that Jon and his fellow representatives were taking to the reconciliation meeting.

"So, it'll have to wait a little while longer, I'm afraid," Jon said, his voice steady but tinged with sympathy when I expressed my frustration once more. "I know you're eager to find out about Helen's death at the hands of Maya, and believe me, I am too. But we can't rush any of this; it affects the future of everyone. I'm sorry, Richard."

With a sense of frustration weighing heavily on my shoulders, I returned home to my family, determined to focus on finalising the alterations we had all been planning. Jennifer, Simon, Earl, and Ankit re-acquainted themselves with the family, and the party we threw felt more genuine than the one we had sprung on Ankit. I was amazed when Simon and Earl helped me arrange a barbecue right in the middle of the dining room! By the time my two friends had finished, it looked like we were on Bondi Beach, the aroma of grilled food wafting through the air, mingling with laughter and chatter.

The general well-being and good feelings that prevailed during that week were infectious. It reminded me of the Christmas periods of my own time, when everyone, for that brief moment, became friends again. I even enjoyed the meetings Jon had arranged for all the Cryogens on 'Earth One' to discuss the proposals they would present to the authorities. True to his word, Jon had let everyone be involved, fostering a sense of unity that felt almost revolutionary.

Finally, the day of the reconciliation meeting arrived, and it was to be broadcast in real-time across the entire system. Rachel insisted we look the part, investing considerable time in choosing the clothes that would make a statement.

I looked down at the suit I was wearing, its fabric shimmering under the lights, and smiled at the thought of the clothes I'd worn to my old school reunion. I certainly wasn't going to get away with an old T.Rex t-shirt today. I made a mental note to ask Rachel if their music still played anywhere.

The conference room appeared twice the size it had the previous week. One entire wall seemed to have vanished, revealing another room beyond it, virtually linked by technology. It might as well have been one room, divided only by the force field used by the hover pods. Unless someone attempted to walk from one side to the other, they would never know that each side of this expanded room belonged to a different planet.

Both sides of the virtual conference room began to fill with representatives from across the system—Cryogens and Manoorans alike. As I scanned the room, I recognised some well-known faces from my past, or at least people wearing their bodies. It crossed my mind that some of the less familiar faces might belong to current celebrities, their identities obscured from me by the passage of time.

I felt a wave of relief wash over me when I realised, I wasn't seated at the top table this time. Public speaking and being the centre of attention had never been my forte. Perhaps it was another of Helen's traits that had rubbed off on me? I didn't know, but I'd never desired fame or recognition, unlike so many of my peers who had chased it relentlessly.

But like many men, I was a big kid when it came to gadgets and technology. I was utterly fascinated by the technology being deployed to bring the people in this meeting together.

As I looked to the front of the room, it was impossible to tell that the representatives on both planets weren't sitting next to each other. Jon occupied a position where the table in this room met the table from the other room, virtually adjacent to the head of the highest Manooran official on the opposite side. From the audience's perspective, it appeared as though they were seated at the centre of one very long table.

When everyone had taken their seats, Jon lifted his arms to quiet the room before giving a general introduction to the people at the top table, particularly the highest-ranking official—a large, elegant man named Bashir Khan, who sat beside him. Jon then outlined the process undertaken over the previous week to arrive at the proposals they would present.

"There will be a need for further meetings to agree on the minutiae of the general proposals we're going to outline now," he said, his voice steady and authoritative. "But today marks the start of a new beginning for us all."

When he finished, he handed the room over to Bashir Khan to deliver the authority's proposals. "Thank you," the official said, standing up and nodding his acknowledgment of Jon. He began to lay out the proposals from the Manooran authorities.

Amongst the most significant of these was a proposal to hand over the Cryogen project to an all-Cryogen team and to accept the revival of biological bodies if that was their wish. "There will be no pressure as to when, or even if, any biological human moves to an artificial body," he stated, his voice resonating with conviction.

A planet was offered to house the future growth of biological humans. "However," Bashir continued, a noticeable break in his voice, "if you ask us to, then all Manooran humans will vacate Earth One." An audible gasp echoed from the Cryogen side of the room. I felt certain they would reject that proposal outright.

"Finally, Cryogens and biological humans will have full representation on all authorities throughout the system."

When he finished and sat down, the applause from the Cryogen side was rapturous. We all knew the proposals exceeded our expectations, and some of us could sense Jon's response brewing.

When he stood up, the room fell silent, and he directed his speech toward the other side. "I'd like to first offer our thanks to you for the proposals that have been put forward today. Before we knew we could revive our race, all we Cryogens wanted was to live in peace without any threat. The opportunity to recreate our race has come as a great comfort to many of us."

"However, a lot of discussions have taken place over many years regarding what we want, not just over the last week. And I can confidently tell you that I represent almost all of us when I say these words." He turned to Bashir. "All we've ever wanted was to live in peace and not feel threatened. All of us living in this solar system are different types of beings than those we started off as. We all have different origins, but it's what we'll become together that will create our common future—a future where we can share a common past."

"We want, as you do, to become one race. And with a little effort from all of us, I am sure we can forget our past differences and achieve that end. The biological expansion that will occur because of those people still preserved will add to the diversity of our race. They will boost our numbers, and it will be up to them when, or if, they decide to move to artificial bodies. I am sure there will be those who choose not to make that transition, forming yet another diverse group within our collection of societies."

"There are those too who wish to explore the universe around them, and I hope we can find it within ourselves to offer this to those inquisitive enough to desire it. The word that should define us from now on should be 'together' because together we can move forward. Taking what we can from the past and creating new art, literature, and music—that will be our future. We can all get what we want from this if we work together, for each other as well as ourselves."

"We propose that any terms other than 'human' as references to describe us are immediately discouraged. We are all human now, so there is no need to vacate planets or set any aside for any reason other than to accommodate the diverse societies that we already live our lives by."

He looked down at the information sheet he was holding, as if reading from it, then looked back at the audience with a smile. "These are the proposals and responses," he paused, "from your fellow humans."

The applause and cheering erupted, echoing through the room for what felt like an eternity. Through his watery eyes, I saw Jon lean forward to shake Bashir's hand as he said, "Here's to our future." I couldn't help but think that this handshake was a symbolic gesture, a bridge between worlds. But the wall was not only able to manipulate images and sound; it could also reshape reality. As Jon held out his hand, it sank into the wall, and the part of the wall in front of Bashir's hand morphed out to take its shape. Bashir shook it!

The system made it appear as if these two men, on different planets, were actually shaking hands. Then, all along the wall, the same phenomenon occurred. The two feet on either side of the virtual walls morphed any object passing into it. As they entered the wall on one side, they emerged out of the opposite side, accepted by the other. It truly felt like magic. *What a wonderful world.*

As people began to leave through the exits on each planet, they received invitations to the evening's celebratory party, which would be held in the same rooms.

It had been a long day for all of us, but my wife and daughter were obviously made of sterner stuff. As we left, Rachel reminded me that they had permission to go to the surface for a picnic. "Why don't you come with us?"

"I wish I could," I replied, "but I've promised to meet with the others to discuss and review the current Cryogen project processes. Make sure you get back home by six o'clock to give yourself time to get ready for the party." As they left, I added, "Don't eat too much."

I didn't bother to change that evening; I was particularly fond of the suit I was wearing and didn't believe anything else could surpass it for the occasion. I didn't even have to ask for a brand new one because all clothing was self-cleaning. A quick shower was all I needed to freshen up. I chuckled to myself, recalling how many times I'd re-worn clothes and underwear in my past. It seemed a man thing. I tried to convince myself it was just a quirk of my gender. Yes, it must have been, even Helen had let me get away with it.

Rachel, however, went overboard, seizing any excuse to get dressed up and preen herself—a definite woman thing. But to me, it was worth it, and she hadn't disappointed tonight. The green satin dress hugged her body like a thin veneer of paint over an exquisite sculpture. Paired with golden shoes that seemed to lift her into the air, she would have knocked any supermodel from my day for six. If I'd ever been able to whistle, I would have.

"You don't think it's too much, do you?" she asked, her expression betraying her absolute confidence.

"Definitely not," I assured her as she admired herself again in the mirror. "I think it'll be perfect for this type of function if it's anything like the ones the bank used to put on." Then I added, "I can't wait to finally meet Amira; it's almost as if she's never existed to me."

"Oh dear, I'm afraid you're going to be disappointed again. I asked Ankit earlier if she was coming, and he confirmed what I suspected. Amira doesn't like going out in public; she's a bit of a recluse. You're going to have to wait until they invite us over to their home."

"Oh right, well that's a shame. I suppose we'll eventually get to meet her when she's ready."

When we arrived at the function, aside from the technology, it turned out to be very much like the events my bank used to host. Everyone was milling about with drinks and food, but instead of human waiters and waitresses, robotic cabinets moved among the guests, offering refreshments. I still couldn't get over that wall when I saw people on one side lean over and take drinks from the opposite side, as if no physical barrier or distance separated them.

Everyone was buzzing with excitement about the outcome of the meeting, and the consensus was that it marked a new beginning for humanity. "I'm just glad I'll finally be able to travel outside the solar system at some stage," Rachel said, her eyes sparkling with anticipation.

After a few hours, I began to feel exhausted. I often felt out of my element at big events like this, and tonight I had a peculiar sense of foreboding that made me long for the comfort of home. So, I went in search of Rachel. She had been deep in conversation with Simon, Earl, and Jennifer, and I caught the tail end of a question being posed by Earl.

"...so, I wonder how we'll deal with the ethnicity issue."

Jennifer tilted her head quizzically. "What do you mean?" she asked.

"Well, most humans are now Asian, but there's virtually no one of that ethnicity awaiting revival. For some reason, hardly any chose to be frozen. On the other hand, there are an equal number of all the other ethnic groups," he paused, looking at Jennifer and Simon.

"Which means?" Simon asked, clearly not understanding where Earl was going.

"Well, it could mean that if the Cryogens who come back in biological form choose to take up artificial bodies representing their own ethnicity after they've had children, then the current ethnic majority today could become the minority of tomorrow. It might be a long way off, but that's how it looks."

"I don't think that sort of thing is an issue anymore, surely?" Rachel interjected.

"I'm afraid that debate will have to wait for another time," I said, putting my arm around her. "I think we need to get back and have an early night. We've got a long day tomorrow, and who knows what surprises it might hold?"

"Yes," she replied in a resigned fashion. Looking up coyly at our friends, she added, "I guess we need to face the truth," and turning back to the others, she said, "We'll finish this conversation another time. Goodnight, everyone."

As I looked at her, a wave of guilt washed over me. Although she was aware of what Ramoon had told me about her mother killing Helen, I hadn't mentioned anything about Jane. I'd been dreading this moment. I knew that soon I would have to confront Helen's death or act on the choice I'd finally made. I just wanted it all to be over; I would need all the courage I could muster. I even considered whether death would be preferable to the life of guilt I felt sure I was facing.

Jon had informed us earlier that we would have full access to the system starting the following day. We could gain access by using the terminals at the library. We both had our own ideas and fears about what we might discover.

When we arrived home, we quietly slipped into Jane's room to check on our daughter before retiring, a ritual we always performed after an evening out. As we crept through the door, trying not to wake her, my attention was drawn to an object standing on her bedside cabinet.

My stomach twisted, and I slowly closed my eyes, as if I could shut out the reality that was attacking my sanity. With the sickening feeling that had become all too familiar, I said, "Where did they come from?" pointing across the room.

'They're what Jane brought back from the surface today. Do you like them?" Rachel whispered.

"They're wildflowers, called Dandelions."

Chapter 41 – An End to the Beginning

I snuck out of our apartment early the following morning, the chill of dawn wrapping around me like a shroud. I couldn't bear the thought of facing Rachel while I delved into the records about Jane. The weight of the truth loomed over me, a dark cloud I wasn't ready to confront. I needed time—time to let the awful reality sink in when it was finally confirmed. A gnawing regret twisted in my gut; I wished I'd asked Ramoon about Jane when he was recounting the details of Helen's death. But there hadn't been time then, and now it felt like it was too late. *How was I going to tell Rachel…?*

The message I left her was simple, almost too simple: I'd gone to Ankit's and would meet her at the library at 10:30 a.m. It didn't give me much time, but then again, it didn't matter how long I had. No amount of time would ever be enough to come to terms with the chaotic mess my life had become. I wished I could just run away, escape this tangled web of confusion and despair.

I had all this time to think, yet I was still lost in a fog of uncertainty. But one thing was clear: I had to uncover the truth about Helen—was she really dead? How had Jane emerged from her? And why? I needed to gather all the facts so I could sit down with Rachel and our daughter, let them weigh the options, and decide our fate together. Just like Jon had advised. It felt only right to let them choose our path forward.

As I walked down the familiar library corridor, memories flooded back—my first time here with my friends, laughter echoing off the walls, the thrill of discovery. It felt like yesterday yet today was shrouded in a heavy haze. Approaching the librarian's station, I had to blink hard, struggling to keep my eyes from popping out of my head.

There she was, the librarian, as large as life, sitting in her seat!!

I stared at her, disbelief coursing through me. "What are you doing here? You're supposed to be dead."

"Ah, you must be one of Nicole's friends?" she replied, her tone casual, as if discussing the weather.

"Who's Nicole?" I asked, my confusion deepening.

"She was the person who worked at this station before me." She searched my face for recognition, but I was utterly lost. "And you're wondering why I look identical to her?"

"Of course," I said, finally relaxing a bit. "Twins?"

"No," she replied flatly. "I never even met her. When I started this job, they told me her template was up for grabs, so I took it. Never liked my old body anyway. Can I help you?"

I slowly closed my gaping mouth, the bizarre nature of this conversation swirling in my mind. I didn't want to know any more about it; it all felt wrong, yet this was a new reality altogether.

"I've got the room at the end of the corridor booked for the morning; my name is Richard Green."

I had to consciously push aside the librarian's unsettling revelation. The only way I could cope was to embrace the idea that anything was possible in this strange new world.

Settling into the room, I took a deep breath, my heart racing as I reached for the vid-screen. I moved my hand forward, to bring up all the records on Jane. I expected to find a direct link to Helen's fate, but to my astonishment, the records revealed a different story. Jane had been a dancer, living on Venus for the last three hundred years with her life partner. He had died in a manner eerily like Rachel's parents, and heartbroken, she had chosen to end her life as she knew it, erasing the heartache that had consumed her.

As I listened to this message left from Jane's earlier self, a chill ran down my spine. Would she heed the plea not to re-integrate to prevent herself from dealing once again with the loss of the love of her life?

But all this meant that Helen was dead. But what about the ring and the dandelions? Confusion swirled in my mind like a tempest. Then a thought struck me.

"How do I know you're not an elaborate fake to deter Jane from re-integrating Helen?" I asked the image floating before me, my voice trembling with uncertainty.

But that line of reasoning crumbled under its own weight. This information was classified, accessible only to Jane and a select few high-ranking officials. No, it had to be true—Helen was gone. It wasn't even a consolation that Jane wasn't Helen. I sank back onto the floor, my mind a whirlwind of thoughts. I needed to search for information about myself and Helen to see if that would lead me anywhere.

Before I could act, a voice behind me jolted me from my reverie. "I thought you were going to wait for me?" Rachel asked, her tone a mix of surprise and disappointment.

I jumped, guilt flooding my system. "I'm sorry! I got here early, so I thought I'd have a quick look."

Her eyes narrowed, disappointment etched on her face. "Richard, you promised me. Please tell me you haven't searched for Helen before I got here."

I reached out, clasping her hand tightly. "No, I haven't. I promise. But come here and sit down. I need to tell you something important. First of all, I haven't searched for Helen yet because I needed to be certain about Jane."

"Jane! Why?"

Her gaze bore into me as I recounted my suspicions about Jane's origins, the ring, and the dandelions in our daughter's room. As I spoke, I watched her expression shift from confusion to shock, recognition dawning in her eyes. Finally, she said to me in a slow faltering voice.

"Richard, that ring is mine! I gave it to Jane... it's what my mother gave me. And she picked those dandelions while we were at our picnic because I told her how much I loved them."

"I don't understand. You're a Manooran... you can't possibly be..." My voice trailed off as we locked eyes, a silent prayer forming in my heart. *Oh please, let it be true.* I knew life rarely offered happy endings, but I desperately wished this time it would be different.

Rachel's brow furrowed as she pieced together the fragments of our reality. "Where are my parent's records?"

As I scrambled to locate Maya and Mazood's records, I could hear her softly muttering to herself, connecting the dots. "And I couldn't access the files at Ankit's, which we originally thought had been blocked to all Cryogens." The pieces of the jigsaw puzzle that had been my life since my revival began to fall into place.

We exchanged a glance, a shared understanding igniting between us, and turned our heads in unison to the vid screen. I thought I'd found a file that fit the bill. It was simply titled *Helen Green*.

Rachel squeezed my hand as she activated the screen, her heart racing alongside mine.

Maya's distraught face appeared before us; her eyes filled with anguish.

"I couldn't do it. That poor woman was staring at me, but Ramoon had told me to kill her. I saw the strength in her eyes, the humanity, and history. She never begged me for anything, but her accusing gaze defeated me as surely as if she'd knocked the gun from my hand and turned it against me.

So, I told her I wouldn't destroy her entirely, but I'd have to get rid of her body, and that I'd arrange for her to be reborn, to give her a chance to live again in the future. She never closed her eyes when I pulled the trigger, just kept staring into mine until she was gone, whispering, 'I love you, Richard, I love you.' Afterward, I took her brain pod and hid it for two years until I could arrange for it to be reborn.

Those accusing eyes have haunted my dreams every night since then. If this record is being accessed, then my husband and I must be dead. So, this is my confession. And if you're listening to this, Rachel, then you've probably guessed that you were that woman. We adopted you and vowed to protect you to repay what I'd done. I'm sorry we had to pretend not to like Richard. But anything less than the way we reacted to him could have raised Ramoon's suspicions. We always wanted you to be reunited with him, but we had to maintain our pretence. And if you're still together now, please accept this knowledge as our final wedding gift. You'll find the information about your previous life attached to these records. We love you both. Goodbye."

Tears streamed down our faces, blurring our vision, but as our emotions reached out across the tiny gap between us, a thousand years dissolved.

For me, it was the answer to all the prayers I'd meant to say—a solution my mind had never dared to dream. For Rachel, a buried fear had been unearthed and transformed into a treasure. Her subconscious worries about her parents, once suppressed, now proved wrong by this fortunate twist of fate.

Eventually, she looked at me, holding my hands tightly. "Come on, Richard. I think it's time for me to reintegrate with my past, and for us both to step out there and meet our future."

And fate, which rarely favoured such happy endings, watched on.

As we walked out of that room and into our future, it continued to shuffle its cards...

It hadn't done with us – yet.

A note from the Author:

If you enjoyed reading this novel as much as I enjoyed writing it, then you might want to read book two of the Cryogen Chronicles entitled 'Living in the Future.' It follows Helen and Richard forward another thousand years when friction between the expanded population of 'Biologs' and 'Artificials' is threatening to destabilise humanity. And some new characters appear, along with a new and more dangerous threat, from a very strange life form that lurks in the hidden depths of another dimension.

Visit www.alexoldham.com to find ways to get the book for your device, or to get a hard copy. If you're reading on an iPad, you can visit the iBooks store (from the iBooks bookshelf) and search for 'Living in the Future.'

I appreciate any feedback from readers so if you feel you'd like to send me any comments you can also do that via my website alexoldham.com

I may not be able to reply to everyone if I receive a lot of comments, so please don't be annoyed at me if I don't respond. I do promise, however, to read and consider everything sent to me.

Thank you again
Alex

All the views expressed in this book are attributed to the characters contained in it. They are not necessarily the views of the author. This is a work of fiction and all characters, names, incidents, organisations and dialogue in this novel are either the products of the author's imagination or are used fictitiously.

I'd like to say thank you to my 'reader number one.' Without whom, this book would be full of mistakes – Janet I'll always be grateful.

I wrote this book for my wonderful and wacky family – but most of all for you Mum and Dad – thank you for my life.

Printed and bound in the United Kingdom
18/12/2025
02021798-0001